STARCRUSH

A NOVEL BY

JUSTINE ERLER

TRIO CAPITAL

First Print Edition: March 2014

The characters and events portrayed in this book are
fictitious. Any similarity to real persons, living or dead,
is coincidental and not intended by the author.

ISBN 978-0-9913676-1-0

For my inspiration child, Jackie,
because you always knew
what mischief we could conspire.

CONTENTS

* * *

PART I

CONTENTS

* * *

PART II

PART I

1. ROCK BAND

It was the first day of auditions. My mother arranged for time at the high school auditorium. From the center aisle, a boy approached — long hair, jeans faded in all the right places. He carried a guitar in his hand, a stack of sheet music in the other.

I noticed his face.

Hmm, I thought. *Not enough for the floor to collapse from under me, barely worth a second thought.*

My mother flashed a look of disapproval. I nudged her away with a drawn-out sigh.

She turned to the boy. "Thanks for answering our ad."

We had placed an ad in the local community paper the week before: *Musicians needed for local band. Show us that you have it: the look, the attitude, the passion. E-mail: ASavoy18@_mail.com.*

"I'm Arielle Savoy," she said. "This is my daughter, Genna."

His eyes met mine. I looked away.

"Wow," he said. "You guys could be sisters."

I caught the accent, rock and roll in a "retro" sort of way.

My mother signaled me to join the conversation, but I was too hung up with a song that wouldn't quit playing in my head.

It's an English accent, Genna, she thought to herself.

My fingers stopped tapping the armrest of my chair like it was a keyboard. In my mind, her voice was clear — as if she was *actually speaking*. She was smiling, still glowing from the complement. She loved it when people said we looked like sisters.

I half-watched as he wrapped a strand of hair behind one ear.

"Nicholas Everett James," he said. "Call me Nick."

The accent made him seem better looking than he actually was, or maybe he *was*, I couldn't decide. He balanced the guitar against a seat and offered his hand. I pretended to be searching for something in my bag.

When I finally did look up, I caught him staring.

Another "flat-line," I thought.

"Flat-line" was how I described boys I couldn't get excited about, which was most of them these days. It was painfully obvious that I'd never have a boyfriend in high school with senior year slipping away.

To myself, I recited the usual rant:

Never had a boyfriend,

Never went on a date,

Never been kissed....

He took back his hand. "How long have you been singing?" he asked.

My fingers locked on a tube of lip gloss. I pulled it out of my bag, ignoring the question like it was background noise. I was thinking about Bill, my Mom's "wanna be" boyfriend. Next to my dad, he was a total loser.

"Since I was three," I eventually answered. "My vocal training is classical but I like to break-out into more edgy stuff."

My mother cut in, "You have your own music?"

She pointed to the sheet music that he seemed to forget he was holding.

"I write lyrics as well," he said, pulling out a single sheet.

"Really," she said; her face curious. "Hop onstage then."

I threw my bag aside and sprang to my feet.

"I meant *him*," she said, waving me back. "First time should be without vocals."

Weighted down by a restless feeling, I stomped back to my seat and brought my legs over the empty chair in front of me. The only distraction was literally at my fingertips. "Speed-texting" was like second nature as if compulsive finger action could burn calories like a treadmill.

My "sometimes" best friend, Trinity, answered back.

Trinity: *OMG, I luv Brit guys.*

Genna: *Totally boring!*

Trinity: *U always say that — even when they're hot*

Genna: *Especially when they're hot !! ;)*

I waited ... two seconds, three seconds....

Trinity: *Just hold him there!*

I was ready to text back an excuse to keep her away, when I sensed the music about to begin. Nick found his position quickly, like he had gone through the motions a hundred times before.

My mother introduced him to Josh — just about the most awesome drummer on the planet. I had to keep reminding myself that we hung in the same crowd since nothing about him felt exceptionally weird.

They talked as Josh steadied a cymbal with his hand. Then Nick turned and signaled "ready." Josh threw me a smile as he raised his sticks. I heard him start the count to himself: *Ready: one, two and three....*

The first blast from Nick's guitar overtook the drums, shearing through the empty space like a razor. Gradually the layers fell away, one chord at a time until he was barely playing, his eyes squeezed shut as if he was forcing the music back ... when the theme rebounded with an explosion of notes too wild to keep down.

Whoa! I slid down my seat.

My mother was already gesturing to cut the music. Nick placed the guitar on a stand and jumped off the stage with one motion, ignoring the row of steps beneath him.

"Anything wrong?" he asked in a voice that knew better.

He was clearly trying to impress while I applied lip gloss without a mirror, trying to look indifferent ... my preferred MO when guys were around.

My mother answered him, "You just worked those chords like a pro."

His mouth twitched into the beginnings of a smile. She was four words away from sealing the deal. I held my breath.

"Welcome to the band," she announced, her arms in the air.

Josh surfaced from behind his drums and slapped him on the shoulder. "Hey dude," he said. "That was awesome."

Awesome was an understatement, but I wasn't ready to join the fan club yet. Instantly Josh winced, as if I had said something to ruin the moment. As always, he was a few seconds ahead of me.

"I'm not so sure about the whole 'stuck in the eighties' thing," I said, slipping my phone back into my bag, leaving Trinity's last text hanging.

The smile fell from Nick's face.

"I'm just saying...," I said unapologetically.

My mother ignored me and turned to Nick, "That 'metal' sound will soften out acoustically once we add strings."

I barely listened as Nick suggested using twin lead guitars, offering to call a friend who might be available.

"Liam is super-talented," he said, his fingers absentmindedly strumming chords.

"Strings...?" I backtracked, the panic rising in my voice. "As in ... violin strings?"

For a moment, the face that popped into my mother's mind belonged to none other than Logan Reed.

"You're *not* serious?" I groaned.

Without answering, she motioned me onstage as if I had been the one holding everyone up.

Give me a break, I thought back.

I snatched the lyrics from Nick's hands and quickly read the first two lines.

"Kinda cool," I said. "It's a love song."

His eyes brightened. I pretended not to notice.

I walked up to the microphone and tapped it a few times until the sound of my own breathing shrieked back, loud and pitchy.

"Testing, testing," I repeated.

It took a moment to slip into the right frame of mind. A few deep breaths and my face went blank, my eyes lowered to my boots. It was better to let the music drive the emotions rather than the other way around.

Nick began shaking his head.

"Hold up," he said with his "almost sexy" accent.

I watched as he brought down his guitar, careful not to whack it against the microphone stand.

"What's that 'thing' you're doing ... with your face?" he asked.

"It's *my thing*," I answered.

"Just relax," he said. "Be yourself and stop looking at the floor. Raise your chin."

Fortunately, I was about to give the performance of my life, or I would have ripped him to shreds.

"Let's go," my mother interrupted with the commanding voice of a drill sergeant.

Next thing I knew she was doing this little conductor's twirl with her hand, giving the cue to start. I lowered my head and then stopped. With a deep sigh, I slowly raised my chin.

It didn't matter that there was no lighting, no special effects and no audience. Instantly, I felt the energy of a concert in full swing. Nick circled me as I sang, chasing me with wild leads, overlapping and repetitive.

Hey, you're crowding my space, I thought to myself.

It was an observation. He seemed to sway into me ... a little too close for comfort, and for a half-second my mind did this little spin and imagined what a kiss might be like.

I caught Josh's eyes as I spun around.

Eavesdropper, I thought.

When it was over, I spoke first. "Too mind-boggling," I said trying to channel the inspirational eighties.

"You're an awesome vocalist, Genna," Nick blurted with enough enthusiasm to nearly knock me down.

Man, I thought. *I encouraged him. There was no stopping him now.*

"I'm from England," he said.

No joke Sherlock, I thought.

"My family just moved here. My Dad was transferred to the New York office."

Okay, I thought, *T.M.I.* (Too Much Information).

My eyes settled on his white T-shirt embossed with a Union Jack flag. Around his neck I noticed the leather cord, a few beads dangling against his collarbone.

"How do you like New Jersey?" my mother asked loudly, interrupting my train of thought so hard it hurt.

I threw her a "say what?" look which she conveniently ignored.

"It's different from what I expected," he answered. "The shore is amazing, so *beautiful.*"

He emphasized the word *beautiful* as he glanced my way. I was still obsessing over his necklace.

My mother giggled. "Glad all those reality shows didn't scare you away."

If he was expecting girls with whiny voices and orange tans, he was in for a big disappointment. Everything about my life shot down the image in the best possible way.

"I like to keep an open mind," he said.

"Cool," I answered. His eyes followed me as I circled. "We're really into *open minds* around here." I glanced behind. "Aren't we Josh?"

No answer.

Josh wasn't in the mood for teasing. His "on-demand" frown made me turn to my mother instead. One look in her direction and I had to force a cough to clear the giggle reflex in my throat.

I turned back to Nick. "It's an inside joke," I explained, managing to straighten myself out by thinking about sad, awful things.

"We have a house nearby in Colts Neck," he said as if he wanted to forget our lapse into silliness. "I have a music studio in the basement. It shouldn't be a problem for us to rehearse there."

"Okay, let's not get ahead of ourselves," my mother said. "I don't want to be a basement band. We're still recruiting musicians. Hopefully we can have our first band practice within a few weeks."

She walked over to Josh. He was packing up his gear.

"Catch you later at the meeting," she said.

I had forgotten about the meeting.

Total bummer, I thought.

Josh threw me a "not so hard to read" stare as he left through the rear stage door. I couldn't help but notice how cute he looked when he was twisted.

Nick strolled over. "Do you have a boyfriend?"

I sensed the question before he asked it, but the directness surprised me all the same.

"Sorry," I answered. "I don't 'do' boyfriends."

Even I was put off by the edge in my voice.

"Hey," I called out as he turned away. "Your music is on fire".

He did a quick "about face."

I broke cover and let him see me smile. "I live nearby ... in Freehold," I said.

My head nodded in the general direction even if I was capable of getting lost in my own backyard.

"Guess that means we're in the same school," he said.

My smile flinched. The last year of high school was moving in slow motion. I just didn't see the point when I was scoring college-level in every standardized test since sixth grade.

"Maybe I can call you ... if you're not doing anything?" he asked, treading lightly, trying to feel me out.

I didn't say "*no,*" but I didn't say "*yes.*" We entered our numbers in each other's phones. I could hear Nick's thoughts. He was thinking about ... what guys usually think about. I don't think that I had to be necessarily *psychic* to pick that one up.

* * *

The last musician who tried out for our band had a problem with his guitar case. The zipper was stuck, and when he yanked at it too hard, the instrument went flying off the stage.

I don't remember moving to help him. I'm sure my mother did while I regretted blowing half the day on mind-numbing auditions.

"We're almost done," my mother said.

Her thoughts drifted along as she pulled together her things, searching for her "to do" list jotted down on a yellow sticky note that was always sticking to something else. I picked it off the floor and stuck it on top of her hand where she couldn't miss it. She peeled it off, but I didn't see what she did with it.

Barely awake, my eyes flickered.

Nicholas Everett James, I thought. *Anybody with a name like that must be a total narcissistic jerk.*

"Nick likes you." My mother's voice whipped out.

I heard myself whimper. If anything, Nick left me even more hopeless. He reminded me how far I'd need to come to feel even a little bit of the spark in his eyes ... light years it seemed.

I waited for her to ransack my thoughts. It was easier than speaking and so much faster.

"If you *didn't* like him, why did you flirt with him?" she asked.

"Stop," I protested, my eyes open now.

"Every time you put him off, you drew him in," she said.

I wondered now if she was talking about Nick or Josh.

"He's the one who flirted with me," I insisted. "Anyway, he's totally hormone-driven."

"You're doing it again," she said with a reproachful finger.

"What?" I asked, defensively.

"You're using your *gift* to judge people," she said. "There's more to him than the few scattered thoughts you just happened to pick up."

"He's *not* like us," I said, sounding more disappointed than I wanted to be.

"Can't have everything," she said; her attitude cynical.

I watched her zip up her bag. Within seconds, she already knew what I didn't mean to say. Her relationship with Bill, the guy who didn't place on any girl's wish list, was strictly off-limits.

"Don't go *there*," she warned.

I headed towards her with an exaggerated pout. She gave me a gentle squeeze and then released me.

"Genna," she suddenly said, as if remembering something that would decide the fate of the world in the next thirty seconds. "Run by the bookstore and grab some sheet music for Berlioz's *Symphonie Fantastique*."

She left me stunned. *No one* could change gears faster than my mother.

"It's a good inspiration piece," she explained before I could ask. "Nick's guitar opens the door to all kinds of possibilities."

I felt myself react to his name. For a split-second, I wondered whether he would really call. The thought passed as I slipped my hand in my pocket and pulled out my car keys. I leaned forward, giving her a quick peck on the cheek before heading for the door.

"You're looking for perfection," she called out after me. "It doesn't exist in this world."

I turned my head while I kept walking. "If it doesn't exist in *this* world," I said. "Then it doesn't exist."

2. Distraction

Traffic was heavy, slowing down the roads until eventually I found myself in a dead-stop by Monmouth Battlefield Park.

The afternoon sun felt good on my face. There was still some autumn color left on the trees. It was the fire-red maples that I liked the most. A single file followed a winding path towards the visitor's center, eventually dispersing around the field, the site of the historic revolutionary war battle.

My thoughts turned to my parents.

"You know that I'll always love you," my father said.

My hand let go of his arm as he reached for his duffel bag.

"Me too," I said, sniffling back tears.

"Tell me something," he said. "Why do you want to live with your mother and not me?"

I didn't see the point in telling him something that he wouldn't believe.

"She gets *me*," I said, my eyes turned to the floor. "I can't totally explain it."

"Your mother," he began, disapproval churning in his voice. "She lives life larger than most people. Just make sure you know the difference between reality ... *and fantasy.*"

Behind me, the shrieking sound of sirens jolted me from my seat. My head hit the visor as an over-sized SUV who thought he owned the road, cut in front of me. We were moving again. I was about to close the gap between myself and the car in front of me when a super-sleek sedan came from literally *nowhere*.

One thought raced through my head: *Seriously — you didn't just almost hit me?*

As he passed my window, the driver whipped his head around like he had heard me. No time to lock eyes, he whizzed by like he had wings ... ahead of two racing SUVs, weaving so frantically that they forced me into the emergency lane.

Five minutes later, totally out of breath, I ran through the mall and into the bookstore. The music section had been recently relocated. Too impatient to find someone to ask, I wandered around ... tossing gel pens and tasseled bookmarks into a shopper's basket.

Eventually, I heard music, a track that was too good to be a free download.

I barely saw the driver that almost side-swiped me, yet somehow I knew that it was *him* standing in the corner with his face buried in a music scorebook.

The book was actually wrong side up. I half-watched for a few seconds as he flipped it sideways, staring at it from different angles as his fingers moved across the page.

Strange, but boring, I thought.

Not as exciting as thumbing through stacks of sheet music looking for *Symphonie Fantastique*.

It was tempting to say it aloud in a flared-out, lip-smacking French accent.

I started searching alphabetically by composer ... first Bach, then Beethoven. My fingers flipped past different versions of the *Ninth Symphony*. Next up: Berlioz. The section seemed thin.

Maybe I should order it online, I thought.

I looked away, mildly frustrated, when I noticed him again. He was wearing dark glasses, a leather jacket and a graphic T-shirt.

Wearing shades indoors ... someone should tell him that the paparazzi already left, I thought. *Man, is he totally stuck on himself.*

Suddenly he lifted his face and turned to me. He tossed the book aside and began to lower his shades.

I resisted the knee-jerk reaction to look away. I had the unreal sensation that all the activity in the store had come to a screeching halt. As the glasses slipped off, his eyes locked on me. The most perfect green eyes I had ever seen.

Wow, I thought to myself.

He tilted his head sideways. His gorgeous eyes widened.

Wow, I heard his voice repeat in my head.

He was looking directly at me, and yet never uttered a word.

With slow, deliberate strides, I felt the weight of each step as I walked towards him. Barely blinking, he watched me approach. I noticed a scarf around his neck. It had a cool design: little gray skulls wearing long bunny ears.

I was suddenly close enough to touch his face, sculpted with sharp, sweeping angles. His hair seemed different without trying too hard — henna-streaked brown, layered in disheveled pieces.

I reached for the scarf and began to slide it off his neck. He let it happen without moving. I imagined what he must feel — the fabric brushing against his skin. His eyes never left me as the scarf came undone. Then with one hand, I caught it and wound it around my neck, tying it loosely into a double knot.

Inside my head, I heard him say his name: *Byron.*

The sound of his inner voice rolled like a wave.

He swept his eyes across my face as if he was trying to memorize the color of my eyes, the shape of my lips. I sensed vulnerability; a sadness about him that I couldn't draw out. I hesitated, letting the impression wash over me until it was *gone.*

I'm Genna, I thought back with my best inner voice.

But your friends call you Gen or Gennie, he thought.

I nodded.

"Hi Gennie," he said.

This time Byron spoke. A restrained smile fell across his lips. The gesture had a devastating effect, making him even more attractive than he already was — *that didn't seem possible.*

Suddenly I realized that my throat was parched. I left my water in the car.

"Let's get you something to drink," he said.

I abandoned my shopping basket, filled with stuff that I didn't need. He led me to the escalator, walking close by my side.

I said nothing, I thought nothing — I was floating.

We walked into the small café on the second floor. I had been there before but now it looked different. The tables, the chairs, everything in the place seemed newer and brighter.

Byron grabbed two flavored waters and motioned for me to sit. He pulled out a chair for me and slipped into the seat beside me. I watched as he twisted off the cap of my water bottle and handed it to me. I took a couple of sips, partly missing my mouth. He was staring, hanging on my every move. He noticed my hand trembling. I steadied it with my other hand.

"Were you born this way?" he asked as if he felt sorry for me.

I began to think out my response when he said: "Please use speech. I want to hear your physical voice."

I swallowed and then reversed the question: "Were *you* born this way?"

Byron didn't answer.

"Are there others like you?" he asked.

I shrugged my shoulders. "At last count, we were a minority," I said. "That's why it's called *a gift.*"

"A gift," he repeated, his eyes narrowing. "What do you do with this gift?"

I lapsed into silence, trying to wrap my head around the question. He was staring so intensely that I felt exposed, as if he was hacking into my most private secrets one by one. I didn't mind so much if he saw through the bigger events in my life. I was more concerned about the little things that happen when you think no one is watching. *No one* has the right to go there!

"What are you doing?" I asked, my shoulders hunching.

Byron's eyes fluttered as if his concentration was waning. I couldn't tell whether he was pulling back or simply giving up. Within seconds, I knew that neither perception was correct.

"Don't," I groaned; my voice uncharacteristically submissive.

I reached for my water, but I couldn't catch my breath long enough to drink. The fact that he knew my thoughts meant that he knew the effect he had on me. That was totally unacceptable.

"Are you okay?" he asked, his stare softened.

I nodded, but he didn't seem convinced.

"I'm sorry," he said. "I wouldn't have pushed so hard, but you were resisting."

"What did you expect?" I asked, still panting.

"I don't know what I expected," he said.

"Most people would have gotten *the message*." I emphasized the jab with my eyes.

"Message?" he asked with a disturbing lack of ability to follow.

"Yeah," I said, "The one that said to back off."

The shadow of a smile crept over his lips.

"Never ask for something you don't want," he said with a bluntness that drew me back.

He was about to repeat the question — the one that I never answered — when I looked up and asked it for him: "What do you do with the gift?"

Byron seemed almost impressed.

"Why should I tell you," I said, annoyed by his intrusiveness.

He waited.

"I don't do anything with it," I reluctantly admitted, "other than eavesdrop on other people's thoughts. I used to think it was an advantage."

"Explain," he said with immediate interest.

"I just don't think that we're meant to hear everything that goes through someone's mind," I said. "There are things that are better left unsaid and unheard."

He listened intently. I liked how he listened, how he focused on every word. I found myself telling him how separated I felt from everyone else.

"You can't really tell people," I whispered, my eyes shifting to anyone in listening range. "They think that you're either crazy or just making it up for attention."

"How do you deal with *that*?" he asked.

"Not very well," I said, wondering why an explanation was needed since he should have known exactly how it felt.

He let me continue. "My dad doesn't believe me," I said. "He thinks that it's a 'power of suggestion' thing and that my mother has somehow convinced me that I can do things that no one should be able to do."

"Name one thing you like best about her?" Byron asked, leaning back in his chair.

The question caught me off guard.

"My mother...?" I asked.

He nodded.

"She drops everything when I need her," I said.

"Okay," he said. "Name another."

"She totally has my back," I said, smiling hard.

"One more," he said.

The scrunched-up look on my face meant that I was thinking. "She brings out the best in me," I finally said.

"So now you understand that it doesn't matter," he said.

I shook my head, confusingly.

"What do you mean?" I asked.

"It doesn't matter if you can't match her skill," he said while his eyes wandered over my face. "She'll never feel any different about you — so stop thinking that you're letting her down."

I wondered if my reaction to the way he was looking at me was showing. If that wasn't bad enough, he had just zeroed in on an intensely personal issue with total accuracy. Suddenly I began to fidget in place, like I wanted to crawl out of my skin.

"Forget what I'm doing," he whispered, "and tell me more."

"We don't have many friends," I said. "It's easier to keep to ourselves."

"That must be hard for you," he said.

I shrugged. "Sometimes I get depressed about stuff."

"What stuff?" Byron asked, looking under my lowered chin.

"It doesn't have to be about anything," I said. "Sometimes it's just easier to hang out in my room, listen to music *or whatever*."

It never occurred to me that I was talking too much. Somehow I felt like I couldn't say anything wrong.

"You're an exceptionally motivated student," he said with a voice that approved. "What are you studying in school this semester?"

"World history," I said, testing him with an outright lie.

"Narrow focus," he answered with a knowing stare.

The confounded look on my face did nothing to deter him as he jumped from one topic to the next. I watched his lips as he spoke. They were dark pink, softly curved and so full that they almost puckered.

Breathe, I thought to myself.

"Do you play music?" I asked, trying to steady myself.

"I don't know," he replied.

I smiled curiously. "Well, either you do, or you don't."

"I do," he said, more convincingly.

Byron returned the smile. Even though I had the feeling that smiling didn't come naturally to him.

"What instrument?" I asked.

An expression came over his face as if he was feeling for the answer.

"Guitar," he suddenly said.

Thoughts of the band began to fill my head when my phone went off. The ringtone made me feel like I was still in middle school — so I practically fell over myself to answer.

The screen flashed: NICK CALLING....

"Hello," I answered, my voice rattling.

Nick was saying something about wishing me a Happy Thanksgiving. I don't think I actually heard the words he used.

"You too," I said absentmindedly.

The phone felt suddenly heavy in my hand while I watched Byron ... watching me. Again I noticed his hair — that wild, messy look that made him look "rock-god" cool.

Nick mentioned Friday night.

I love Fridays, Byron whispered into my thoughts.

Me too, I thought back. Friday was awesome and so beyond Thursday.

"Do you like Indian food?" Nick asked.

Byron leaned across the table. Underneath his jacket, I glimpsed his T-shirt, a tour schedule printed across it for a band that always sold out before tickets went on sale.

"No," I answered without thinking.

"We can go somewhere else," Nick offered.

"Yes," I stammered. "Um ... I mean — I love Indian food."

I watched as Byron's fingers ran along the grooves of my water bottle, the eco-friendly kind that uses less plastic.

"There's a good place in Colts Neck," Nick said.

I knew the place, and it was better than good. Josh had taken me there on one of our "non-date" nights.

"My Dad might be coming in from Maryland," I said. "I'll have to check with my mother."

Byron reached for the scarf, still wrapped around my neck. I felt a playful tug as his fingers weaved through the fringe. He flashed a brilliant smile — so openly inviting that I had to stop talking. His eyes crinkled when he smiled, and I noticed dimples at the corners of his mouth.

The next thing I knew, the phone was slipping through my fingers. It happened so fast, as if every muscle in my hand decided to let go. I barely caught it before it hit the floor.

"Hello, hello." I heard Nick's voice through the phone.

I had accidentally pressed the speaker, and now I couldn't find the button to switch it off.

"Sorry, I almost dropped my phone," I said. "Listen, I'll see you at the next round of auditions, okay?"

I ended the call before he could answer.

"Do you like using *that*?" Byron pointed to my phone.

He took it from my hand. I watched him run his fingers across the cover. A photo of the earth from space was on the lock screen.

"Excuse me?" I asked; my face astonished.

If he was teasing, it didn't show. If he was deluded, I'd rather find out now.

"You carry this everywhere you go?" he asked.

"Pretty much," I said, rolling my eyes.

I felt sure he was messing with me. Even my mother relied on an unlimited text plan, the kind with free internet service and nine hundred cable channels.

He passed the phone back to me. I couldn't help but notice his hand moving alongside mine.

"You're a good singer," he said, flipping the topic again.

My face tried to look unimpressed, but the scary truth was that I couldn't keep up with him. No matter how hard I tried, I was barely hearing any of his thoughts except those that were specifically directed to me.

For a moment, the idea flashed through my head that he was *blocking*, preventing me from reading his thoughts while he picked through mine — a sort of one-way conversation. The odds of an asteroid hitting were infinitely better.

"You should audition for our band," I said trying to think of something that might distract him from probing deeper.

"I'm *not* from around here," he said. "I won't be here very long. In fact, I should have been home by now."

Suddenly it felt like he had already left.

"That's too bad," I said, my voice deflating like a balloon. "We're holding auditions over the weekend."

Then I remembered the sheet music. I had completely forgotten the reason I came to the mall in the first place.

"Come walk with me, Gennie," he said in a casual way.

He picked up my water bottle and handed it to me. My thoughts went racing.

Say my name again, I thought.

When he said my name, it sounded like he knew something about me that I didn't know. I had to wonder if it was something worth knowing.

"Gennie," he called out.

This time, the sound of each syllable fell apart, gliding over his tongue like warm honey. I felt a gush of excitement in the center of my chest as he gestured with his hand for me to follow.

"This way," he said.

We walked through the store and towards the case holding the sheet music. He reached out his hand as we passed and pulled a copy of music from the case without stopping or even looking.

"Berlioz," he said as he handed it to me.

"Must have missed it," I said.

We walked out into the mall. The light was brighter in the sky-lit atrium. I noticed the hollows beneath his cheekbones, the squared lines of his jaw. His eyes held a moody perfection that was near impossible to resist.

"Medical school is the right choice for you," he said. "Your father will be pleased that you're willing to follow in his footsteps. But the 'band thing' is going to be a problem."

"Man," I said. "You don't miss a trick."

"Does that upset you?" he asked with a slight upturn of his lips.

"I'm just not used to that kind of accuracy," I said, "except when my mother does it."

In general, family members and close friends were easier to read than strangers, the connections were shorter to bridge. Most of the time, I struggled to pick up bits and pieces of what was going on in an unfamiliar mind. If strong emotions were involved, it didn't matter because I couldn't read at all.

"What about you?" I asked as I felt a dull ache move across my eyes. "Are you following in your dad's footsteps?"

"*Not* really." Byron hesitated. "My father has a very large footprint. I don't think I'll ever be able to follow him."

His striking eyes seemed to wander.

"Does your family understand your abilities?" I asked.

"*My family* is very different from most," he answered.

"Everyone thinks *that*," I said.

He cocked his head and gave me a puzzled look. We stopped walking.

"My mother and I belong to a local psychic group," I said. "There's a meeting tonight at my house."

I regretted the way it sounded, like an event better than a music awards after-party.

"Psychic," he repeated, as if the word were unknown.

He was likely too serious about the gift to accept labels, more popular than accurate when used to describe a wide range of extrasensory skills.

"I know," I agreed with my own assumption. "I don't like the word either."

For a moment, I held back unsure of what to say.

"We meet every Wednesday night," I began. "The time allows us to exchange thoughts free of outside interference."

His eyes encouraged me to continue.

"The idea is to be totally immersed in each other's thought patterns," I explained. "It's easier to develop our skills in a supportive environment."

"How's that working for you?" He grinned knowingly.

"The others are way better," I admitted. "Sometimes I think that I would be better off without the gift since the little I have doesn't count for much."

Byron's eyes narrowed. "What does Level 3 mean?"

He had picked up on my unofficial rank.

"On a scale from one to ten...," I sighed. "Level 3 is just a notch up from educated guessing which is why I find a reason to go missing on meeting night." My face mirrored his faint smile. "If you're around," I fished. "Maybe you want to stop by and check it out."

The words stumbled out before I realized that I had set myself up for rejection.

I waited for it.

"Why would I do *that*?" he said. "There's no reason why I should come."

His eyes turned distant, instantly cold.

Okay, I thought. *That's a little more honesty than was necessary.*

An unfamiliar twinge of emotion made me turn away. Ordinarily, I was the one who did the rejecting and *not* the other way around. Even so, there's something uniquely obnoxious about someone who gets into your private thoughts, and then lets you know with an extreme lack of tact … that he's not interested.

"Once I leave," he said. "I won't be back this way again."

The finality of the statement threw me back.

"Point taken," I whispered under my breath.

I didn't remember moving, but I must have because I wasn't in the same place when I found him facing me again. His eyes had softened into a pool of dusky green, but his lips were still *unsmiling*.

"I said that *I shouldn't* come tonight," he breathed, his mouth leaning into my ear. "I didn't say that I didn't want to come."

Just when I thought he was leaving, he motioned for me to follow. I told him about my parent's separation. He told me that his family was from somewhere north of here. He was staying with an uncle in Pennington. He mentioned family problems, the reason why he was here, but nothing more specific. He was a year older than me — eighteen.

We found our way outside.

"I'm parked over there." I pointed towards the blue section on the far right. "I know you're leaving …," I said, practically biting my lip.

"I don't have a phone," he jumped in, his eyes fixed with a gold starburst etched in each pupil. "Did you want me to call you?"

My lips flexed into an awkward smile. The aversion to electronics seemed ridiculous especially when most guys, psychic or *not*, couldn't get enough. Then it occurred to me that maybe this was a way to back out without faking a promise to call.

"Stay vocal," he interrupted. "You keep too much inside. You make mistakes, jump to the wrong conclusions."

"That's way too judgmental," I said pressing my fingers to my temples.

"I wish I could stay to help you," he said, unfettered by my reaction. "Those walls you surround yourself with — they need to come down."

I took a deep breath, trying to control my reaction. I noticed his face, still chasing after me with those amazing pixel-green eyes.

"Don't look at me that way," I snapped. "Who do you think *you are* that you can say stuff like that to me?"

"Who I am has nothing to do with it ...," he began.

Here it comes— the next line, I thought, *the one that blames me.*

"It is you, Gennie," he answered plainly. "If you can't see yourself, then you can't see much and the gift will never develop into anything useful."

Anger rushed in, my thoughts more cutting than anything physical speech could deliver and yet I wanted the last word.

"By the way," I said. "Watch the speed limit around here. You never know when you might hit someone."

He seemed vaguely amused, still processing my remark when I started to back away. Then suddenly I remembered the scarf. Quickly I pulled it from my neck and bunched it up in my hands.

I never saw it move through the air. I never saw him catch it. Suddenly the scarf was in his hand and with one swift movement he replaced it around my neck. My hand felt for the scarf as he adjusted the loop to fall just below my collarbone, his sleeve brushing against my face.

Our eyes met again. When he was done, he flashed a barely-there smile. His feral eyes, deliciously detached ... shimmered in the late afternoon sun.

"I'm glad we met this afternoon and not this morning," he said.

"Why?" I asked unthinkingly; caught in the depth of his stare.

"Because then I would have to wait longer to *see you again*, Gennie."

3. Lost Cause

I took the long way home, the scenic route along a winding road. The laminated sign hanging in my windshield said "*no text zone*," a reminder to ignore my buzzing phone tucked safely away in my bag.

It couldn't be Byron anyway. He never took my number. He didn't have a cell. How technophobic and totally lame was *that*?

Up ahead, I spotted detour signs. No worries when I listening to my favorite satellite station even if thoughts of him kept intruding, standing there in the mall with the smoldering eyes and fleeting smile.

The orange and black arrows that were supposed to get me to the highway suddenly disappeared. Left with one option, I followed the road past a lonely stretch of farmland that eventually opened to the other side of Battlefield Park.

"Are you kidding me?" I grumbled.

My mother's truck was parked at the top of our driveway at a weird angle, practically blocking me. With some effort, I managed to squeeze by without scraping my door.

"It doesn't feel like the holidays," I told Trinity.

I talked first even though *she was the one who called*.

"Where are you?" she asked, hearing the music.

"Sitting in my driveway," I said, preferring to shout instead of lowering the volume.

"It never feels like the holidays," she backtracked. "Totally messed up when my parents split too, but think of it this way — no more arguing, no more pressure to take sides."

I didn't answer. My fingers cut the engine, leaving the key dangling in place.

Daylight was fading. The soft light from the window candles settled on the harvest decorations, revealing the front steps strewn with crimson, gold and plum-colored leaves.

"What's the story with 'Brit guy'?" she asked.

The munching sounds from her mouth reminded me that I had skipped both breakfast and lunch. I dug into my hip pocket and pulled out a guitar pick. Nick dropped it during the audition. I flipped it over and noticed the details: fire-red, mother-of-pearl and curved into a wide triangle ... as if it had the power to fly out of my hand.

"His name is Nick," I said.

My answer veered off into a sigh. She was still talking when I ended the call, the phone dragging down to my lap as my eyes closed. For a moment, I wanted nothing more than to watch the swirling patterns behind my lids. Then a soft breeze blew across my face like a wakening touch. The guitar pick fell from my hand — and my fingers opened around Byron's scarf.

My mother called out as I galloped upstairs, two steps at a time. Stumbling in the dark, I turned on the music before the lights and then jumped across my bed, over a pile of clothes too clean to wash, but too dirty to put away. The sound of an incoming text made me kick away my blanket and reach for my phone. Three texts, and all from Trinity trying to get me to ditch tonight's meeting. Any other time, it would have been the best idea.

I texted back: *Can't :(See u later.*

It wasn't as if I believed Byron was coming. He didn't know where I lived. All that flip-flopping back and forth — one minute he was saying good-bye and the next he was saying, I don't know — something else.

My fingers reclaimed the scarf as if I was warding off a chill, while I faced my mirror, the full-length kind that swiveled back for a better view. The smoky eyes stopped short of extreme, unlike my new favorite lipstick, super-dark, the color of dried blood and probably over-the-top even for me. I stepped in closer and then back again. The metallic-washed jeans and leather bracelets might have been on-trend, but the way I wore them practically screamed: "I'm in the band."

"Total supermodel," my mom interrupted.

She was standing in the doorway.

"Sure," I said sarcastically.

"Hope that memory of him is exaggerated," she said with a growing smile. "Because if that's the real deal — OMG."

"Do you have to use text language when you're *not* texting?" I groaned.

Subconsciously, there was a natural tendency to upgrade the way we remembered stuff; minimizing what we didn't like, enhancing what we did — mostly to keep from being bored to death.

Man, if that's what happened here, I thought to myself. *I totally over-killed it!*

"Can I have a little privacy here?" I yelped.

"I'm *not* prying," my mother insisted. "You're carrying his image in your head like a poster. I can't help but get it."

I started to back away.

"What's this?" she asked, grabbing the scarf from my neck.

"Give it back," I snapped.

"Someone's in a testy mood," she said. Her fingers sank into the fibers, as her nose sniffed out his scent.

I spoke while caught in a daydream, "Did you ever get close to something that you knew was almost perfect ... and then watched it slip through your fingers?"

"Actually NO!" she said.

I avoided her eyes. "He can see through every thought in my head," I said, my voice drifting. "It's like we're playing a guessing game compared to the things he can do."

"Just one problem," she said handing the scarf back to me.

I didn't want to hear about the problem. I knew about the problem.

"Why are we even talking about him?" I complained.

"Oh, I don't know," she teased. "Totally gorgeous, totally hip — a mind-shattering psychic — you know, the kind of thing that you run into every day."

"Okay, just say it," I sighed, impatiently.

"He's leaving," she said, her smile gone, "like his life depended on it."

I began mouthing the words to a song on my playlist. I didn't actually know the lyrics, so I had to fill in what I thought the words sounded like which probably wasn't anything close to the real ones. I stopped somewhere in the middle while my mother stared at me like I was going to break.

"He's completely rocked out," I said.

It was my final opinion and the one that seemed to count above anything else I might be tempted to say.

"He's rocked out all right," she said, musing over the extreme close-up flashing through my head. "He's so rocked out he belongs in a quarry."

"Here's your Berlioz." I handed her the sheet music.

"Thanks," she said, expecting it two hours ago.

"Tell me *more*," I pleaded.

"Sorry," she said. "It doesn't always work that way. Besides, for some reason I'm drawing a blank ... unless he's blocking."

I couldn't tell if she was serious.

Better chance of hitting the *Jersey Lottery*.

* * *

The sound of the doorbell made me jump, like the pipes of a church organ on mood-altering drugs.

My mother raised her eyebrow suspiciously, but I didn't dare wait for her to figure it out. I ran to the door as fast as I could on heels, released the lock and turned the knob.

"When are you going to do something about that bell?" my father grumbled.

I flew into his arms so hard that I almost threw us both over.

"It's nice to see you too, Jack." My mother startled him.

"Hey," he said, removing his jacket. "You know, I almost hit your truck in the driveway. You're sticking out too far."

"Sorry," she said like she didn't mean it. "What are you doing here anyway?"

I started to back away, slowly and carefully so they wouldn't notice.

"You invited me," my father said.

My mother's eyes deadened.

"You said that you couldn't wait for me to get here," he insisted with a clueless smirk.

She caught my arm before I could run.

"All right ...," I yelped, trying to break free. "When I texted him to come over, I might have accidentally used your cell."

She sighed dramatically, shaking her head.

My latest "parent trap" stunt was backfiring faster than usual. Especially since my father had managed to say all the wrong things while still in the doorway. Like a faithful puppy, he followed us to the kitchen. I caught the aroma of tomato sauce simmering on the stove. My mother positioned a long wooden pepper mill over the pot and began to grind.

"Listen Arielle," he said while helping himself to a cup of coffee that couldn't be fresh. "I'm here now — so we might as well have dinner tonight."

He's losing her, I thought. *He's treading too hard.*

"Tonight's our meeting," she said.

"Oh, that's right," he said, pretending to seriously care. "I forgot that Wednesday night is freak-night."

"Dad," I snapped. "Remember *last time* when we said that we weren't going to do *that*."

"Of course he remembers," my mother mumbled.

"Skip the meeting," he insisted.

"I can't do that," she said. "Bill and I are working on a case."

I was hoping she wouldn't mention Bill.

My father wrinkled his face.

"A veteran detective who did two tours in Iraq actually believes that you can find a missing girl," he said. "Get real, Arielle. Even your lucky hunches won't find her."

"Okay guys," I said with my hands up.

"Besides, he's only hanging around because he likes you," my father said as he took his first sip of coffee, bitter enough to spit out. "Now you have my daughter thinking that she's some sort of mind reader in-training."

"Don't talk about me like I'm *not* here," I said. I hated it when they did that.

My mother kept her eyes on the stove. "We found a guitar player today," she said as if he had actually asked. "He's not one of us."

I cringed, nearly choking on the organic soy milk I had just poured myself.

"Looks like this rock band idea has already gone too far," he said.

Extracurricular activities never satisfied my creative side, especially when I felt pressured to sign up for stuff that I didn't want to do. Music was different. I didn't have to try hard. I didn't have to stress. All I had to do was feel it.

"Maybe you need to stop trying to be her best friend," he remarked. My mother grimaced, mocking his scowl with practiced perfection.

"She's *not* my best friend," I quickly corrected. "She's *better* than my best friend."

The warmth of my mother's smile reached across the room.

"You are studying?" he asked, eager for confirmation after just being blind-sided.

"Every night," I assured him. "How else can I get into medical school?" A mixture of relief and pride crossed his face. The best part was that I meant every word.

"That reminds me," he said, his mouth breaking into a hefty smile. "I enrolled you in a college-prep program at Rumson University next semester. It's designed to fast-track honor students."

"That's so cool," I said, my voice super-excited.

My father had managed to redeem himself by finding a way for me to finish high school early. The spring semester was my last before graduation. Now all I had to do was get through the last few weeks before winter break, and I was practically in college.

"Sounds good," my mother followed in a neutral voice.

She replaced the cover on the pot. My father looked at her sheepishly. Then I heard him invite himself to dinner again. Maybe without meaning to, I might have suggested the idea to his subconscious.

Ask her again, ask her again ...

My mother quietly agreed, as she threw a sharp glance my way.

"I have to get back to the city now," he said, "but I'll be back later."

"Dad," I called to him as he walked away. He turned his head.

"How's the conference?" I asked.

The color drained from his face, and that "deer in the headlights look" that I missed so much came into his eyes.

My mother followed him to the door.

"You didn't mention a conference, did you?" she gloated.

"No," he stammered. "She must have reasoned it out." He shrugged his shoulders. "It's a good guess that I was in town for a medical conference."

"Dad, don't forget your phone," I said as I made my way upstairs, gulping my milk. "You left it at the hotel." I watched as he frantically patted his jacket pockets trying to feel for the device.

My mother flashed me a huge ear-to-ear grin.

Show off, she thought back.

4. MIND GAMES

I didn't eat dessert. Trinity and I had planned to grab a frozen yogurt after the meeting. It was a chance to gossip about all the hideous things that people did when they thought we didn't notice.

The doorbell rang non-stop as people arrived. In between, a tap on the door got my attention.

I heard my mom greet *him* with her cheery, hostess voice.

You're skimming again, I thought loud enough for her to hear.

"Skimming" was a way of picking up on obvious thoughts, one part psychic ability and two parts ordinary assumption. Either way she was "scary" good at it.

"Genna has told me so much about you," she said.

I knew what she was thinking ... that my memory didn't do him justice. He was so much better looking.

I tiptoed behind them, half-hoping to catch him unaware.

"I didn't tell her anything that she didn't already know," I said, watching unseen for a few seconds before speaking.

"Gennie," Byron said unsurprised, while he spun around as if he couldn't turn fast enough.

Wow — you're pretty. His voice melted into my head.

My mother didn't react. She hadn't heard him. I struggled to maintain composure. The word *pretty* was ringing in my head louder than my name. I never thought to ask him how he found my house or knew when to arrive exactly on time.

We moved to the sofa. He took a seat beside me. I tried to act natural even though sitting next to him that closely was a pulse-racing event.

Gradually, the rest of our crew trickled in. The moment I heard Josh's voice, my temples began to pound, which meant that his mother had already stepped into the room.

Serena Remi was a mind-purging, and sometimes over-rated, Level 9 telepath. Her presence had an immediate effect on me. The simplest explanation that I could come up with is that she made me sick.

"Hey Genna," Josh said. He hurried past his mother. "I didn't think you were showing up tonight."

I shrugged my shoulders, catching Remi's unwanted attention as she walked by, her sari sweeping the floor with the familiar rustle of silk.

Suddenly she stopped; her eyes on Byron. What little smile she had crumbled into a thin, hard line. Then without saying a word, she sat in her favorite chair, compulsively arranging the folds of her sari while her head turned looking for my mother.

Music would have relieved the more awkward moments, but I could only imagine the reaction if I played something on my phone.

So instead, I ran the music through my head.

"I can *still* hear it," Remi quipped.

Josh slipped out of his jacket and took a seat across from us. I noticed his basic polo with a button down collar, not the rock-worthy shirt he had been wearing earlier, covered with feathered wings and motorcycles.

"I'll be back in a minute," I told Byron.

I didn't want to leave, but Josh was sending signals that he wanted to meet in the kitchen. He was already behind me when his mother's hand forced him back, probably the same hand that chose his clothes for the meeting.

I would have welcomed almost any diversion — anything that is, except for the fourth-grade twins, Chloe and Cassie. Their mother, Lexa-Rose, was busy chasing them around, trying to hold her phone in the process.

The last thing she expected was Byron.

"Are you okay?" Josh asked her.

The yelp was loud enough to hear from the basement. Apparently, Lexa didn't see the ottoman when she reached for Chloe while watching Byron.

She sent me one thought: *Super-cute — is there an app for that?*

I looked away, pretending not to hear.

"We talk to dead people," said little Cassie, batting her prepubescent eyes his way.

"They're mediums," I whispered, just in case he wanted to know.

Lexa, still flustered, straightened herself out while sneaking glances at Byron when she thought I wasn't looking.

Harris, her "techie" boyfriend, was relatively clueless while he ranted about traffic on the Jersey side of the tunnel. In the space of five minutes, he also whined about the weather, no bars on his cell and missing lunch at his favorite sushi place.

I slid the cookie tray over as he opened his laptop, some clunky version that almost no one used.

"And what's with that doorbell?" Harris asked like it was my idea. "It's like a warning siren for the zombie apocalypse."

"Clairvoyant," I mumbled to Byron. "Don't let the un-cool exterior fool you. When you dig deeper, you'll find out that he's even more, un-cool."

Harris narrowed his eyes, ready to comment when he suddenly looked around and asked if anyone had seen Emerson.

Somehow *she* managed to float past us like something made of air, tucking into the window seat with a fleece blanket thrown over her legs, her head darting back and forth as if in communion with unseen beings.

She returned to our existential plane only when someone mentioned Logan.

"Logan's not here," Emerson answered, looking my way. "Hey Genna, you should know that I totally feel it..." She smiled. "You're on your way to a killer band."

Remi scoffed while her eyes scoured the room for the missing one. Trinity was late. If she had any virtues, punctuality wasn't one of them.

"Hey sister," Trinity said, just walking in.

If we "styled" the same, it was because she copied me down to the best accessories. I waited as her eyes moved from what I was wearing — to the new guy sitting next to me. One look at Byron, and suddenly her entire face lit up like she struck gold.

"Man," she said in an uninhibited way. "...And to think that I almost missed this tonight."

"Trinity," Remi barked. "We're ready to start."

Preparing for a meeting was like yoga class: eyes closed, deep breathing and mind emptied of all distractions. All but one — Byron was still in the room.

I whispered to him, "They'll be hard on you if you don't participate."

He tilted his face toward my cheek. "Trust me. I intend to participate."

My hand jumped to my face — to the place where I felt his breath when he answered me. Maybe I didn't expect him to get that close because it was suddenly difficult to join the group as they repeated the words in unison: "Inhale, exhale...."

One of Trinity's eyes opened. I sensed the movement without seeing it. She was watching Byron. She was still wondering about Nick. I had forgotten about Nick. I was still wondering why Josh was twisted tighter than a pretzel. Whatever it was, I was sure that it wasn't my fault.

"Enough!" Remi scolded.

Finally, one last, deep breath and slowly we opened our eyes.

"I'm Trinity," said my "fallen from grace" girlfriend, immediately unleashing on Byron.

I reeled back as she leaned across like I wasn't there.

"Haven't I seen you in school?" she asked, knowing that if she had, she'd be in class a lot more.

He didn't answer. In fact, he remained perfectly motionless, like he was duck-taped to the back of the sofa.

Lexa leaned across the table. "I'm Lexa-Rose," she said. "I'd love to read you sometime."

Trinity rolled her eyes, thinking: *Total cougar.*

Meanwhile, my mother was about to introduce Byron when she realized that she didn't have his last name. He never mentioned one.

"Scott," he said. "Byron Scott."

One of my mother's friends cheerfully remarked that her son's first name was Scott.

Byron didn't turn or raise his eyes. "I know," he said.

"Members only, Arielle," Remi snapped. Before my mother could respond, Bill walked in.

"I'm *not* psychic," Bill said as he roughly grabbed Byron's hand. He made sure to get that point across right off. "I'm a detective with the Marlboro Police Department."

He took a seat beside my mother (a.k.a.: psychic detective). The unofficial title referred to her ability to multi-task between extrasensory skills, making her the undisputed favorite with the local police department.

I didn't notice at what point the conversation took off. When I found myself listening, half the group was using telepathy.

Byron apparently had nothing to say — at least nothing that I heard. He appeared to be at his best when he was seemingly brooding, deep in his own thoughts whatever those thoughts might be. Just as well because the twins were making flirty faces at him and giggling into one another's ear.

If I had a watch, I would be stealing glances by now, trying to think of any excuse to cut the night short. I turned to Emerson, her always-nimble mind capable of cutting through the chatty nonsense and heavy silences of our ill-fated get-togethers.

Say something Emerson, I thought. *Please say something.*

She had been more remote than usual. Now I noticed that she had moved herself from the window seat and sat awkwardly balanced on the edge of a chair, unanimated as a piece of wood with her dark eyes set on Byron.

With one look, Remi let the others know that she was above his influence. Maybe he was used to turning heads with his handsome face, disturbingly appealing in a shallow sort of way. But of one thing she was certain. She wouldn't allow a newcomer to hijack the meeting.

She whipped herself around like a predator ready to charge, and addressed him in her lovely sing-song accent. "You're not especially communicative, are you young man?"

He didn't respond, confirming her observation.

Harris giggled. "Is that his dead man's pose?"

Byron blinked to life just as Bill began talking.

"First I want to thank everyone for working on the case," Bill said. My mother's eyes closed, sensing the inevitable. "But without any new leads..." he sighed. "I'm forced to close the file on this one."

The announcement was hardly a surprise. The case had run cold ages ago, and still there were disappointed rumblings and long sighs of regret — until Byron suddenly turned to my mother with a calm but decisive look in his eye.

"You've missed it," he said plainly.

An immediate buzz took over the room. The others drew near, awaiting a scuffle.

"Excuse me," my mother answered in a protracted tone that emphasized her annoyance. He had caught her off guard, and I never supposed that it was possible to do.

"The girl is alive," he calmly announced.

My mother quickly stood up, almost dropping the coffee cup that had been resting on her lap.

Remi's eyes flew to Byron. "You've come out of your catatonic hibernation to tell us this," she said her voice seething. "You're nothing more than an upstart who should confine his abilities to card tricks."

Byron looked directly at my mother, ignoring the drama unfolding around him. "You've been looking for a red barn where she was last seen," he said.

"That's correct," Bill chimed in. "We checked all the surrounding townships and counties and turned up nothing. Not even a tool shed matching that description."

"That's because it's *not* a structure," Byron said. "It's a place called Red Barn Road."

His eyes were unblinking, as if the image of the street sign was locked in his sight.

"There's *no* such location," Bill said disappointedly. "We covered that lead thoroughly. That's why we're looking for an actual building."

"Over two hundred years ago, it was called Red Barn Road," Byron explained. "The name existed during the revolutionary war and up until the late nineteenth century. It hasn't been called by that name in over one hundred years. You would have known that if you checked the historical record."

I watched Bill retrieve a small notebook from his jacket pocket. I had seen him do this a hundred times before. He clicked his pen.

"Can you tell us what it's called today?" he asked.

"Somerset Road." Byron answered, without hesitation.

An agitated look passed between my mother and Remi.

It was a major route within the area of interest but had been overlooked because the name didn't match, and there was no other evidence to support investigating further.

"A neighbor has her," Byron said. "She's unharmed but you have to act fast."

"You'll need an object," my mother said anxiously. She opened her clue box. "Let me get you a possession, some clothing, a hair tie maybe — it'll help you be more precise."

He shook his head. "I don't need props."

Bill passed him his pen and pad. He held the pen awkwardly between his fingers and wrote down the house number.

"The back door leads to the basement," he said, drawing a rough diagram. "She's in the storage area behind the pantry."

Bill was already on his cell directing police units to the address.

Remi grabbed her smart phone and began downloading maps of the area. She was grappling with the fact that Somerset Road went on for miles and across two town lines, yet Byron had pinpointed an exact address.

"I'm so sorry." My mother handed Bill his jacket. "I've wasted so much time by leading you in the wrong directions."

She seemed on the verge of tearing up. He put his hand on her shoulder. I pulled my eyes away when I saw her respond. I was waiting for my dad to come barreling through the room. I wondered if Bill knew that he was in the house.

"You brought us close," he told her. "That's more than anyone else was able to do up to now."

He stopped short of kissing her forehead when he saw me staring again.

She returned to the living room, looking as if the air had been sucked out of her. Byron remained seated on the sofa, quietly unaffected.

The group was already in the midst of a heated debate, trading ruthless remarks. Worst of all, they were focusing their energies against him — to put him in his place or the place where they thought he should be. Any normal person would have collapsed to the floor and crawled his way out, faster than the door would open.

"I'm getting hungry," Byron said, eyeing the cookie tray on the table.

Remi pushed his hand away just as he was about to reach for one.

"Amazing skill *or* amazing luck," she said. "But before we congratulate you, I'd like to know why I can't hear your thoughts — or is your mind as silent as your mouth?"

I thought that it was just me. Now it was clear that even a veteran reader like Serena Remi had no access to his mind. And my mother — she hadn't picked up on his telepathic exchange either.

I didn't notice who it was that shouted: "He's blocking."

Remi acted as if she never considered the possibility.

"Nonsense," she said with a flighty gesture of her hand. "I would know if he was blocking."

"Absolutely," Harris snickered.

"You must think we're fools," Remi said, turning back to Byron. "I urge you to remember that quite the opposite is true."

"In that case," Byron said. "Why bother challenging when there's no possible way for you to win."

My mouth dropped open. The gasp my mother intended to muffle with her closed fist let go. Lexa faked a need for coffee. Harris followed. The twins ran upstairs, probably to my room, but I was too caught up in the moment to race after them.

Remi, who had a high regard for her abilities, interpreted his defiance as an act of war.

"Let's cool down," my mother advised. "You caught us by surprise," she said, her eyes on Byron. "We didn't expect a serious demonstration of talent tonight."

Angry voices rose up.

"Talent is difficult to deny." My mother spoke in a louder voice as she locked eyes with the best in the group. "On the other hand, modesty might make it easier to accept."

The last part of her remark was directed to Byron.

His face was unreadable as he left his seat and walked towards my mother, taking the seat that Bill had vacated moments ago. "I want to offer my apology," he said in a carefully polite voice.

My mother's lips curved into an accepting smile. His gentle manners had the instant effect of relaxing the crease across her brow.

"I know the extent of your abilities and I didn't mean to suggest...," he continued.

"Apology accepted." My mom stopped him, before he ran the risk of saying something that could get him into trouble again.

The others remained reluctantly silent. Remi was indignant.

"Gennie," he said, turning to me. "I thought we were going to watch some videos?" *Did I say that?* I couldn't remember. The sound of my name made me soar. The next thing I knew, we were in the basement. The vibration of footsteps creaking the ceiling meant that the group was leaving.

"The last season," I said, handing him a box set of DVDs. It was a popular sci-fi series and one that I didn't mind seeing again.

"Very cool," he said as he looked them over.

I lowered the lights, but I couldn't get the video system to work. He stepped in and pushed a button or two and re-inserted the disk. Almost instantly, the picture flashed across the screen as the sound of jetting star-fighters blasted through the speakers.

I caught the shadow of his smile through the darkness. I felt his movements as he turned, but my eyes didn't dare leave the screen.

"Gennie," he whispered ... and there was no way not to look.

My mother shouting from upstairs shattered the moment. The lights turned on from a switch at the top of the stairs.

"Getting late," she called out.

We stood in the doorway.

"Happy Thanksgiving," I said with lips that weren't sure whether they should be smiling.

"Oh, that's right," he said.

My eyes narrowed. "Aren't you going to have dinner with your uncle?"

It seemed plausible since he was living there.

"I don't think he's going to be around," he said.

I denied the impulse to invite him, already sensing another rejection. He read my thoughts faster than I could take them back.

"I can't Gennie," he said. His face darkened. "This will have to be good-bye."

For the second time today, I felt like a weight had been thrown across my chest.

"Thank you for tonight," he said.

"You're the one we should be thanking," I said with a voice that seemed like it was in a freefall slide. "You may have saved that little girl."

He lowered his head as if I was embarrassing him.

"Why did you come tonight?" I asked him.

"I don't know," he said in a voice that felt honest. "I tried to stop myself and then I thought: how would it change anything, who would it hurt if I spent just a few hours here with you...?"

The side of my head leaned against the door, when for an instant I thought I felt the sensation of touch across my cheek. It was impossible of course, because his hands remained fully visible at his side. All the same I reacted — by jumping back.

"You've been leaving since this afternoon," I said. "So why not just leave?"

The sharpness in my voice unsettled us both. I followed the words with a wave of my hand as if I had the power to make him disappear on the spot. It was the last thing I wanted.

He leaned closer and then hesitated.

"Good night Gennie," he said.

5. BOYFRIENDS

There's something about uncertainty ... when things can go either way that makes you secretly hope for the whole thing to somehow self-destruct.

My eyes could barely focus when Nick's name popped up on my phone. I checked the time before I opened the text. No self-respecting rock musician should be up so early *and* on Thanksgiving.

Getting lost in the shower seemed like the best idea, worth the feeling of soft, vanilla-scented skin. I ate around the turkey, the one day a year that my mother served a non-vegan dish. It was late afternoon when I found myself driving in Colts Neck, freely abandoned to a new song.

Nick's address was off the beaten path. My GPS re-calculated twice before it led me up a steep hill. The road split into smaller, inlet roads before I finally reached the top — a place so isolated that the only sound was the whistling wind.

The house was set back, a sprawling estate that looked like a celebrity crib, large enough to hold three houses like mine. An elaborate iron gate at the entrance startled me as it suddenly cranked open. I had just turned around the front of the house when the sound of metal gears made me brake. I glanced in my rear view mirror, towards the end of the driveway. Something about the gate made me wish it wasn't there.

Everything else about the place screamed "fairytale" like the twin sports cars in the driveway, seriously expensive and capable of violating every posted speed limit in New Jersey. I waited for someone to answer the door. The stables were behind the tennis courts, fenced in by a row of spruce trees. Behind the pool and gardens, there was so much land that I couldn't see any sign of neighbors.

The woman caught me off guard when the door finally opened. She wasn't wearing a uniform; just a plain white smock over straight-legged pants but her demeanor was formal enough to make her position in the household understood.

"Good Afternoon," she said, reacting to my outfit, a little edgy in a striving for "rock royalty" kind of way. "Is Nicholas expecting you?"

"Probably," I said. "Can you tell him I'm here?"

She nodded and motioned me inside. The house was spacious and modern, with white sofas that looked more like sculpture than furniture. The woman disappeared behind a closed door.

I sat down in a chair that cupped around me like an open hand. My eyes were drawn to the artwork on the walls, abstract and blue. Somewhere below, I heard the synthesized beat of music, turned up so high that it made the three-story glass walls shudder.

Nick suddenly appeared.

"Genna," he said.

I half-wondered if he shouldn't go back to whatever he was doing, and I shouldn't just leave. The way he said my name fell flat and gave me the feeling that I had just been exiled to this lonely island; a place where no one would ever be able to mesh with my thoughts again.

"Hey," I said trying to wiggle out of the chair.

He held his hand out and pulled me up. He was slow to release it.

"I'm glad you came," he said in a bright voice.

I noticed that he was wearing dog tags, hanging from a black rhodium chain, the monogram of a famous Italian designer inverted so the letters interlocked like a double embrace.

"My parents are at the house," I said, still gawking at his necklace. "It's tense between them." He listened without pressing for details. "It's only a matter of time and they'll get back together again."

"I'm sorry Genna," he said.

"Are your parents around?" I asked. I couldn't see beyond the room where we were standing.

"Somewhere," he said.

It was hard to believe that the house was so big that you could actually lose a couple of parents.

"Come have a look downstairs," he said, motioning towards a set of mirrored doors that at first looked like a closet.

"Totally cool," I said, stepping in. "An elevator in your house."

"You haven't seen anything yet," he said.

The basement was set-up for some serious jamming. Two other boys were there, friends of his he said. He introduced them, but I had to turn my back and pretend I was interested in the autographed concert poster hanging on the wall because they were staring at me so hard that they made me feel self-conscious.

I heard the stuff they were whispering, even the stuff they were thinking. There were comparisons to actresses who I thought looked nothing like me and then some reference to a model who posed in a lingerie catalogue.

Nick did his best to get rid of them, practically pushing them out the door. But they circled around him and got back in. They had every reason to stay. The session wasn't over yet. They wanted to hear me sing. The guy wearing "destroyed" denim jeans and a wallet chain was scheduled to audition for the band.

"This is Liam," Nick said.

I barely smiled before turning away.

"Sorry about that," Nick said when they were finally gone. "Have a look around."

I toured several rooms, full of vintage guitars and rock memorabilia. He flipped on some music that had to be the most outrageous surround-sound *ever*. It was only natural to fall in-sync with the rhythm, especially when the song seemed to know my own feelings.

"What are you up to?" he asked, deliberately moving himself into my space.

My arms fell around his neck as the beat picked up.

"If I asked you to dance with me all night — would you?" I asked.

"Is that a trick question?" His face was in my hair.

I suppressed a giggle.

"If I said no," he whispered; his voice careful. "Then I'm a liar."

"But if you said YES?" I teased, waiting for him to admit to something that I could fault.

"Then I don't deserve you," he answered.

Feeling unexpectedly out-smarted, I stopped dancing. The music stopped with me.

"Have you had dessert yet?" he asked.

I shook my head.

"Come with me," he said, tugging my arm.

I ate the pie in small, slow bites trying to make it last; the thinnest possible slice that could be cut without breaking apart. As far as I could tell, it was the best pumpkin pie ever. He laughed when he saw me push it away and then take it back again.

Back on the elevator, voice command glided us to the top floor. I peeked around the corner into his room equipped with everything that a boy of his age could possibly want.

"It's okay," he said, as I pulled back.

"Can we leave the door open?" I asked.

"No problem," he said, flinging the door open as wide as it would allow.

Once in the room, he grabbed the closest guitar — there were so many of them. He settled down on the floor next to me.

"Do you play?" he asked.

"Very little," I said.

"Let me show you."

He placed the guitar in my hands and pulled himself around. His fingers moved mine in the correct position.

"Just like that," he said pressing my forefinger in place. "The guitar does this ..." He worked the scale off the low E string. "And you do this..." Now he was playing the exact same tune but from the flat third string.

My fingers fell limply on the fret. "Again," I said.

I felt the weight of the guitar ease away as he took hold of the instrument like he was born with it in his hand. I watched him play the tune again but when he switched position to the lower chords, I started singing, following the scale like I was hooked on a wave.

"That's really nice," he said. "Let's try it again."

My hand moved over the guitar. This time it felt more natural.

"I just finished writing this song." He covered my hand with his and strummed out the chords.

Without the synthesizers, the sound was raw. He sang just the first verse but in my mind, the lyrics unfolded ... and I saw what he was doing when he wrote it. I saw the pen in his mouth as he worked the strings, breaking time only to jot it down on paper.

"How do you do this?" I asked, musing. "How do you write music?"

His response was a kiss on the side of my cheek. I wondered how long I had been smiling.

"I have to go," I suddenly blurted.

I grabbed my bag and phone. If they weren't so close to me, I might have left without them.

"Genna," he called after me. "Did I do something wrong?"

Nothing was wrong, but nothing was right.

I ignored the elevator and took the stairs instead, whipping around two landings on my way down. I slowed to a fast walk when I heard the bleep from the elevator. His hand reached over mine, holding onto the doorknob and preventing me from turning it.

"Is it Josh?" he asked. "I thought there was something going on at the audition but I wasn't sure."

"It's *not* Josh," I said just as a text from him buzzed on my phone.

"It's *no one.*"

* * *

I heard his musical voice from downstairs before I had my clothes on. For a guy who was determined to leave, he had a strange way of showing up.

I heard my mother say: "Go on up. She should be dressed by now."

Instantly, I scrambled as the sound of boots pounded the stairs.

On the other side of the door, I heard a light tapping. I flew through the air, my hand over-reaching in order to lock the door as quietly as I could.

Then I backed away.

"Who is it?" I called out, pretending not to know.

It gave me a few extra seconds to try for that "just fell onto the catwalk" look.

"It's Byron," he said.

"Who...?" I shouted while messing up my hair so that it fell in all the right places.

Finally, I released the lock and pulled the door open. There he was — larger than life, luminous eyes framed by softly-arched brows. In the morning light, a sweep of long lashes created a shadow around his lids as good as liquid eyeliner.

He had a single, long-stemmed white rose in his hand.

"It's white," he said waiting for my reaction.

The sight of my favorite flower rendered me speechless. With hesitant fingers, I accepted it from his hand. My eyes closed as the scent filled my head.

"Tell me why it's your favorite?" he asked, tapping his head against mine. "Tell me because it's more fun *that way.*"

I opened my eyes, suddenly aware that he was dangerously close.

"I'm not sure," I said, momentarily obsessed with the smile lines around his mouth like tiny parentheses.

"Is it because it's white?" He pressed me.

No one had ever asked me, and now he was going to force me to think about it.

A quick grin flashed across his lips. "Think extremes," he said.

Extremes were so *me*. Despite my affinity for white, I always wore black or some variation of black — like blue so dark it might as well be black or red so red that it fought to be as good as black.

He sat on my messy bed with one leg crossed over the other. Quickly, I slipped beside him; positioned to conceal a pair of panties, part of yesterday's outfit caught between the sheets.

"It's just easier to see everything else against white," I said.

My fingers twirled the stem while I studied the petals — edged in pink; the color that you wouldn't notice was there if it wasn't reflected by white.

"Tell me more." His eyes moved attentively across my face.

"The petals curve in," I said. "See how they fold in around the center."

"Like a beautiful universe," he said.

Suddenly every word spoken, every subtle gesture seemed oddly poetic.

Byron even looked the part, the kind of guy that should be dressed in a long, flowing ruffled shirt, tortured and dreamy, thinking about things that could only please me.

My mother's voice announcing breakfast interrupted.

My father was already seated at the kitchen table pouring coffee. He had talked my mother into letting him stay the weekend giving her "the holiday traffic excuse" for not driving back.

Byron and I split a bagel. Dad looked up from his paper, giving him a sour grin.

"You were at the meeting," he said while scanning the front page.

"Yes," Byron answered.

"Must mean you're one of them." He flipped the page and folded the paper into a neat rectangle.

We caught each other's smile. When my father said "one of them," I felt like we had just oozed out of a pod in some old-time, black and white horror movie. My mother giggled until a familiar look came into her eyes. She had turned towards the door seconds *before* the bell rang.

My father winced as he covered his ears. "*That* doorbell again," he shrieked.

"Maybe you better get that, Gen," my mother said, her voice uneasy.

"Sorry." "I turned to Byron. "I'll just be a few minutes."

"You can't help *him*," he answered, his face displeased.

My father glanced up from his reading and sighed. I left my crumpled napkin on the table and backed out of the kitchen ... with Byron's eyes tracking me until I was out of view.

Josh was back in cool clothes. He had rescued one of those Chinese take-out menus stuck in the crack of the door. I took it from him with a disinterested hand and invited him in.

He faltered when he sensed Byron in the house.

"Gen — he's *not* for real," he blurted. "Something about him is way too perfect."

"I'm completely aware," I said, defensively. "Is that all you came here to say?"

I wondered if jealousy was fueling his reaction or his mother's wicked opinion. Either way, I knew what was happening when he looked at me that certain way.

"If you try to read me when you're upset," I said, blocking him with my hand. "You'll get your signals crossed."

"Okay," he said. "Then tell me why I should still believe in *us*?"

I started to answer, but he cut me off. "And what's the deal with Nick?"

"There is no deal," I said. "There's nothing."

"Nothing," he repeated sarcastically. "The guy's half in love with you, which you might notice if you weren't so tripped up by mister psychic superstar in the other room."

"That's not fair," I said, my face lowered.

"Tell me something." Josh raised my chin. "How many times do you need to hear that you're beautiful? How many times does it take... to feel alive? Because, deep down you really don't feel anything for *anyone* — do you?"

"Okay, that's just too mean." I cringed.

"I thought we were friends," he said, dropping his hand.

"We are," I insisted. "That can't change."

"Genna," he groaned helplessly. "What do you want from me?"

"I didn't mean to hurt you," I said, overwhelmed.

"Wow," he reproached himself. "My mother and the rest — they were right. I didn't see it because my emotions kept getting in the way."

"I wouldn't blame you if you never wanted to see me again," I said, waiting for a make-up smile, a friendly hug.

When it didn't happen, I reached for his arm.

"I still want to be in the band," Josh said, pulling back as if my fingers had seared him. "But we'll never be friends again."

When the door closed, it felt final like something had ended that I had no hope of getting back.

Byron found me in the hallway, sitting on the bottom step. He sat beside me.

"What are you doing here?" I asked, wiping away a stray tear. "Why do you keep coming back?"

Josh might have been love-sick; he might have been manipulated by his mother, but on one point he was right — maybe Byron wasn't for real.

"This place isn't important," he said, his eyes motioning to the room. "It only means something because I'm here with you."

It was an intensely romantic thing to say and yet I wasn't satisfied.

"Okay, I said, my voice flustered. "Why are you here with me?"

"Change of plans," Byron said; his voice suddenly buoyant. "I'm not leaving; at least *not right now*."

My face must have brightened, but I resisted any reaction that would make me seem deliriously happy. He wasn't leaving now, which was practically the same as staying *indefinitely*.

"Maybe I could audition for your band," he said. "You haven't found another guitar player yet."

I trembled as his hand wandered to mine. He stopped before it got there. Then as if it was happening to someone else, I watched as he slowly and gently lifted it in his.

"What are you thinking?" he asked with a sly smile.

I flexed my fingers and let his hand mold to mine.

"I'm thinking about the last time I prayed," I said. "It was when my dad left."

"And what are you praying for now?" he asked in a hushed voice.

I wasn't in the habit of asking for divine intervention, unless of course circumstances demanded it. Maybe this was one of those times because what I wanted now — what I needed now — was to be with him. I didn't want him to go back to wherever it was where he came from ... to wherever it was he called home. The reason he was here no longer mattered. Maybe meeting him had changed that ... forever.

Suddenly his eyes froze. I felt my hand fall to my lap; my fingers separated and stunned.

"*Don't* come any closer," he said a voice so sharp that it splintered through me. "Stay away from me."

6. Second Chances

Trinity was on the phone. I huddled in-place, prepared for a long conversation, too full of details to text without making a hundred mistakes.

"What's he like?" she asked.

At first I couldn't tell who she meant — Nick *or* Josh. Then I realized that it couldn't be Nick because she never met him. I knew that it wasn't Josh because she knew him well enough that there would be no point in asking.

That left Byron.

I didn't want to talk about him. What was there to say?

Should I say he was almost perfect — that I couldn't imagine anyone so perfect, fiercely perceptive with the face of a prince gone rock-rebel...?

Or should I say that he could turn on me faster than I could blink, take back every sweet word he ever said so ruthlessly that he couldn't have meant it in the first place.

"I think he 'broke up' with me last night," I blurted.

The idea of breaking up may have missed the point. In order for something to end, it had to begin. Regardless, I expected my "sometimes" best friend to say something sympathetic, something encouraging. Instead, she was determined to grill me over my "near miss" boyfriend, with the hope that circumstances would somehow turn in her favor.

I decided to dispense with the easy questions first.

Q. "Where did you meet him?"

A. "Bookstore."

Q. "Who does he know that *I know*?"

A. "Um," I hesitated. "Let's see ... probably no one."

Q. "Did he say anything about *me*?"

I walked to the sofa and plopped myself down between two pillows. My knees flexed to my chest as if I was trying to make myself small and inconspicuous.

"Like what?" I asked, flipping my hair aside.

"I don't know — just anything," she said.

"No Trinity," I sighed with the last bit of patience I had left. "He didn't say anything about you."

"So what's he like?"

She returned to her first-impulse question; the one I had to think hard about in order to answer.

"He's like...," I said. "Zero to Romeo in less than six seconds."

There was dead silence.

"Are you still there?" I asked.

"Yeah," she gasped, her mind unable to let go of the visuals.

My eyes flew toward the front door. The phone slipped down my cheek as I abandoned the sofa.

"Can I come in?" Byron said.

I held the door barely open, my body wedged between so he couldn't get through.

"Please, Gennie," he insisted.

A thin stream of sunlight fell across his face. He seemed pale, his eyes drawn like he was worried or upset.

I shrugged my shoulders and stepped aside, just enough for him to squeeze by.

"I'm sorry," he said, his voice intense.

He watched as I walked wordlessly past him, through the hall and into the living room.

"Gennie, I'm really sorry," he said again, following.

I collapsed on the sofa, my legs dangling over the sides and my eyes fixed on the ceiling. The clouds floated past the skylights; wispy white islands tinged with blue. When the sun threatened to peek through, I blinked hard — my eyes still swollen from crying half the night.

"The sky is amazing," he said looking with me.

He lifted my legs and sat down beside me, resting my calves across his lap. I reached for my phone wedged between the cushions and tossed it inside my messenger bag.

"What does that mean?" he asked.

His hand had latched onto my bag; his fingers slowly traced the raised letters printed across the flap. They spelled: *Gotta Be Green*.

"Tell me something?" I asked, yanking the bag away from him. "Were you dropped on the planet yesterday?"

"And *your point*?" he asked.

Byron's sense of humor, if you could call it that, was super-weird. He liked to play with words so that you thought that he meant "this" when he could have meant "that."

"I'm into environmental issues," I explained.

He smiled playfully as he began tracing the letters on my hand with the lightest touch of his fingertips. First the capital letter "G" and then the small case "o." The contact of his skin against mine made it hard to concentrate.

"I don't understand ... environmental issues." He fumbled the pronunciation.

"What's to understand?" I asked, expecting a challenge.

The pressure of his touch increased.

"You have heard of recycling?" I asked, mildly disturbed.

Byron smiled again, barely shifting focus from his fingers moving across my hand. "Is that what the blue bin in your garage is for?"

Suddenly I grew impatient. The "green talk" was on track if only I could get past his attitude last night.

"When I'm with you," he said. "I forget so easily what I should remember."

"Yeah, well," I said abruptly. "Wish I could forget."

"I already apologized," he said, reading my thoughts. "It isn't fair to bring it up again."

I sighed, unwilling to accept a reprimand.

"Do you remember learning about second chances?" he asked.

"How do you know what I learned?" My voice subtly mocked him.

"I just do," he said.

We suddenly locked eyes.

"Do you know more about me than I know?" I asked. The restrained smile across his mouth made me rephrase, "how much *do you know*?"

He moved a strand of hair away from my face and let his hand drift across my cheek.

"Everything," he said. "I know everything about you."

* * *

A faraway sound drifted closer.

Barely awake, I shifted position. Byron responded by opening his arms around my shoulders as my hand reached across his chest.

I yelled out one word for my mother to hear: "Phone!"

I had no intention of moving because the side of my cheek fit so perfectly in the space below his throat. Besides if the call was for me, whoever it was would have tried my cell first. It was just too un-cool to ring the house. Unless I didn't answer my cell because I had fallen asleep sitting on the sofa, and in that case, there would be a "missed call" on my screen.

I was right. My phone, which had been lying on my lap suddenly lit up with two missed calls. Finally, my mother answered from another room. I pieced together the conversation from her thoughts since all I actually heard were clipped one-word responses.

Nick had called, asking if auditions could be held at his house rather than the high school auditorium; something about having to watch his little brother. Despite my mother's aversion to basement bands, she agreed.

An hour later, Byron and I were driving in Colts Neck. My mother had picked up Logan and was following behind.

They were passing through the "monster" gate when we pulled around Nick's driveway.

Logan pulled me towards her in a tight squeeze that made me cringe, my shoulders reaching high enough to touch my ears.

Where do you even find clothes like that? I asked myself.

Strictly speaking, we didn't "style" the same, and yet there was one thing we shared that should have drawn us closer had we liked each other in the least: pathetically weak, undeveloped extrasensory skills.

"Hey Genna," she said.

I didn't answer, still trying to recover from the bear-hug.

"Love the fedora," she said pointing to my black felt hat. "It's *fedorable.*"

Leave it to Logan to use some corny, made-up adjective to describe an accessory that was seriously trending.

"Did you happen to show up at last week's meeting?" she whispered.

I sighed, and then shook my head.

"You know what I think," she said. "If you can't be the best at something then why bother."

I didn't completely disagree but at least I never gave it up, *not totally.* At least I showed up at the meetings, *now and then.*

Logan turned to Byron.

"Hi there," she said in a girly-girl voice.

Trying to be sexy when she wasn't — that didn't bother me. It was how she leaned into him that made me instantly imagine her falling into the hedge behind us. I couldn't tell whether it was a vision or just wishful thinking because when I looked again, I saw her covered in mulch and broken pine needles.

Byron tucked his hand in mine, pulling me along faster than I wanted to go with my arm stretched out all the way.

"I thought you didn't have a boyfriend?" Nick's voice whipped out low and harsh as we descended to the basement.

All I could manage was a blank stare while my mother and I took refuge in the back of the studio, perched high on two stools that were perfect for viewing.

Logan pulled out her music and played something traditional, nothing more than a warm-up piece. My mother stopped me from yawning. Then Nick handed her the music for a tune that I had heard only bits and pieces of before.

"It's a work in progress," he said, "but give it a try."

She positioned her instrument under her chin and signaled "ready."

It was obvious that no one expected her to adapt so easily, least of all her. As far as I could tell, the sound hit the mark, scratchy with a cool gypsy style.

My mother commented first, "The violin adds a whole new dimension." She tapped her forefinger to her lips. "What do you think Nick?"

"No question that it works," he said, trying to be enthusiastic while his eyes moved from Byron to me, and then back again.

Logan placed her violin into its case and took a seat by my mother. I could read her like an 18-point font. She was psyched over her audition but mostly ... she was thinking about Byron, and wondering if her ability to morph into a rock violinist had his attention.

Or not, I thought back.

The auditions continued. Nick's idea of staging twin lead guitars was a trend from another decade, each instrument synchronized with harmonious riffs for a more powerful effect. Liam was up first. It barely took a minute of working the chords to see that he was super-skilled. In fact, with the exception of Nick, I couldn't imagine that there was better.

Byron's turn next.

"Where's your guitar?" Nick asked.

I didn't notice until now that he had no instrument.

"I forgot it," Byron said.

"You came to audition without an instrument," Nick scoffed. "Never mind — let's just get this over with." He opened a glass case and pulled out a guitar. "Just be careful," he said. "It's practically priceless."

"He can use mine," Liam offered.

Nick held his friend back with a firm glare. If I read him right, the vintage guitar was a whole lot trickier to play. Before I could intervene, Byron willingly accepted Nick's guitar, his hand spinning it awkwardly, upside-down and then wrong-side around — like he had no idea how to hold it. After a little rougher handling, he finally found the correct position.

Liam and Josh locked eyes. I was seriously worried that Byron was about to embarrass himself.

"How long have you been playing?" Nick snickered.

Byron ignored the question. "I'm ready," he announced.

"So are we." Nick grinned, expecting the worse.

The first sounds didn't disappoint either. They were spine-wrenching, ear-splitting "fingernails on a blackboard" chords. Nick was propped up against a wall with his arms folded across his chest; rolling his eyes in my direction as if I needed him to tell me that it was worse than bad.

Josh hid behind his drums as if they were a sound-proof shield. Logan cupped her hands over her ears, pretending to adjust her earrings. I watched my mother wince from across the room. She began to raise her hand to cut the music, a gesture that was more like a defense maneuver than a stage direction — when the chords seemed to flow into a semblance of order.

Suddenly, the guitar sang in Byron's hands with skillfully raw, appropriately distorted riffs, the kind of rapid playing worthy of rock legends.

My mother moved in closer. She had been worried that we wouldn't find another lead guitarist that could keep up with Nick. Now her eyes were glued to Byron as if he was channeling an interactive video game — the Pro Edition.

"Thanks," Byron said, returning the guitar to Nick's waiting hand. "I'm sure that I can play bass too."

The expression on Nick's face was a combination of shock and disgust. "Where in the world did you come from…?" he blurted so loudly that his accent almost disappeared.

Byron walked over to where I had been watching.

"Don't worry," he said, blotting the sweat from his face. "I'm in the band now and there's nothing Nick can do about it."

7. STRANGER

I hate it when I lose my phone, and I'm forced to ring it from a land line and hope that I can hear it. It was ringing somewhere in the living room, the sound bouncing off the walls. Desperate, I resorted to a slow crawl across the carpet until my head bumped his knees.

"Looking for this?" Byron asked, my cell in his hand, the word "Home" in bold letters across the screen.

"Thanks," I said as he released the phone into my hand and slowly stood me up.

"Hi," he whispered with a growing smile.

His hands slipped into mine.

"Hi," I repeated.

His lips brushed my eyelids, forcing my eyes closed. To myself I began counting, hoping he would still be there when I reached ... *ten.*

In my mind, I had a definite idea of how a guy should look, how he should feel. There was never a time when I didn't feel let down in some major way. Either they looked all wrong — buzz cuts and flip-flops were the ultimate turn-off. Or they acted so immaturely that it was embarrassing just to be standing next to them.

"Ten," I said aloud ... like I was daring him to evaporate from the visible plane.

My eyes opened and there he was — knockdown, out-of-this-world gorgeous. He wore a black suit with a thin tie loosened at the collar. His hair was flawlessly disheveled, and a barely-there beard shadow covered his face.

"Let me look at you," he said.

I stood back, craving the attention, yet embarrassed by it at the same time. The dress was black, not especially revealing, but form-fitting with leather lace-ups that ran along the sides like a corset.

The plan was to meet my parents in New York. My father made dinner reservations at The Museum of Modern Art. I was so proud of him for coming up with the suggestion, since being the sole mastermind of "Operation: Get Back Together" was beginning to wear me out.

"Have you been to this museum?" I asked Byron.

In a city with museums on every corner, this one had to be hands-down the coolest.

"I don't think so," he answered.

I watched helplessly as he lifted my right hand it to his lips … just shy of actually making contact. The longer he held back, the more intense it felt.

"I can let you hear what I'm thinking," he said. "But it's better if I just tell you."

"What?" I asked, too distracted to hear right.

"You're so beautiful, Gennie," he answered.

I didn't dare blink when he leaned in and kissed my cheek. I don't think that I actually tripped or stumbled. I simply veered off my gladiator stilettos falling slightly into him. He steadied me with his arms, slipping them around my waist for support.

"All right?" he asked.

His eyes melted into mine, liquid green.

"Yeah," I said, dazed.

We lingered for a moment before my mother walked in to remind us that we had better leave soon if we wanted museum time before dinner. We instantly pulled apart although I was pretty sure it wasn't fast enough. She knitted her brow as she walked away.

"Almost forgot," I said as I grabbed my bag.

It felt heavier than usual because I was carrying a second phone.

"Hang onto this," I told him.

"What's this?" he asked, taking the phone reluctantly from my hand.

"It's one of those disposable phones," I said.

He smirked.

"Honestly," I said. "What's the big deal?"

"What should I do with it?' he asked, looking at it like it was a useless toy.

"Uh ... use it," I said. There was an awkward moment during which, I seriously regretted getting it for him. "I mean ... if you ever want to call me — ever."

"Oh," he said, as if the thought never occurred to him.

"You know," I said, totally annoyed. "If you're not going to use it — then I'll just take it back."

"Thank you," he said, keeping the phone from my snatching hand. "I'd really like to have it — *please*."

* * *

Busy people with busy lives rushed through congested streets. We ran with the pace, skipping over steamy manhole covers and zigzagging between crawling cabs and buses. Twice we got separated, swarmed by fast-moving crowds spilling onto the sidewalks.

It was obvious that he wasn't used to the city. He moved awkwardly, spinning around to gawk at stuff that wasn't worth noticing. The expression on his face was always the same, distant and preoccupied, even if his eyes occasionally betrayed the slightest fascination.

A gust of cold air chased us down the last block towards the museum entrance. Given the fact that it was already mid-afternoon, it made sense to see the new exhibitions. The permanent galleries would have to wait for another time.

I so wanted another time.

"Nineteenth Century European Impressionism," I said in a low voice, reading from the sign in the lobby.

A collection of paintings was on display in a small gallery on the second floor. We headed towards the escalator.

"I use the names of famous artists for passwords on my computers," I said like it was the best idea ever. "Monet, Van Gogh, Cezanne..."

"Good to know," he said, suppressing a giggle.

I took hold of his sleeve and pulled him away from the first painting to an appropriate viewing distance.

"Impressionism works best when you stand back," I said. "If you're too close the images get lost."

Another step back and the painting suddenly flashed into focus: tall cathedrals washed in pink, white and blue; some doused in sunlight, and others muted by shadows.

"There's more," I whispered, moving to the water lily paintings.

The three panels, mounted side-by-side on the wall, were painted in sheer, luminous veils of blue and green with thick swirls of white rounding out the shape of floating petals.

"I like the reflections in the water," he said, trying for a smile.

"Hey," I said, watching him. "Tell me what's wrong?"

"Nothing Gennie," he said with his eyes immersed in the painting. "Right here, right now it's hard to believe that anything could be wrong."

I noticed the gift shop.

"Last time I was here on a class trip there wasn't time to stop," I said. "I was so bummed out because they have the coolest stuff."

"Wait here," he said, giving me a slow kiss on my forehead that left me stunned.

I watched him walk towards the shop until he was out of sight. Somehow, the warmth in the room left with him. Maybe it was my insecurity, or maybe it was something else ... like the man standing next to me, giving off the weirdest vibes.

I backed away and found a bench opposite an awesome painting that reminded me of spring. The landscape was iridescent green with thick brushstrokes that seemed to run in opposite directions.

Suddenly I felt the cushion depress as someone sat beside me … someone large, weighted down by heavy garments. I took a peripheral peek and noticed an umbrella, the pointed tip scratching against the marble floor.

"Are you with the docent tour?" he asked.

The man had a museum guide in his hand, but I got the feeling that he had just found it lying somewhere.

"No," I answered, resenting the interruption.

"I'm *not* a mind-reader," he said. "But I'm willing to bet that you really like that painting over there."

I shifted uncomfortably as my eyes moved to the entrance where Byron would eventually emerge.

"Claude Monet painted that one in Paris," he said, tilting his head.

The Eiffel tower flashed through my mind as I turned to a painting of a woman with a large feathered hat walking under a wispy, winter sky.

"Monet's wildflower garden," he said, pointing to another painting. "It was done at his country house."

I checked the time on my cell.

"You strike me as the kind that would go in for the more avant-garde stuff," he said.

I sighed heavily hoping that he would get the message.

"I don't like stepping away from convention," he continued. "It makes me uncomfortable."

My stomach clenched with a sudden uneasiness and for whatever reason, I disliked the man. Maybe it was his sarcasm-tinged speech or the way he seemed to sneer and taunt with an exaggerated self-importance. He probably meant no harm, and yet the childhood warning to avoid strangers was so perfectly instilled in me.

"When I was young," he said, "I was more interested in football than in art." He expanded his chest to demonstrate physical strength that was no longer there. "Later on I transferred to a military academy."

I smiled at a woman who recognized the disinterested look in my eyes.

"The way I saw it...," he said. "The interest of the country superseded my own personal interests. It still does in a way."

Without saying a word, I picked myself up and walked to the other side of the gallery. The guard was standing against the wall. A small group gathered in front of a painting that hung alone, surrounded by rope to keep people from getting too close.

"Beautiful girl like you shouldn't be here on your own," he whispered.

The sudden heat of his breath against my face made me turn so fast that I almost lost my balance.

The movement alerted the guard. "Anything wrong?" he said walking over, his eyes moving between us.

Before I could answer, the stranger spoke but *not* to the guard who was waiting for a reply. *He spoke to me.*

"He's back now," he said.

I turned to find Byron walking through the gallery.

I glanced back at the guard to tell him that I was fine, when suddenly I realized that the stranger was already gone.

The touch of a hand on my shoulder made me jump, knocking my handbag to the ground.

"It's only me," Byron said, retrieving my bag from the floor. "Are you okay?"

"Yeah, I'm fine," I said taking my bag from his hand. "It's just that my head hurts."

The first twinge of pain had reached my temples.

"You're upset," he said.

I shook my head. "It's nothing."

"Really?" he asked, unconvinced. It was obvious that his psychic prowess would make it impossible for me to dodge him.

"There was this older guy — really creepy," I began. "He spooked me out a little and then bolted when the guard came over."

I couldn't help but notice how his smile faded while his eyes scanned the gallery.

"I'm sorry I took so long," he said, turning back to me. "There was a huge line."

My continued wincing roused his concern. He took my arm and led me to a seating area in the center of the atrium lobby. I squeezed into a slim space, shoulder to shoulder with mostly tourists. There wasn't enough room for him to sit, so he knelt down instead, with his arms balanced on my lap.

"I'm sensitive around people that I don't like," I confessed.

Byron's hand pressed the side of my head. The pressure felt good against the pain.

"You have good instincts," he said.

"The others in the group ... they say their minds are too powerful for me to handle," I said. "They say that I haven't built up enough resistance."

"Remi?" he asked.

"She's totally toxic," I said. "She latches onto my thoughts and I can't spring free."

"I'll teach you ways around that," he said.

Suddenly we realized that, despite our hushed voices, people were listening. They may have been sitting back, staring into cell phones, but they caught enough "wild talk" to lock eyes with us— and *not* in a good way.

The lady next to me grabbed her things and abruptly vacated her seat.

I turned to Byron, "Is that for me?"

"I almost forgot," he said. He slipped beside me and placed the bag on my lap.

"Looks like you raided the gift shop," I said reaching inside and pulling out art calendars, postcards and magnets. "How did you know that I totally love this kind of stuff?"

"Lucky guess," he said.

* * *

My parents called to say that they were running late.

The hostess behind the reception desk turned the pages of a leather-bound book, checking for the reservation. She would have found it faster if she could manage to take her eyes off of Byron.

We were already seated when my mother came barreling through the dining room complaining about something my father said when she told him to go right, and he went left.

"We're late because you made me follow the navigation, and it was wrong," my father accused, defensively.

"Oh, excuse me," she said. "The GPS is wrong and you're right!"

Byron and I locked eyes.

I whispered. "Do you ever wish that you could run away?"

"Actually, yes," he said, catching my hand under the table.

After the first two courses, my parents ran out of things to fight about. The conversation moved from the menu to museum exhibits to college plans next year.

"What are your plans?" my father asked Byron.

"My father and I haven't talked about it," he said. "He's been a little preoccupied with my sister."

It was the first time he mentioned siblings.

"I hope everything's okay?" my mother asked.

He gave her an unreadable look. It was probably a sensitive subject and neither one of us wanted to force him to answer a lot of awkward questions. Although the obvious problems popped into my head: drug problems, unintended pregnancy.

"Genna has the advantage of being an only child," my father said.

I gave the statement careful thought. If my mom decided to re-marry, I could lose my first-child status. I'd be someone's "big sister," a built-in babysitter for my mother and her new husband which under the worse scenario could be Bill. I suppressed a giggle, realizing that I was getting worked-up about nothing because there was no way she was getting pregnant. She was way too old.

My mother jabbed me with a sharp look, cleared her throat and changed the subject.

"I have some exciting news," she said as dessert was being served.

It would have been nice to hear that my dad was moving back in and that all the petty nonsense between them was over. Another sharp look caught my eye as she repressed the reprimand that she thought I deserved.

"I booked our first live show at the new club down the shore," she said, digging her spoon into my custard ... until half the serving was lifted from my plate.

"Hey!" I complained.

"The club on Ocean Avenue?" my father asked.

He seemed skeptical.

"That's the one," she said, licking the back of her spoon. "The owner was so impressed when he heard the promo CD. He just couldn't believe Byron's solo."

As usual, there wasn't a noticeable reaction registering on Byron's face. Most bands lived and died by the vocals, but I was only too happy that he set us apart, amongst tough competition, the kind that made the Jersey Shore home to more than a few high-profile bands.

"There's so much to do," my mother said.

"There's nothing to do if you call the whole thing off," my father jeered.

No one was listening.

"Of course, we'll have to rehearse," she said, whipping out her phone.

"No worries," Byron reassured. "You can count on me."

8. STAGE FRIGHT

I didn't want to be *that girl* — the one in a state of torment because he didn't call. The last time we talked was two nights ago, long enough to convince myself that I might never see him again. To make matters worse, I was fighting back a sudden case of stage fright.

"It's not like you'll be out there alone," my mother reminded. "The band will be there."

Some band, I thought.

Except for Nick, we were a band of outsiders — all gifted with what most people called a "sixth sense." While I could depend on them musically, I wondered if there was anything else to keep us together. I couldn't stand the sight of Logan. Josh was barely speaking to me, and Byron was missing in action.

Nick was the only one who wasn't acting like a total jerk.

"It's our first show," my mother said, glancing at her watch. "He'll be here."

I couldn't tell if she believed herself. She pressed her lips to my forehead and told me that she would be back later.

Now I was in countdown-mode with less than an hour before the doors opened. I decided to check for messages. That annoying, mechanical voice triggered when I tapped my password: *No Messages.*

I scrolled down my contact list until I found his name. It would be a good time to call him, assuming he actually had the phone I gave him.

But what if he answered ... what then?

Maybe I could say something like: "Hey, what's up? I'm here at the club for sound-check, and you're *not.*"

I wasn't sure if I was capable of being casually calm. No matter what I said, the frustration would leak into my voice and make me sound desperate.

I decided to wait it out, lose myself in the sound of chords raging through an amplifier. Nick was sitting cross-legged on the edge of a drum case, playing with the upper fret of his guitar.

I flapped my hand to let him know that I saw him.

He gave me a smile, the kind that had a good chance of breaking into a giggle *if I could only hear him*. It was impossible to hear anything above Josh's drums, reminding me with every crash of the symbols, how our last conversation went.

"We'll never be friends."

Nick looked up again from his guitar, his fingers mindlessly strumming.

Nick was all about the music. While Byron was mostly indifferent, skipping rehearsals and band meetings without a single thought. Then when no one was watching, he would suddenly reach for his guitar like it belonged in his hand.

"You know the song," he said after one of his scorching solos. "You know how it begins but you can't tell how it will end."

He was right. I didn't know how it would end. Maybe I had an idea though. Maybe the band was just a distraction for him — something to do while he waited around, until it was time for him to finally leave.

I abandoned the thought and moved center stage. My voice ran through scales until the sound engineer gave me a "thumbs up." The warm-up relaxed me enough to sing a few lines from one of Nick's three-minute love songs. Instantly, he looked up with the kind of approval that made me feel strong again. I walked towards him but not for his reassurance or for the way he had of making me feel safe and normal. I walked towards him because he would listen, and what I wanted to do now was vent.

"I can't look at *her*," I said as if I expected him to know.

Logan sat on a speaker stack with rolling wheels. She lowered her violin and rested it on her lap.

"What's on your mind?" she asked; her tone already defensive.

Nick placed his guitar down. "What's going on?"

"Tell him," I said, staring at her. "It's time to drop the innocent act."

My voice was loud enough to end Josh's battle with his drums.

"What are you talking about?" she asked, her eyes fluttering.

"I logged on to my computer last night," I said.

She shrugged. "And...?"

"And...," I snapped. "You won't get away with it."

"If you have something to say," Logan said. "Just say it!"

Josh leaned back whistling part of his solo while he balanced a stick between his fingers like a baton.

"Save it until after the concert," he said, rescuing the stick out of a spin.

The cold way he put me off made me pounce on her.

"How could you post that stuff about me all over the internet," I said.

At first she threw me a blank look. For a second, I believed her ... that she didn't know what I was talking about.

"Whatever you think," she said. "You're wrong." She paused. "It wouldn't be the first time."

"Guess not," I mumbled. "At least I didn't give up. You don't even try to *read* unless it's text."

"That bothers you, Genna?" she asked. "All this time I thought you felt exactly the same way."

I couldn't say why I faulted her for rejecting the whole "paranormal thing;" maybe because I couldn't ... *not* completely. As much as I didn't want to admit, it was part of who I was.

"If I want to know something about someone," Logan said with wide eyes. "I'll do what comes naturally — I'll ask."

"Whoa," I said sarcastically. "Why didn't I think of that?"

Josh's sticks fell to the floor ... as if to remind us that we were in "mixed" company. Nick wasn't one of us. Not that it mattered, since he was more likely to think that we were stark-raving crazy than consider anything even close to the truth. Already there was a look in his eyes that felt like he trying to rewind the conversation in order to think back to what he thought he had missed.

"Uh...you've lost me here," Nick said, shaking his head.

"Don't mess with me." I warned Logan. "I know it was you."

"Chill out," Nick said, suddenly standing behind me.

Josh bolted from the stage with Logan towing behind.

"Hey," he whispered in my ear. "Whatever she posted online — we'll find a way to get it off."

I felt his fingers press my shoulders.

"It's going to be fine," he said, turning me around. "I'll make it fine."

His arms were a safe place to land. I felt my head roll against his chest while whispered assurances gave way to a kiss, the slightest pressure — very quick on the side of my cheek. But before the smile set on my lips, he suddenly straightened up.

My head bounced up like I had been doused with ice water. Byron was staring us down, a hard frown distorting his mouth.

"You're late," Nick said, holding me tighter.

"Looks like I got here just in time," Byron snapped.

Nick reluctantly released me, and then disappeared behind the stage muttering something that wasn't meant for me to hear.

"What's going on?" Byron asked.

"I've never performed for a live audience," I stammered. "I have stage fright."

I wanted to linger while that bothered look was still on his face. Payback for every time he made me feel like it could be the last.

"How convenient," he snarled. "That Nick was around to take the edge off."

"Don't read into it," I said.

Suddenly his eyes seemed more hurt than angry.

I resisted the feeling of wanting to stand on a high place and scream out to the world: "How can I be in a relationship that isn't?" A relationship that seemed as temporary as a full moon, and yet intense enough to make we feel like it was forever.

Byron followed me backstage.

"Is that outfit 'street legal'?" Logan taunted.

I was leaning over a mirror framed with yellow incandescent bulbs, the kind that highlighted every imperfection.

"Why don't you call the fashion police," I snapped.

Before I knew it, someone said it was time. We mumbled a few words of encouragement to each other. Even Josh threw me a smile.

The stage dimmed as we found our places. The music crept in slowly. Once I heard the cue for vocals, I jumped in and instantly forgot about the audience. The guitars and drums came alive like a high-energy explosion.

I sang the first verse and then leaned away from the microphone. The vocal breaks gave way to some seriously awesome solos.

Byron held his guitar like an axe, wielding it up and down, and then side to side. He played scrunched down on his knees. He played with one leg balanced on an amp, his face focused on the finger-play, agile and super-fast. Then he ran across the stage and up a flight of steps that were half-hidden in purple fog. The guitar screamed as he jumped off a speaker stack, ending up somewhere between Nick and me.

The audience roared.

Had we rehearsed that? I asked myself. *We never rehearsed that.*

Next Nick moved to center stage, his hair hanging in his face while he phased in with highly-controlled riffs. Byron's guitar responded when it should have been silent. Note for note, he tracked the rhythm ... and virtually stole Nick's solo.

We finished up with two encores and headed backstage.

Byron's face was flushed as if he had just run laps. I pushed away a soaking strand of hair and let the moisture run down my wrists, between my triple-wrapped bracelets, layered to my elbows.

"Dance with me," he said, panting wildly.

Something was different. Something I wasn't used to seeing. He was smiling hugely and with his entire face.

I didn't have the best dance moves, but suddenly I wanted to learn. Besides, everyone I practically knew was on the dance floor — people from school, the rest of the band — some of who couldn't dance to save their lives. Even my mother and Bill were out there, which was just too weird for words.

Byron slipped his arms around my waist and drew me towards him. Our faces were so close that if someone had bumped me from behind, the kiss would be inevitable. Suddenly a switch in tempo made us reel apart. For a moment, neither one of us knew what to do.

I looked up and saw Trinity dancing with Josh.

When did that happen? I thought.

Then the song took off with a burst of colored lights. I spun around with my arms in the air. Byron mirrored my moves as I shimmied low and then came up again. The second spin was faster. My hair whipped across my face as I turned, just about to face him again when I saw Nick there instead.

I skipped backwards and then stopped. Byron pushed him back with both hands. Nick quickly reversed direction and rammed into him. For a moment, the action slowed, like a storm gathering momentum. A crowd was closing in around us. Byron flashed a sadistic smile ... and with one easy motion, flung his arm against Nick and nearly knocked him to his feet.

The gasping sounds from my throat were drowned by the music. I felt only the vibration when I screamed: "Stop!"

My mother was already there, standing beside me. Bill had managed to wedge himself between Byron and Nick, each of them practically jumping over him to reach the other.

Now was the time my mother chose to reveal her ordinary hero — from the time Bill played quarterback in college. Some of the images were hard to take, like the time he was running from sniper fire in Iraq and couldn't save his best friend. There were proud moments too ... when he stood at attention waiting to accept the Silver Star for valor ... and then private moments alone in his bedroom, sitting on the foot of the bed when his wife died.

"You guys are either going to break it up now, or we'll end this in the police station," Bill shouted.

The force of his voice detached me from my mother's thoughts. So much was happening that it felt like a traffic jam inside my head. People had started to take sides. The lights were still extreme, flashing like laser beams while the music pitched high.

I began backing away ... when I felt a shove from behind. All at once, my foot slipped. Bill caught me before I went down.

The fighting stopped.

"Are you okay?" my mother asked.

"Someone pushed me," I cried.

When I glanced over, I saw the two girls who were standing there, side by side. My eyes went to Trinity, and then to Logan. If I had to bet, I was betting on the cyber-bully.

"Sorry," Logan said. "If I did ... I didn't mean to."

Not that it excused her in the least, but the boots I was wearing were super-high. Theoretically, a stiff breeze could have sent me flying.

"Sure you did," I responded. "You meant it."

I watched her stomp away in a fit of tears. Josh disappeared into the crowd after her.

"You're getting ahead of yourself," Byron said. "With Logan I mean."

"Now you're defending her?" I snapped.

"No, of course not," he said, "but wanting to believe something doesn't make it true."

"I suppose you know the truth," I said.

He didn't answer.

My mother interrupted with an invitation to join her and Bill at the diner, something about having breakfast at midnight. Nick wanted to catch a late movie.

"No," I said to both.

When I turned to say good-night, Byron was gone. My eyes searched around, but I knew better. He had left without a word.

"I'll follow you to the house," Nick said.

Trinity was still there, standing behind him and looking at me strangely.

"Thanks," I said. "But I'll be fine."

I threw my arms around my mother and then Bill, who seemed genuinely stunned that the girl who wanted nothing to do with him because he wasn't her dad had suddenly behaved ... almost human.

"Be careful, Gen," Bill said. "We'll see you back at the house."

I worked my way towards the lobby. That was when I saw *him*. The man was just a blip in a sea of faces ... only his face didn't belong. He wasn't young; he wasn't hip. He was only familiar because I had seen him before. He looked my way for a second and then he was gone, absorbed in the moving crowd as they drifted towards the exit.

9. Night Vision

The music was jamming in my head before the song came on.

I followed the road carefully, my two hands clutching the steering wheel, shoulders leaning in and eyes squinting into the windshield like someone's grandmother.

The turn was hard to miss because of the old Tennent church. From a distance, the steeple rose above the trees, glistening white against a starry sky.

Slowly, my hand relaxed off the steering wheel as I came to a stop. The night was cold. A frosty drizzle had begun to stick to my windshield. I wondered about Nick. By now, I should have heard the rumble of his engine.

My eyes circled uneasily.

The intersection was deserted except for the SUV braking behind me with dark windows. Luckily, the light turned, but before I could react, he flashed his high beams.

Driving faster than I should on a winding road, I wondered if I wasn't imagining it when he seemed to turn when I turned — weaving in and out of lanes around me. At one point, he even ran a red light when I made it through before he did. Two miles later and he was still there, sitting alongside me at another light, revving up his engine like he was daring me to race.

Dude, you seriously need to get a life, I said to myself.

Then I went for it.

I hit the accelerator without waiting for the light. The front of his vehicle resembled an angry face with the lights slanted on either side of the hood.

The sleet powered by wind slapped across my windshield while my eyes narrowed on a flashing light, swinging wildly in the wind. There was a fork in the road. I immediately signaled a right turn and then — at the last possible second — I turned left. My tires screeched ... the turn so insanely sharp that I screamed.

He reacted quickly, running over the divider and looping around. Behind me, his headlights cut harsh cones, as I whizzed past boarded-up sheds and old farm equipment. I was headed for the detour — the one that wasn't on any map, the one that led through Battlefield Park.

Eventually, I saw it, illuminated by moonlight as a passing cloud slipped away. The graveyard stretched over higher ground. The older headstones, discolored and worn, sloped down the hill towards the street.

The fence was the picket kind, draped with pine garland and ribbons, with posts driven in the ground every few feet. On the north side, there was a service gate that exited on a side road, leading to the park. The divider was down, so I had to drive over gravel and dirt to get through.

My mind was considerably sharper under the influence of music, so I turned the radio up until it was deafening. This way I didn't have to hear the noise my tires made when they left the asphalt. I couldn't even hear myself imagine what my mother would say if she saw me now, because I was about to break one of her cardinal rules about cell phones and driving.

With one hand, I frantically searched my bag for my phone. But just as I pulled it out, the combination of off-road driving and limited visibility proved too much, and it slipped from my fingers. Crouched down while still driving, I scoured the floor mat. In my mind, I went over the things I wouldn't do. I wouldn't hit the brakes. I wouldn't unfasten my seat belt or unlock my doors. And above all, I wouldn't get out of my car.

If it wasn't for *the vision*! It struck like a bright light with fast moving frames.

At first glimpse, I didn't see myself going through the normal routine of getting home, pulling into my driveway, opening the garage door. At some point, I was still trying to get away ... when my car clipped the trunk of a gnarled tree. There was an explosive sound as the front seat air bags inflated, compressing my chest and tangling my arms over my head.

Then I felt it, a trickle of warm blood sliding down my cheek. One glance in my mirror and I saw the blurred image of the vehicle. It had come to a full stop, parked sideways to block me — as if there was a way to escape, because my door was wedged against the tree, and I couldn't get it opened ... no matter how hard I tried.

I felt the gasp in my throat as the driver's door opened. A figure jumped out; the details lost in the darkness as he walked towards me with purpose. Then like a reliable nightmare, the *vision* fizzled out, just before he got close enough.

There was no time to think it over, no time to talk myself out if it. I bolted from the car, leaving the engine running and the door open.

I ran clumsily on heels with my arms flailing through the air.

"What do you want?" I cried out.

It felt like I was covering distance until I realized that I still heard the music streaming through my car speakers. That was when I seriously doubted that I was running fast enough to get away.

Darting shadows flashed in the woods, between silhouettes of crowded trees. The white powder dusting the ground wasn't enough to cut through the darkness. I was tired. I was wet. I was too busy looking behind to notice what was ahead. My body slammed against him.

I screamed.

And then I fell into his arms with all the force of my weight.

"It's okay," Byron said, bracing my shoulders.

"Someone was chasing me." I managed to get the words out with barely enough breath to spare. "I saw myself crash into a tree. I was trapped inside my car ... and he was coming for me."

"Shhh," he said, cradling my head against his chest. "I'm here now."

I stayed still for a moment and then raised my eyes as he wiped away the tears. Part of me expected more of a reaction from him, maybe something along the lines of:

"OMG ... how did this happen? Are you okay?"

As usual he was unfazed, except for the serious look on his face that was near-constant.

"It wasn't Logan who posted that stuff about you on the internet," he said pulling my hair away from my face. "It was Trinity."

I shook my head. "No way," I said. "That can't be. She wouldn't do something like to me."

"She bumped you at the club ... *not* Logan."

"Why would she do that?" I blurted, more shocked than angry.

"It's about Josh."

"Josh!" I almost laughed. "She doesn't like Josh — *not* in that way," I said. "Besides, I was never into him other than just being friends."

"You're wrong about her feelings," he insisted. "You never noticed because you were focused on how he felt about you."

Byron's arms closed around me while he pressed his lips to my head, but his eyes were open on the woods ... chasing the wind.

"You never told me what you're doing here...in the park," I said.

"I didn't?" His voice was distracted as he stared into the distance. Slowly his eyes returned to me.

"You left the club without saying anything," I said.

"I felt your movements," he said. "So I followed you here. Now I'm glad that I did."

If he was following, he should have been braking at the same four-minute lights, I thought.

"Didn't you see him then?" I asked. "He was racing towards Colts Neck in this huge SUV with blacked-out windows?"

"No," he said, devoid of curiosity.

"How can that be?" I asked. "You didn't see the guy chasing me and I didn't see you. And where was Nick?"

"Are you disappointed that Nick isn't here?" he asked.

I drew out a deep breath that was as good as "No." His hand circled my face until I almost forgot what we were talking about.

"I didn't see anyone," he insisted with a softer voice, his fingers moving behind my ear.

I gave him a wary look that went only so far because I didn't want him to stop doing what he was doing. Then my mind switched gears as I remembered the face in the crowd — the one that seemed out of place, the one that I thought I had seen before. Thinking about it now, it was more likely that it was someone else, some old guy who worked for the club's road crew, hired to roll equipment from the stage.

"Whoever he was, he must have seen you leave the club," Byron said.

My eyes widened. "Are you sure about the 'he' part?"

Trinity's face popped into my head. Her father's new truck had a stereo upgrade, but she couldn't drive it to school because the parking spaces only fit compact cars.

"Guess you like the feeling of being bigger than everyone else," I said, sliding into the front passenger seat after yoga class one day.

She took my band's CD from my hand and slipped it into the audio slot. The sound quality was impressive but not worth the price of gas.

Trinity — she was the one trashing me on social media. It had to be her, especially since she drove the same super-sized SUV.

"So do lots of people," Byron replied, his expression blank as he read my thoughts with un-hesitating precision.

* * *

The visitor's center was part of the museum, run by the local historical society to preserve artifacts excavated from the battle. An American flag hung in the outside courtyard just above the New Jersey State flag.

There was something eerie, yet beautiful about it ... the chime of the pole as the flags flapped in the wind like a bell ringing in an empty church. We walked past the cannon, part of the resources brought by Washington to defeat the British; a marker staked in the ground commemorated the battle.

The viewing arc at the top of the hill overlooked the actual battlefield, nothing more than a flat depression surrounded by trees. In the distance, a wooden bridge caught my eye. Without the need for words, Byron led the way.

As we crossed the field, our steps sank into a fresh layer of soft snow. My boots were already ruined, scuffed and scraped while fleeing an unknown predator. What was left of the sculptured heel pounded the ground ... like the steps of hundreds as they marched away, withdrawing to higher ground.

Suddenly, Byron stopped and turned. A distressed look invaded his eyes.

"More than anything, I want to be the person you need me to be," he said, his voice competing with the wind.

If this was a rejection, he'd have to try harder because the emotions behind his eyes led me to believe otherwise. My face said what my mind was thinking. He moved towards me with a purpose that made me lower my eyes. Then I felt his hand across my cheek. The snowflakes clung to our hair and clothes. I brushed a few from his jacket and then kept my hand there, braced on his chest.

"I've always been drawn to this place," I said, glancing around us. "No matter how lost I am on these roads, somehow I find my way here ... and I don't know why."

The faintest smile brightened his face.

"I can show you," he said, as he adjusted my scarf.

"Show me what?"

"Look towards the center of the field," he said.

He kept his eyes on me as I turned … as if my reaction was more important than what he was trying to show me.

The snow fell faster, the trees branches already bending with heavy frost, but the field was drenched in sun. And the grass … it wasn't withered and frozen. It was green.

"It was June when it happened," he said, his eyes still on me.

"When what happened…?"

I was looking at a photo of summer cropped into a wintry night-time scene.

"The battle," he said.

That was when I heard it — the sounds of engagement.

* * *

"Emerson … are you awake?"

My question came in the form of as high-pitched whisper, deliberate and insistent.

"I am *now*," she said blinking into her computer screen.

"Sorry, I didn't mean to wake you," I said, trying to be convincing.

"It's two in the morning!" she groaned, wiping her eyes with closed fists.

"We were at the battlefield," I said.

"The battlefield," she repeated. "What were you doing there?"

"Some creep tried to follow me home after the concert, so I detoured into the park to get away."

"Oh no," she said, holding back a yawn. "Are you okay?'

"Yeah, I'm fine," I said.

Somehow everything that happened since made the chase feel less traumatic.

"Probably some psycho fan," she said. "Maybe you should report it to the police. Did you get a license number?"

"I couldn't see a thing," I said. "I ran from my car and somehow I ran into Byron."

"Are you serious?" she asked. "He showed up — just like that?"

"What do you mean?" I resented the suspicion in her voice.

"Maybe it was him, Genna," she said. "Maybe he tracked you there so that he could be the one who rescued you."

I rolled over on my pillow as if to squash the idea.

"That's totally sick," I said. "Besides it wasn't even his car."

If I wanted to grab at straws, I could probably suspect almost anyone in the band. One way or the other, they all had something against me except for Nick.

"Anyway," I said. "There's something else. I saw the battle."

"I can't believe I missed that," she said, stretching her arms.

Logan had texted her about the fight between Nick and Byron, probably while it was happening.

"*Not* that battle," I clarified. "I meant The Battle of Monmouth."

"What?" she blurted.

"It happened in June," I said.

"Yeah," she said, her voice spiking high. "June 1778."

"Snow was coming down around us," I began. "Byron pointed to the field. I looked once, and there was nothing. I looked again, and the battle was playing out in real time."

"Genna, normally I would give you the benefit of the doubt — you know that," she said. "But that's too wild even between friends."

"I saw it Emerson," I insisted. "It was a live event ... just for a few minutes and then it faded out. The grass wilted away, and the sun dimmed. When I looked again, it was night, snow over the ground and an empty field."

"Man, how cool is that!" she said, sounding less skeptical. "Last Halloween some of us went up for fun. There's that hidden entrance in the graveyard that opens near the field. The woods are teeming with ghosts."

"They weren't apparitions," I said. "It was like the place was imprinted with the memory of what had happened."

"Hmm ...," she deliberated.

"There was so much going on," I said. "There was a little boy, maybe eleven or twelve. He looked so lost and scared. He was carrying a bucket of water to the Patriot line and for a moment I thought he made eye contact with me."

Emerson twitched. "Hey Genna," she suddenly said, pressing her nose to her computer screen. "I just picked up on it."

"I knew you would if I concentrated hard enough," I said, excitedly.

"It's like a photo album," she said, browsing my thoughts. "You can't interact with what has passed. So they can't see you *or* hear you."

"I know," I said. "I asked Byron and he said that I would have to be happy with watching the action from my own existence plane. He didn't have the ability to merge the two."

Emerson's face turned serious. "Where did you say you met this guy?"

"In the Mall," I said. "Why?"

"The guy's a freaking wizard, Genna," she snapped. "Keep away from him."

10. Separation Anxiety

I was sprawled across the sofa with a bunch of magazines, pulling out scented flaps, "try me" ads for the latest perfumes. By the time I heard wheels crunching leaves in the driveway, I was into some seriously awesome aromatherapy.

Byron stood on the other side of the door, out of breath like he had just run up the hill. I noticed his car running, the headlights blazing a path to the house. The driver's side door was open, the radio blasting the coolest music.

Before I could ask him in, he rushed past me. I shut the door. Then I saw the state he was in — his face drawn as if he hadn't slept, his eyes moist, as if holding back tears. Without looking away, he blotted the sweat off his lip with a shaky forearm.

My eyes widened as if to ask: "What's wrong?"

The silence made me uncomfortable. I thought about taking his jacket, asking him if he wanted something to drink.

He shook his head and swallowed. "There isn't time."

Then he stepped forward with an urgency that startled me.

"I love you," he said.

I forced myself to blink. He was still there, but I was somewhere else — plunged into a surreal moment that made me wonder if I was dreaming.

"*I love you so much,*" he said, more insistently.

This time the words struck hard. I didn't think about how it sounded — like he was resisting himself. Another moment and the serious look on his face erupted into a smile, the saddest, most beautiful smile I had ever seen. His hand reached for my face, and I wondered truly if I would ever breathe again.

I watched him toss back a strand of choppy hair.

"It's okay," he breathed. "You don't have to say it. I know how you feel."

"How can you?" I stared at him. "Sometimes I don't even know who I am ... who I'm supposed to be."

"Let me help with *that*," he said as his fingers swept over my face. "You're the part of me that I didn't know was there."

As far as I can tell, there's a rushing sound that happens when oxygen leaves the room. It made me dizzy. It made me quit fighting. I watched his eyes respond as my hand fell behind his neck, as my cheek touched his and for the first time, I felt like he was mine.

The feelings were scary and wonderful at the same time.

"I'm here with you," he said, pressing his fingers to my lips. "And I'm scared too."

I could still hear the heartbeat of the world when he said my name.

"Gennie," he said, his voice almost choking. "I have to leave tonight."

My eyes opened on his, and all at once I straightened up like I had been poked from behind.

A one-word response reverberated in my head: *Liar!*

I didn't feel the steps as I took them backwards, my head shaking as if to deny him the chance to explain.

"How can you say stuff like that to me and then just leave," I said.

I put up my hand to block his approach. I didn't want an answer. There was no answer that could satisfy me. Within a matter of seconds, he had managed to reverse every beautiful word, every perfect thought.

I felt my back touch the staircase railing.

He stopped.

"I need a few days at the most," he explained.

Hearing the details now made it feel more real. A sense of dread filled the space between us — as I looked into his eyes and knew that he might never come back. Not in a few days, not in a few weeks ... *not ever.*

Holding my stomach, my fingers dug in deep...through skin and muscle, trying to find the place where it hurt the most.

"Don't leave," I said, hardly recognizing the sound of my own voice. "Please stay. Don't go."

I found myself crouching on the floor, trying to fend off a sick feeling. My eyes shifted towards the bathroom which seemed too far away to reach in time. He lowered himself to my level and braced me with his hands.

"Don't do this," he said in a voice too wounded to speak.

My shoulders hunched in a half-hearted attempt to break away.

"Just say it," I said, impatiently.

I waited to hear what I already thought — *we were officially over!*

"No," he said.

"Say it," I demanded.

"I'm trying to be everything you want," he said. "I promise that I won't let you down."

I felt myself double over, dying inside — a little bit at a time or all at once; I couldn't tell.

"It'll be okay," he said, coming closer.

"Stay away from me." I collapsed on the bottom step with my hands over my face.

He squeezed himself next to me.

"My father sent me here," he began. "I never wanted to come." His voice trailed off as if he was recalling an exact moment. "Things didn't go according to plan and now I'm going fix it before he does."

"Let him," I said, my voice pleading. "Let him help you with whatever it is."

His eyes pressed mine. "If he comes here or sends someone, Gennie," he began, "I'll be forced to go back and we'll never see each other again. But if I do this on my own, he won't bother coming just to bring me back. I'm *not* that important to him."

"There's more," I said. "What aren't you telling me?"

"I'll be back soon," he said, avoiding the question with the same proficiency that he avoided every question.

"I don't believe you," I said with a twisted grin.

It never occurred to me that the "mystery problem" could involve another girl. Somehow it didn't matter that I couldn't get inside his head, because if someone else was between us, there would no way that I wouldn't know, no way that I wouldn't feel it.

"Do you trust me, Gennie?" he asked.

"You wouldn't want to give me just a little idea about what we're talking about?" I asked.

"That wouldn't be my first choice."

"Why?" I asked.

He shrugged his shoulders. "It's not the easiest thing to explain."

"Try," I dared him.

"You won't look at me the same way," he said. "You'll be afraid."

"What have you done?" I asked, fearing the worst.

"It's not what I've done," he said. "It's what I'm going to do."

"How do I know that you're coming back?"

His cryptic smile flashed.

"You're here," he said. "There's nowhere else I can be."

Suddenly I needed air. My parka was hanging over the banister. I zipped up and stepped out on the backyard deck. The frigid air was saturated with moisture, and there was a thin halo around the moon.

Byron followed.

"The stars are out," I said.

He giggled through the anguish in his face. "They're always out, Gennie."

I watched him lift his head towards the night sky. The green in his eyes seemed to flicker with the stars.

A few days to handle a family issue — it didn't sound unreasonable, it didn't sound excessively long. Yet without him, the moments would stick together like lifeless grains of sand pouring through the neck of an hourglass.

"Can I go with you?" I asked.

"No." His response was immediate. "I have to do this alone."

"Why?" I asked.

The smile refreshed on his lips. "Believe in us," he said, lifting my chin with his forefinger. "And no matter what…don't give up."

I nodded uneasily, trying to hold back tears. "Are you going to call me?" I asked.

I knew that he wasn't into high-tech, but there was no reason why he shouldn't use the phone I gave him.

"I'll probably be out of range," he said.

The answer sounded like a lame excuse.

"Gennie," he said, as if he was about to confess some long-held secret. "I really did like playing in the band and I'm sorry that it worried you when I wasn't around enough."

"You're scaring me," I said.

My eyes suddenly lowered to his hand which held a CD in a cellophane sleeve. Written across the top, in oddly-perfect penmanship was my name.

He placed it my hand.

"If, for some reason, I'm not back within a week," he said, "promise me you'll play it."

The freaked-out look on my face forced him to explain.

"Just in case there's an unforeseeable delay."

Had he purposely left something out, the part that might have said: "Or, in case I don't come back."

"I'll be back," he reassured.

"I don't know," I said, staring at the disk in my hand.

"All you need to know … is that I love you."

My tongue began to slide. It took everything I had to hold back. I knew what he wanted to hear, but how could I say it now. It would be better to tell him when he got back. This way if the unthinkable happened, I'd be glad that I didn't make a total fool out of myself.

Gradually he turned away, the punished look on his face enough to keep me up all night. I watched him walk to his car, sensing when it was time to go back inside the house.

I wasn't sure if I called out to him before I ran, or the other way around.

With my hair blowing in all directions, I flew down the driveway, rushing into his arms as he turned. His embrace was immediate and unrestrained. I felt his kisses, soft kisses, over my neck and face before he stopped short of my lips. For an instant, his eyes held mine and then with one movement of his hand, he drew my chin to his face.

That was when I stopped him. Acting on instinct, I pulled away and kept what would have been my first kiss from being a kiss good-bye.

* * *

Absence makes the heart grow fonder — or, out of sight, out of mind. The long week of waiting was officially up, so there I sat loading the CD for the seventh time, knowing in my heart that he could never be out of my mind.

Byron's stunning face popped up on my computer screen.

"Gennie," he said.

My heart sank again when I heard my name.

"If you're watching this, I probably should have been back by now."

His face moved closer as he reached out, fingers spread apart. I did the same, pressing my fingers against the screen to line up with his.

"Do you feel me, Gennie?" he asked. "Promise me that you won't give up on us."

I powered-down and tossed my laptop aside.

It was the kind of night that made me excessively aware of stuff that wouldn't be nearly as freaky when the sun was up. If I had waited until morning, I was sure that I would have never called.

I remember thinking: what if he doesn't pick up? What if his phone just rings endlessly because I didn't set up voicemail — and I doubted that he would have...? Another possibility: what if he answered? What if I woke him, my voice desperate enough to drive him away...?

I hesitated, sitting up in bed, hugging my knees for support. Then I pulled my phone from under pillow and stared at it like it was something dangerous.

The phone rang maybe, three or four times. My heart fluttered when I heard it pick up, the connection open long enough for someone to say something. I called his name twice. Against the sound of breathing, I heard movement in the background and maybe other voices.

The next sound was a fast click. He had hung up.

I knew that I would never call again not even when he was gone *twice as long.*

* * *

Trinity drifted into the kitchen.

"Hey," she said. "What are you doing?" Her eyes went to my drawstring PJ bottoms and fuzzy slipper-boots.

I pretended that I didn't hear her.

"Genna, wake up," she said, snapping her fingers. "It's Wednesday night. The meeting is about to start."

"Already," I said, stretching my arms.

Our eyes met for just a second and then I looked away.

"I can't believe you're still mad at me," she said. "I took down the videos. I deleted the messages on your page even though no one actually believed it was you."

"I just don't feel like talking," I said.

"Byron is such a major troublemaker," she snipped. "If he bothered to read me, he would have known that it was just a joke."

Emerson strolled in with Logan trailing behind.

"Cyber-bulling is *no joke*," Logan snapped. "People got hurt and I'm the one who got blamed."

Logan eventually accepted my apology when I wrongly accused her of being responsible. Still it didn't change the fact that we never really liked each other. Now I guess we just liked each other a little less.

Emerson gave me a hug which I gladly returned. "So what are you going to do?' she asked. "Spend your life in the house, in pajamas until he comes back?"

"Maybe," I said with a listless voice. "I don't know."

"Genna, you have to know that saying it back would have made no difference," she said. "His mind was made up before he met you. He would have still left."

I tried not to second guess myself but in the back of my mind, I wondered.

Then my phone went off, and I nearly fell over.

"Hey angel voice," Nick said. "I miss you."

I tried not to sound disappointed. I wasn't really.

"I miss you too," I said, nearly crying.

"I'm on my way," he said.

I happened to catch a glimpse of my face in a stainless steel appliance, tear-stained, no makeup. I couldn't even remember the last time I brushed my hair.

"*Not* tonight Nick," I said. "There's a bunch of my mom's friends over here and the energy is super-weird."

"How weird could it be?" he asked.

"Don't even go there," I said. "Trust me."

From the living room, I heard Remi's voice calling everyone together. Even without leaving the kitchen, most of the conversation was audible.

"All along," Remi began. "I had deep suspicions that he was blocking."

"Actually you never did," Lexa answered. "You said it was impossible."

"Since when do you keep track of everything I say," Remi said.

"No one believed he was blocking." I heard my mother's voice. "It would an extraordinary feat to push other telepaths from your mind."

"Decoy thoughts," Lexa proposed. "They're put out there to distract from the truth."

"Maybe he's a handler." Harris spoke with his mouth full. "You know ... someone with superior ability who manages the thoughts of everyone around them, while shielding their own inner musings."

"That's blocking sweet face," Lexa said. "Haven't you been listening?"

"Twice I tried to communicate with his mind," Remi said. "I heard nothing but an incoherent buzzing sound. The closer I got, the more organized it became."

"What did it sound like?" Harris asked.

"I don't know," Remi answered. "Like music ... I think."

Lexa laughed. "You're all trying to fit him into this box based on what we know or think we know," she said. "What if there's more to it?"

"Like what?" Harris asked. "He's no more gifted than anyone else. He's just a guy trying to impress a girl."

"By the way," Remi asked my mother. "How is your daughter?"

I didn't hear my mother's response.

The twins bolted into the kitchen in a frenzy of giggles.

Chloe or maybe, it was Cassie climbed onto my lap and started braiding my hair. Ordinarily, I would fling her hand away but the attention felt good, so I closed my eyes and let her work.

"Don't be sad, Genna," she said. "Byron's thinking about you."

Startled, I opened my eyes. "Cassie," I said, pushing her away. "Don't do that. It's too mean."

"Byron's thinking about you, Genna," she repeated.

I took hold of her shoulders, probably harder than I should have. "You can't tease me like that — do you hear me?"

"Sorry, Genna," she said, threatening to cry.

"It's not your fault," I said in a feeble voice. "It's not anyone's fault that he didn't come back."

Great, I thought. *Now I'm explaining my love life to a ten year old.*

She jumped off my lap and walked towards the refrigerator. I watched her hand fumble through the items stuck to the door: my school calendar, cat photos and car wash coupons. Finally, her nimble fingers snatched an art magnet, one of the gifts Byron had bought from the museum.

"This is why he can't come back," she said.

I sighed deeply as I took it from her hand.

"Byron can't come back because of a magnet, I said. "Thank you, Cassie. I feel so much better now."

I should have guessed that sarcasm would have no effect on her. She pushed the magnet in my face with fierce determination.

"Okay, Cassie," I said, reeling back. "Let's try this again. Byron can't come back because of a magnet?"

It was typical of her to become non-verbal when she was fixated on something. She flipped the magnet over and forced me to touch it. The other side, the one worth looking at, was a laminated photo of a water lily painting.

Suddenly, I felt guilty for riding her.

"Oh Cassie," I said inviting her into my arms. "I really wish that explained it."

"I'm Chloe." She corrected me with an adult voice. "Cassie is my sister … and it does explain it perfectly."

11. FLIGHT RISK

My mother's truck was pulled into the driveway as if she had just stopped short of ramming the garage. I parked behind her and that was when I noticed the "stick figure" family decals on her back window. The "dad figure" looked like it had been scraped off, bits of white still flaky on the glass.

I entered the house through the back door and then raced through the first floor looking for her.

"You can't do that!" I shouted. "You can't just rub him out of our lives."

I found my mother huddled in a chair, her nose in a book.

"*Oh that,*" she said casually, unwilling to look up. "Maybe we can get a pet or something to fill the space."

"Mom...!" I snapped, ready to tear up.

She tossed the book aside and waved me closer. I squeezed beside her, although the chair wasn't wide enough for the two of us.

"I haven't forgotten that your father is part of our lives." She tugged my hair playfully. "What are you getting so upset about?'

I guess it wasn't the stickers. It was more the idea that my parents weren't getting back together. *They were never getting back together.*

"It's Christmas," I whimpered, my eyes lingering on the pre-lit blue spruce standing by the window.

"I have a surprise," she said, excitedly. "You'll be spending the holiday at your dad's place in Maryland."

I was almost happy until I remembered.

"I can't go," I said. "I can't leave until Byron gets back."

Her arms pulled away as I wandered over to the window, parting the curtains as if I expected him to pull up any minute.

"The change of scenery will help," she said. "It'll get your mind off of things."

How can it do that? I thought. *How can leaving make me miss him any less?*

"I don't want to go," I whined.

Now I sounded as loyal as an army wife.

"I'll call you if he comes by," she said.

My response was delayed.

"What do you mean you'll call me?" I asked, confused. "I'm not going without you."

"Tell you what," she began, her mind racing through options. "You fly down tomorrow and I'll meet you there on Christmas Eve."

I rolled my eyes as if to say "maybe."

"Flying is easier," she persuaded.

I sighed under pressure. For sure the drive down was totally boring and would probably take twice as long with holiday traffic.

"I can always forward the house phone to my cell," she said. "In case he calls."

Suddenly it dawned on me as if for the first time that *he never called*. Not even after my cell number showed up on his phone as a recent call.

"I can leave a note on the door," she said. "Would that make you feel better?"

"I guess," I said, my voice falling flat.

The fact that I hadn't heard from him should have been proof-positive that we were over. Still I was stuck in a kind of waiting mode.

I almost changed my mind about leaving when my father called. He sounded too happy to disappoint.

Something in his voice told me that he was holding out for a chance to reconnect with my mother.

"I'll e-mail you the travel arrangements," he said.

He had unused miles on an aircraft timeshare that he had bought when he and my mother were still together.

"This is a real plane?" I asked him.

"No. It's a crop-duster Gen," he kidded. "Of course it's a real plane."

* * *

I should have been grateful, since flying commercial was such a pain these days. At least I wouldn't have to deal with security — shoes off at the gate, walk through slowly and then walk back a second time after my "rock glam" jewelry sets off the metal detectors.

Bill was helping himself to coffee when I wheeled a set of three matching suitcases through the kitchen. I used both hands, but the turns were a little tough to navigate, especially on heels.

"Hey princess," he said. "Let me give you a hand with that. Are you sure that's it?"

He was teasing. My makeup kit alone could delay every domestic flight departing Newark Liberty.

"I'm not checking luggage," I said. "So it doesn't matter."

"Yeah," he said. "I heard that your dad was flying you down on a private plane."

I picked up the edge in his voice. He wasn't thinking about my first-class ride — he was thinking about my mother spending the holidays with her ex.

"Mom is driving me to the airport," I said, pulling up a chair next to him.

I watched him drink his coffee while he checked his phone for messages. Actually, I braced my chin with my hand so that my head stayed perfectly still while I stared him down. He looked up a few times, his eyes fluttering uneasily until he nearly gagged on his coffee.

"Can you do me a favor?" I asked, smiling.

When I wanted something, tact wasn't exactly my strong point.

"Uh ... sure," he said with a wary look.

"Okay," I said. "Can you find Byron?"

"Ah ... Gen," he said, wrinkling his nose. "The guy's nothing but trouble. Even your friends think he's weird — and that's a stretch."

My lips inflated into a pout. A few minutes elapsed without a word. From the corner of my eye, I caught him fidgeting. Once or twice he began to speak and then held back.

"What can you tell me about him?" he finally said, ashamed that he had given in.

I knew he was serious when his pen and notebook came out.

"Practically nothing," I said. "He has an uncle in Pennington."

"I'm sure lots of people do," he chuckled.

My mother walked in. "What about his car?" she asked.

For a moment, my detective's attention wandered. My mother was reaching for a cup in a pair of skinny jeans.

"I need a plate number," he said forcing himself to look away.

"I can tell you the make and model," my mother said. "But I never saw the plate."

I wouldn't have noticed either. When Byron was around, it was impossible to notice anything, much less a stupid license plate. Yet maybe it was true what Emerson once told me about never actually forgetting something once you've seen it.

I closed my eyes, trying to lock on the image of the car sitting in my driveway, remembering the first time I saw it, when he nearly plowed into me by the mall. It was a trendy gun-metal color ... an expensive European brand with spoke tires. The yellow plate had the graphic of a lighthouse; black letters scrolled across: *New Jersey — Shore to Please.*

"The first letter is like 'house' or 'H,'" I suddenly said.

I pressed my fist to my head and grunted a few times, but it was no use. I couldn't go further. My mother drew nearer. She was hooked into my thought pattern and intended to stay there until she had the rest. The heavy sigh meant that she was struggling. Bill handed her his pen and pad. Sometimes it was easier to access information by going through the physical motions of writing it down:

HT-EMC2

She slid the pad across the table and dropped the pen like the exercise had drained her.

"Okay," Bill said. "Let me run it through and see what turns up."

* * *

Nick called twice on the way to the airport trying to convince me to stay.

"Just wish you weren't going," he said. I pressed the phone against my cheek and closed my eyes. "By the way," he said. "I think the guy's a total jerk."

I wasn't in the mood to hear him trash-talk Byron again, so I made him think that I was losing the signal. Afterwards, I felt guilty. I hated lies, even the little white lies, but I didn't want to admit that I was hurting and that his gloating was pushing me further away from him, *not* closer like he wanted.

Nick had been all over the "Byron leaving and never coming back" situation from the moment he left. At his insistence, Liam quickly replaced Byron.

"He's talented, and he's normal," Nick remarked during our last band meeting. "Not like some 'solo-stealing' rock superhero that doesn't have his head on straight."

Nick worked hard promoting the idea that Byron was stranger than strange. By now it was so deeply rooted that there was nothing I could say to change anyone's mind. How could I defend him anyway? He left the band without a word. He left me and never came back.

We arrived at the departure gates a few minutes early. My mother held me tight. I tried to break away twice, only to have her pull me back.

"What is it?" I asked.

"I love you," she whispered in my ear, emphasizing each word.

"Hey," I said. "Are you crying?"

"I'll miss you," she said. "You're the best daughter."

I walked backwards, with my eyes still on her standing in the terminal. The pilot was waiting for me at the gate, at the point where only passengers were allowed. He said something about good weather and grabbed my over-sized duffel bag from my buckling arm. I motioned to the suitcases that he didn't notice sitting on the ground. With a grin that stopped short of laughing, he hoisted them on a luggage cart.

It felt strange, not necessarily in a good way, to have the entire plane to myself. The size of the cabin, with about twelve seats, made me feel mildly claustrophobic. I found myself compulsively switching seats before finally settling into a window seat two rows from the cockpit.

The hum of the engines on stand-by lulled me into a light sleep. The dream was always the same: Byron in the bookstore. Through the loudspeaker, the pilot's voice overlapped his dream voice.

"We're cleared for take-off," he said through a crackle of static. "Fasten your seatbelt and enjoy the ride."

My eyes squeezed shut as we taxied and then jerked to a stop. The engines roared as they throttled back, and suddenly we were racing down the runway. Less than ninety seconds in the air and we were already over Manhattan. I leaned sideways and squinted through the window. The skyline was one of those views that never got old, no matter how many times I flew over it.

The pilot's voice again: "On short flights we don't get up that high so don't be concerned if it gets a little bumpy. We'll level off at about 15,000 feet."

I returned to my dream, repeating the motions of sliding the scarf from his neck. Then the music cut in and the bookstore became the stage with Byron sprinting around me, his eyes lifeless as the guitar exploded in his hands.

The music stopped when the dream did. I wasn't sure why my eyes opened. It was as if I was bracing myself, my hands gripping the arm rests. Two or three seconds later, the vibration hit.

Around me, the cabin shuddered like the plane was breaking apart. I bolted upright, panting heavily and ready to scream. My seat belt restrained me as I leaned forward, my eyes on the closed door to the cockpit.

The noise that followed was a series of rib-shaking roars ... one after another hissing by the right side of the plane at incredible speed. Then another sound, like a high-pitched squeal, forced me to cover my ears.

The plane dipped. And this time, I screamed.

The loudspeaker switched on.

"Whoa ... looks like we got military aircraft up here," the pilot said. It felt good to hear his voice. "No worries. They're probably fighter jets on their way to McGuire Air Force Base or Pax River."

I shifted nervously in my seat. There was a clear view of the buildings and roads below. It was a cloudless day. Thin rays of yellow sunlight streamed through the cabin. Somehow the natural light felt reassuring. I couldn't imagine anything going wrong as long as the sun was shining.

Eventually, I got tired of trying to keep track of flight noises. Anything I heard or didn't hear was completely normal. The plane climbed higher in gradual increments before settling at cruising altitude. My head fell back. The release of the weight from my shoulders forced my eyes shut.

I opened them again when I sensed the light change, a dark shadow moving over us blocking the sun. The overhead lighting began to flicker; the news show on the TV screen flashed out with a sizzle.

"What's going on?" I shouted.

The emergency lighting sparked on.

"Stay in your seat," the pilot said over the speaker. "There's something just above us. Something enormous and it's *not* maintaining distance."

Safety instructions were tucked into a pocket on the back of the seat in front of me. I pulled out the pamphlet and ran my finger across the schematic of the plane. I located the nearest exit. There were only two.

Okay. Now what do I do, I thought.

As I asked myself the question, the plane began to shimmy sideways, as if we were about to roll. Gradually the motion became more intense until it felt like the walls of the plane were being beaten down. Then there was an abrupt, violent descent — that had to be the most terrifying feeling that I've ever felt.

My mouth must have opened, but I couldn't hear the scream. It was overcome by a sinking feeling in the pit of my stomach and a wave of nausea. The plane pitched wildly. I lunged forward still held by my seat belt. Around us, there was a swooshing sound — as if other planes were up there with us, closing in from all sides and sending us down faster.

"Stay with me Genna," the pilot said as the shrill sound of an alarm went off from the cockpit.

Then I heard him say something else, his voice distorted as he struggled to keep the plane in the air. I watched my oxygen mask drop. My hand reached for it instinctively.

Breathe normally, I thought. *Is that what they tell you to do?*

"Mayday, Mayday. This is flight 585," he said in a mechanical voice, forgetting that the speaker was still on. "I'm declaring an emergency, over."

A calm voice from the control tower spliced through the static: "State your emergency, 585, over."

"I think." The pilot hesitated. "There's military activity in my flight path, over."

"Affirmative 585, over. Verified on radar, over."

"Too close," the pilot said. "I don't know ... they spun us around ... can't recover, over."

I thought back to earlier that morning. My mother held me longer than she should have, but if I was really going to die, there's no way she wouldn't feel it. My eyes suddenly reacted to my phone screen. Quickly, I accepted the call.

My mother's voice came rushing through, shouting and wailing.

"Genna…," she choked. "I was in the shower and all of a sudden I had the most awful feeling…"

I was crying too hard to say more than: "Love you."

"Listen to me," she said forcefully. "Don't give up. I love you too much for you to give up."

"Mom…," I gasped, talking past the time that I lost the connection. "I'm so scared."

"Head down!" the pilot shouted. "Head down, prepare for impact!"

I kissed the dark phone screen as if it was her face. These last words: "prepare for impact" seemed to reach me through a tunnel. The images around me began melting into a kind of hazy syrup. Then the endorphins kicked in, the chemicals your body produces to get you through.

We were plunging towards the ground in an almost vertical spiral. Above me, suitcases broke free from the overhead compartments, the contents flying into the air. I watched it happen, but it no longer meant anything to me. My breathing slowed. I even stopped screaming.

Maybe, I thought. *The struggle was worse than the dreaded outcome.*

Then my mind backtracked to my mother's last words about not giving up — to Byron's last words about never giving up on us.

So I brought down my head as far down as I could, straining my muscles to get there. Through the noise, I heard a voice in my head, clear and perfect. I wasn't alone.

He spoke to me.

"Genna…"

"Byron," I called out. "Byron, are you there?"

* * *

"Don't leave me," I said.

"Hey," he said, moving a strand of hair from my face. "Take it easy. You're okay."

My mother's voice followed. "We're here baby."

My eyes opened. The people standing over me were my parents. The place was a hospital. And I was lying on an extremely uncomfortable bed with scratchy sheets.

"You gave us quite a scare." Bill walked around my mother and leaned over the bed.

My dad glanced up at the monitor. "Looking good," he said; his voice clinical.

I watched the steady peaks of bright green pulses and bleeps. And then suddenly I bolted up ... remembering.

"The plane...!" I screamed.

"Okay now," my mother said easing me down, adjusting my blanket. "It's over now and you're going to be fine."

"The plane went down in Havre de Grace," my father explained.

The name was familiar. It was a quaint colonial-era seaport town outside of Annapolis. We had stopped for lunch once on our way to Washington.

"The pilot...?" I asked, remembering.

"He has a concussion and a few broken ribs, but that's about it," my father said. "He'll be fine but you were way luckier, sweetheart. Not a scratch. It's a miracle."

"Genna, there's someone outside from the Transportation Safety Board," Bill said. "The pilot is unable to give them an official statement right now. They want to talk to you. Do you remember what happened before...?" He hesitated, unwilling to say the "crash" word.

I nodded. "Can I tell you first?"

"Sure," my father said. "Take your time."

I closed my eyes trying to recall.

"Everything was fine," I said. "Then there were loud vibrations and the plane started losing altitude." I cupped my hands over my ears like I heard it again. "There was something huge ... no sound just speed. It came over us. I felt a drag, like we were being pulled down ... and the cabin lost pressure."

I sat up in the bed as the sensation of falling came back. My mother wrapped her arm around me.

"The pilot mentioned that there was military activity in his flight path," my father said.

"He radioed the tower that the planes were too close," Bill said.

"Someone was with me on the ground," I said. "It was Byron."

I watched my mother's face go blank.

"Byron's away, honey," she said. "Remember...?"

"Yeah, I remember," I said. "He should have been back weeks ago."

"Too bad it didn't work out," Bill said. "We have another case that's running cold and I could use his help."

My dad, the eternal skeptic, rolled his eyes and sighed.

"Someone was holding me on the ground." I turned to my mother. "It was Byron."

"Maybe an EMT," Bill said. "They were the first responders on the scene."

My dad contradicted him. "You were unconscious when you were brought into the Emergency Room."

I looked at my mother and sent her my thoughts loud and clear: *Someone was with me ... I know that it was Byron. I felt the connection.*

She thought back: *What kind of connection?*

This time I spoke. "The only kind that matters...."

I don't know why, but then I turned to my father, "There's a college prep program at Princeton."

"Princeton...?" My father looked surprised. "That's a bit out of the way."

"It's a great place," I said.

"No argument there," he said. "But what changed your mind?"

"I don't know," I said. "Maybe because Josh just got accepted for pre-med next fall."

"He did?" my mother asked. "Remi didn't mention it."

"She doesn't know," I said. "The acceptance letter hasn't come yet."

Part II

1. Princeton

Heads turned with that "check the new girl out" look as I walked through the science building, making my way to the physics department. Random bits of conversation followed as I caught the thoughts of strangers ... with seemingly unnerving precision.

"Coming into your own," Remi had called it.

She was referring to my sudden improvement in psychic ability, the equivalent of an extrasensory growth spurt.

My eyes turned to the old photos of Albert Einstein on the walls. They reminded me of those famous theories, the ones printed across T-shirts in the campus store. A student in one of the study lounges told me that Dr. Tashimoto's office was down the hall, the third on the left.

"Everyone calls him Tash for short," he said.

I managed an awkward smile while his thoughts streamed in. Somehow it felt wrong — the easy access into his personal life.

"Welcome to Princeton," he said.

I looked past him without answering. The room had a cyber-slick vibe, quirky and high-tech with energy drinks edging close to electronic devices ... the kind that barely felt like anything in your hand, but could probably re-program a satellite on-demand.

There was something else too, more than what my eyes could see. An attitude that announced itself like writing on the wall: *Whatever you think you know – think again, because you're probably wrong.*

What I knew *or* didn't know wasn't the point. It was what I wanted to believe that mattered. So for the second time today, my mind cut away to the fantasy ... to the perfect image of Byron with his guarded gaze and fleeting smile.

Suddenly I was holding back what was by now an involuntary reflex, sadness welling up inside, choking me to tears.

"I'll be glad to show you around," the student said, slinging a backpack over his shoulder. "I'm heading towards Tash's office now."

"Thanks, but I can find it."

Without thinking, I let his name slip; forgetting that he never told me. I didn't stick around long enough to catch that "she must be psychic" look in his eyes.

When I reached the office, the door was closed. A brass plaque told me I was in the right place: Henry J. Tashimoto, Ph.D., Associate Professor of Astrophysics.

Carefully, my fingers ran over the raised letters one at a time, the metal cool to the touch. Almost instantly, a series of disconnected images moved through me: his life on campus, late nights spent juggling mathematical problems. Then there were bits and pieces of his home life: his sons, soccer on the weekends.

Slowly I lifted my hand, breaking the connection as quickly as hitting the power button on the TV remote.

Awesome, I thought, staring at my open hand like it belonged to someone else.

When I raised it again, ready to tap on the door, I heard voices — nothing distinct, just an impression of an argument. I hesitated, about to walk away when the voices turned silent.

Reluctantly, I knocked. The door opened slowly and then, barely halfway. The man peeking around the door startled. I was interrupting something after all.

I easily recognized him from the slide show that had just run through my head. He was middle-aged but actually very cool for a Professor. He wore a dark red turtleneck under his favorite sport coat, the kind with suede elbow patches. His slightly graying hair was longish and pulled back from his face, wrapped neatly around his ears. His eyes were kind, but drawn with fatigue.

"Professor Tashimoto?" I asked.

"Yes," he replied, his voice distracted.

A moving chain of math problems reached me, highly technical, they meant nothing to me but apparently something was missing. Something he couldn't find.

"Hi, my name is Genna Savoy," I introduced myself. "I'm in your undergraduate prep-course: Intro to General Physics 101."

I was reasonably sure he hadn't noticed me hiding in the back of the lecture hall, tucked into an aisle seat, my jacket purposely draped on the seat beside me in order to discourage some overly-interested boy from sitting there.

I waited while he glanced behind his shoulder. His eyes returned to me when I spoke again.

"I was reading ahead in the textbook," I said. "And then I realized after the first couple of chapters that I was stuck on the math."

His face warmed as he pulled the door open a bit more.

"Ah, Ms. Savoy," he said. "I remember seeing your name on my class list. Your profile said that you're headed for a life science major — pre-med, right?"

"I'll be majoring in biology this fall," I confirmed with a weak smile.

Something in the way he said "life science major" made me feel like an intellectual light-weight.

"I'm available during my regular office hours from three to five, but unfortunately...," he apologized, "I'm in a meeting right now."

The afternoon time wasn't convenient. I started to back away when a voice from inside the office called out, "Tash, don't turn her away. I'll help her."

The voice was bright, strangely uplifting.

Professor Tashimoto made little effort to disguise his irritation, sighing heavily as he flung the door open. He stepped away as he gestured for me to enter.

A boy was seated at the only desk in the room. His legs were outstretched across the top, over papers and folders. I noticed his dark-washed jeans, fashionably torn across the knees.

The music playing in his head quickly reached me, while he read aloud from a science magazine ... the kind you usually find in a doctor's office. Held up with one hand, it just about blocked his face. His other hand was busily stroking the head of a striped cat, the motion of his fingers in-time with the music.

"You know Tash," he said matter-of-factly. "That new telescope, it can look back to the big bang almost 13 billion years ago ... *imagine that!*"

"You're reading an old magazine," Tash snapped, his tone sharp enough to send my eyes between them, until they finally settled on the boy.

He waved the magazine across his face like a fan. The quick glimpses teased and startled, until he finally tossed the magazine aside. Freeing his hands, he stretched his arms wide ... and fell back against the chair in a state of absolute contentment.

I barely noticed the cat as it jumped from his lap. All I saw was his eyes as they locked on mine ... large, oval and razor blue.

There was a directness about him that made me want to step back. I felt my arms tighten around my books as the rest of his features fell into view, almost too beautiful to take in at once: perfect skin over a strong, well defined face. His hair was dark, slightly wavy and worn long, just below the collarbone. He reminded me of that statue. I had seen it once in Italy.

I began to turn away when he flashed a smile, the most amazing smile I had ever seen. Huge and playful, it filled his entire face with light. The feeling I had was as if we were celebrating — something.

"My name is Elon," he said softly, his lips held the smile, bold and beautiful.

The books against my chest felt weightless like the rest of me.

"Elon is my graduate assistant," Tash said.

Graduate Assistant, I thought. *He looks so young; he couldn't be more than nineteen.*

Tash turned to him; his politeness forced.

"Elon, this is Genna Savoy," he said. "She's taking a college prep course in physics."

Somewhere between smiles I had heard his last name, tangled in oddly-placed consonants and impossible to remember.

He came around the desk. Even the way he walked made my heart beat faster.

"Hi," he answered sprightly.

His arms were folded across his chest, his gaze unwavering as if nothing could be more important at that moment than exactly what he was doing ... *talking to me.*

"Hi," I repeated back in this fragile, little girl's voice that I didn't know I had.

Just as I felt my thoughts wander, he removed the "feather-weight" books from my arms and placed them on the desk. With nothing else to ground me, my arms fell to my side like two floppy rubber bands. Suddenly I was daydreaming. I was down the shore, and the sun was floating high in the sky, warm as July.

"You know, Tash," he said without looking away from me. "I should get her started on those equations — you're way too busy today."

The sense of authority in his voice returned me to the moment.

"Okay, then." Tash agreed, reluctantly.

"This is amazing!" Elon pointed to a cup of what smelled like coffee. The lightness in his voice came rushing back, more upbeat than before. "Can I get you some?" he asked.

I shook my head.

Man, I thought. *How can anyone get that excited about coffee?!*

"I could use some more … coffee." He stalled in mid-sentence, as if he had forgotten what it was called. "Then afterwards, we'll find a quiet place to work."

I drifted into silence as my eyes fell over him, the way he leaned against the desk, chilled to the extreme. Yet there was something overpowering about him. That "easy does it, rule the world"' attitude felt good to be around but just now I couldn't decide whether this made him the most incredible guy I ever met — *or* the most obnoxious. I was relatively sure that the answer was not somewhere in between.

"Why don't you guys get some miracle coffee," Tash said with his eyes on his phone. "I have a lecture in ten minutes."

Elon turned to me. "We were out partying all night, so he's a little touchy." His eyes shifted. "Aren't you Tash..?"

If they were sharing an inside joke, only one seemed amused. My natural curiosity made it difficult to stand by without fishing for details, but each time I tried to read either one, I drew a blank.

It seemed that the slightest bit of tension was enough to render my insight practically useless, while Elon stood by unaffected; rattling his teacher like he knew that he could totally get away with it.

Unaffected and uninhibited, he was looking at me now so closely that I wondered if my "morning face" could hold up to the scrutiny. That concern didn't last when I caught the glint in his eye, an "in your face, ready for anything" look that screamed: FUN!

Dancing all night in a club FUN; skiing down a white mega-slope FUN. His perfect smile widened and then he laughed … as if to seal the promise.

I had to wonder what he'd do next.

With his eyes still on me, he leaned over and scooped up the tiger-cat, as it scurried from some unseen place.

"Elon, if you don't mind," Tash said impatiently, as he motioned towards the door. "I'd like my desk back, my magazine — my cat."

He pulled the protesting animal from Elon's arms.

"Come on Genna," Elon said as he grabbed my forgotten books from the table. "We'll leave Tash alone for now."

His tone was insolent. But when he said my name, I heard nothing else, different from Byron and yet *the same*.

I stood deliberately still, baiting him to say it again.

Wait for it, I thought.

"Genna," he repeated softer this time, the last syllable drawn out as if he was reaching across a distance, "Are you okay?"

He giggled as I almost walked into the door.

"Fine," I answered, holding my eyes shut for an instant.

I wasn't fine.

I was so *not* fine.

Just as I managed to get the door open, he swung around. His extended arm, revealing perfectly-pumped biceps, blocked my way.

"I'll walk you to the library," he insisted.

I ducked under his elbow; my chin carefully lowered to avoid another look at that face — so "smoking hot" that it had no right to show itself in public.

"Can I meet you there?" I asked.

"Okay," he hesitated.

I turned towards the nearest bathroom: a quick mirror-check, time to cool down, time to mess up my hair until it fell right. As long as no one else was in there, I could do what I wanted to do — scream!

"I'll wait for you," he said.

I jerked to a stop.

He looped around and faced me again.

The words buzzed in my head like my favorite song, like one mind talking.

"What's your favorite place?" he asked.

I noticed how he rolled his R's — man, I so loved that!

"I guess the beach," I said.

"After we're done, we'll go to the beach."

I followed him into the hallway, as if I had a choice. Tash dropped his head and closed his door behind us.

"The beach," I said, my reaction delayed. "We're in New Jersey. It's January."

He turned his face, close to mine. I thought I'd faint.

"I want to feel the wind," he said.

2. Anti-Flirt

Elon was the type of guy that when he looked at you, the adrenaline rushed in faster than bungee jumping without the cord.

He found me sitting in the back of the library, in a chair wedged between a bookcase and a wall. He ignored the empty seats around the table as he pulled my jacket off the seat beside me, the seat he wasn't supposed to take. He opened the textbook to the first chapter and began reading aloud, hardly glancing at the page. I felt his eyes close in. Then there was that "too cool to play by the rules" smirk that wouldn't quit.

I realized now how much energy it took to intentionally ignore someone — much less someone like him. Everything about him demanded attention. Then I remembered something that Trinity told me. Trinity, who liked every boy she met so that liking anyone was meaningless.

"Someday that 'anti-flirt' act will turn against you," she warned. "You're so hooked into playing 'hard to get' that all that energy comes right back at you."

Okay, I thought as I whipped out my phone. What better way to "zone out" than to text everyone on my contact list!

From the corner of my eye, I saw Elon pick up a ruled pad and write down a series of equations. I heard him explain the theories, but my attention kept drifting — to the sharp angles of his face, to the pirate-hip sideburns under his hair and to that blue stare that made me feel like I was floating off the ground.

My eyes pulled away — as if they had inadvertently glimpsed something indecent. I had just one way to level the playing field. I focused harder than should have been necessary to hear his thoughts, but all I got were math equations, numbers and symbols streaming by like breaking news.

If that was all he was about, there wasn't any point in looking further.

The guy's a total geek, I thought; *Super-hot but a geek all the same.*

"Now," he said, "you solve the equation."

He offered the pencil to me. I slipped my phone back into my bag. This was going to be embarrassing. I had lost track of what he was saying. My hand overlapped his as I took the pencil. I felt a slight flutter, deep inside, like a pair of beating wings.

Man, I thought, *I'm crushing on him big time.*

I dropped my eyes.

My head was suddenly swimming away from me like it was caught in a rip tide, while I spent the longest minute staring at my dark blue fingernails.

Then I heard myself whimper aloud, "I'm feeling sick."

It was my voice but somehow strange. Slowly I laid the pencil down and began to lift out of my chair. The image of Byron in the bookstore flashed through my mind.

"Sorry," Elon said, "let me take you home."

"No, that's fine." I stumbled on my words like liars do.

"It's not a problem," he said.

"I have my car," I explained, my books already off the table. Before he could talk me out of it, I was through the library and out the exit doors.

"Wait up, Genna."

I heard him call from behind as I broke through the crowd, moving as fast as possible without attracting attention. All the way his voice gave chase, growing louder as he came steadily closer. It was tempting to glance behind but for fear of slowing down, I kept my focus ahead, following the signs that led to campus parking.

Once outside, I realized that I didn't remember where I had parked.

My head bobbed up and down while I tried to see over vehicles, as I pointed and pressed my key in random directions. Finally, I ran a winding path towards a flash of headlights — to where I heard the familiar sound of doors unlocking.

I spotted my car further in, sandwiched between two neon Minis — and the boy leaning against the driver's door waiting for me ... my jacket beside him, draped across the hood.

Instinctively, I whipped my head around. Seconds ago, he had been close enough to pull me around. How was it possible that he got past me? I wasn't even sure where I had parked!

He looked pleased with himself as I walked over, his arms folded against his chest like he was forever waiting.

"Way too freaky," I said, my voice pitching high with astonishment.

"You forgot your jacket," he said casually.

"How did you know where I parked?" I asked, still trying to catch my breath.

"Lucky guess," he said. "Looked like the kind of car you might drive — a hybrid."

I felt his eyes draw me in.

"You're in my way," I said looking past him, past his riveting blue eyes.

He didn't move.

"Guess I'll have to call security," I lamely threatened, pulling my phone from my bag.

He flung my jacket to me. I caught it with one hand as he opened my car door and stepped behind it.

The door slammed shut just as my seat belt fastened. As I drove away, I looked back in my rear view mirror expecting to see him still standing there, forlorn and rejected, but he was gone ... in the blink of an eye.

Just as well, I thought.

* * *

Been there, done that ... there was something about him, something in the way he moved that felt familiar.

I knew how impossible that was because IF I had met him, even in passing, there would be no forgetting — eyes the color of sapphires, the way his lips teased when he smiled, one corner curving higher than the other.

He's bad, I kept telling myself; *too bad to be good.*

He's so full of himself that there's no room for anyone else.

My mother's truck was parked in the driveway like she had been coming and going all day and couldn't bother straightening out. The moment I turned the key, I heard voices from the living room.

"We didn't cover much ground," he said. "Maybe if she's feeling up to it, we can finish the chapter."

I walked into the room. My mother was sitting on the sofa. Elon had a fizzy drink in his hand, one of my favorites and probably the last one in the fridge.

"Hey," he said, stretching his arms like he had been lounging in the same position all day. "Feeling better?"

I wondered if that incorrigible smile ever left his face.

No one is that happy, I thought.

"I'm okay," I said cautiously.

Man he looked so good it hurt!

"I have some things to do," my mother said as she rose from the sofa, making no effort to hide the smirk on her lips.

I could tell that she saw through my invented illness and still she did nothing to help me get rid of him.

Help me get rid of him, I signaled her.

"Staying for dinner?" she asked him, jabbing me with another smirk.

My eyes widened as I answered "NO" at the same time; Elon answered "YES."

My mother's only reaction was the "eye roll thing" she always did when she thought that I was being a pain in the "you know what."

No time to argue. I pitched her only one thought: *Later!*

She shrugged her shoulders, figuring that the story was already a trilogy, and left the room.

"How did you find me?" I asked straight-up.

"Tash gave me your address," he answered.

"There should be rules against that," I said. "How did you get here so fast?"

He threw me a blank expression as if English was suddenly a foreign language.

"Where's your car?" I asked. "It's not parked in my driveway."

He didn't respond.

"How did you get here?" My eyes widened, insisting on an answer.

"Genna," he said, instantly rousing my attention. "Tell me why you're so freaked over math."

"I'm *not*," I said defensively. "It's just new."

"New is good," he said. "Learning to think in a new way requires a certain amount of cooperation on your part. So let's get back to work — or you'll find yourself falling behind."

I frowned. Now he sounded like any teacher I ever had.

He tossed me my textbook.

"That is — if you're feeling better," he said with a sly grin.

I imitated my mother's "psychic sleuth" face as I slipped out of my jacket, still trying to break through the wall I was hitting whenever I tried to read him.

A few minutes of hard concentration and the only thing I got was his seriously juvenile obsession over chocolate mint cookies. Now I was forced to accept the images of pulling apart wafers to get to the cream filling, knowing that it was happening again ... like one mind talking.

His brain might be impenetrable, yet when a stray thought came crashing through, I seemed to own it like a bruise. It meshed with my own thoughts until I couldn't tell which one of us was actually doing the thinking.

I sat on the sofa, at the extreme end of where he was sitting. I didn't know what to do with my hands, so I placed them at my sides, braced flat against the cushion.

"Where are you from?" I asked, trying to absorb the taste of chocolate in my mouth.

"I told you," he said.

I raised my eyebrow. "No, you didn't."

"California," he said after a few seconds. "That's on the West Coast."

"Really," I said with grinding attitude.

"Look at me." His voice beckoned almost as much as his smile.

I fought myself harder than I wanted to fight him. Unlikely as it seemed, he was striking the same feelings — the ones I thought I had for Byron. I hated him for that. I hated him more than I could have loved Byron.

"I am looking at you," I insisted, my eyes wandering.

"I won't bite." He handed me his drink.

I took hold of the glass with hesitant fingers. He watched as I set my mouth on the edge of the glass where there was still a smudge-print from his lips. I finished what was left in one gulp.

The smile on his lips began pulling at the corners of my mouth. I tried not to feel it ... that tugging feeling I felt when he was around. The more he pushed, the more I pulled back, and the better it felt.

"Every action has an equal and opposite reaction," he said.

"Excuse me," I said just becoming aware of the edge of the sofa.

"Newton's Third Law of Motion." He pointed to the bold type under the chapter heading. He set the book on my lap. "Were you thinking about something else?"

His eyes blinked at me precociously.

"No," I said awkwardly.

My hands pressed deeper into the sofa, my butt barely hanging on to the cushion. If I moved any further away, I'd be on the floor. He removed a pillow from the sofa and tossed it on my mother's rug, my anticipated landing site if I kept inching over.

"Just in case...." He grinned.

I felt a nervous, breathy giggle enter my throat as he pulled me back towards the center of the seat. The gentle pressure of his fingers against my wrist passed through me like an electrical charge.

My eyes shut tightly — you can't feel this stuff and keep your eyes open at the same time.

"I think my Mom is making spinach lasagna tonight," I said struggling to say the words without shrieking. "We're vegan," I explained. "No meat, dairy, eggs."

"Perfect," he said.

3. REALITY CHECK

There was a kind of destructive excitement about him that was fueling my lust-hate. It made me feel like I could get away with anything — like flying through open air, or like running around the Jersey Shore in the dead of winter, in the middle of the night.

"Why are we here?" My voice scattered as the first blast of frigid air whipped around my face — so cold that it startled me stiff.

"Whoa!" He surveyed the distance with his hands on his hips. "This is so cool."

Cool? I thought. *He must have meant frozen solid.*

I followed his eyes to a line of city lights twinkling on the other side of the water.

"That's Manhattan," I pointed with my eyes.

Suddenly I was fighting the urge to ditch the suburbs. His eyes flew to mine, as if he was responding, but I didn't say anything. I was only thinking.

Thinking now of what to say next....

"First time at the Jersey Shore...?" My voice fought to be heard over the wind.

"Yeah, but I've traveled a lot here and there," he said laughing. "Mostly *there*."

My eyes widened. The teasing was too strange, especially when I was struggling to stay with the conversation, jumping in-place while trying to keep warm in a cropped leather jacket.

He removed his coat and draped it over my shoulders. Underneath, he had nothing but a black T-shirt on. Staring at him, the way I was staring at him, I almost didn't notice the text printed across his perfectly-molded chest: *I Bring Everything to the Table.*

Hmm, I thought. *So humility wasn't his best quality!*

"What are you doing?" I asked. "You'll freeze to death."

If it wasn't for the cold, I could have easily stood there while he slowly adjusted the coat around me, moving to free my hair caught under the collar.

"I'll be fine," he said as he lifted his eyes towards the sky.

The night was a smoky violet-blue. The crescent moon cast just enough light to cut through the shadows so that I could still make out the outline of his face and that heart-stopping smile.

"Over there," he said pointing up, his warm breath misting in the air. "That's Orion, the Hunter." His eyes widened. "And there on the right — that's Jupiter."

I followed his moving finger, trying to connect the dots like a planetarium sky, but all the while it was his eyes that took me back, shining brighter than the stars.

"C'mon," he said turning to me. "Let's go."

I shrank back when I saw his hand open for mine, motioning me onto the beach. Just the sight of the water plunged my body temperature another ten degrees.

I rushed to pull up my zipper. My favorite top underneath, splattered with rebel-rock lyrics was probably too sheer even with the lace bandeau underneath.

His eyes lowered. "No wonder you're cold."

"Fashion is like music," I explained. "It can't be afraid to take risks."

"Really," he said, sliding my zipper higher. "Even when you won't?"

He was obviously still trying to get me down to the water.

"My band is playing here next week," I changed the subject.

The club was just behind us, closed for the night. The glass walls facing the boardwalk reflected the ocean.

"Gotta stop by and check it out," he said, like the invite was already in his hands.

"Sure," I said, trying to appease him. "Let's just head back now before we freeze out here."

"I thought you liked the beach," he said, missing the point.

He flashed a huge smile as he waved me on, the sparkle in his eyes persuading me to follow.

I looked down at my four-inch platform boots, knowing for sure that I'd sink into the sand if I tried it. While I hesitated, he threw his arms under my legs and effortlessly lifted me up; carrying me off the boardwalk, down the steps and about one hundred feet out to the water.

The tide was coming in fast, foam-edged waves washing over the sand with that steady, hypnotic swishing sound like a spa-music track.

"Still cold?" he asked.

I nodded my head while his face moved closer.

"The water is warm," he said, his voice certain.

"Warm!" I repeated, sarcastically. "Yeah, warm like hypothermia."

Still holding onto me, he managed to pull off my boots, my thick sport socks pulled off with them. I winced as the freezing cold air hit my bare feet, numbing them up within seconds. The only thing I was thankful for was the fresh pedicure and the dark, vamped-up polish that looked good even at night.

I felt his grip release. He stood me up on the wet sand just as a thrashing wave came on shore. I screamed so hard that my rib cage rattled, as the frothy water raced towards me, running fast between my toes.

"No way," I said as the water splashed high above my ankles, so warm that it felt like bath water.

"Are you having fun, Genna?" he asked, exploding into bright laughter.

He was sprinting around me, teasing me with an orbit-like motion that put me in the center of his view. As I turned he turned, stalking me with his spectacular eyes.

He had said my name, and for a moment I almost didn't care about what was real and what wasn't — or the fact that he had so easily cornered me into a position where he could block my every move to get away.

"Are you having fun?" he asked again.

Suddenly I noticed that he was farther away, much farther. He was walking the shoreline with his hands in his pockets as if he hadn't a care in the world. Seagulls clustered at the water's edge, glowing whiter than the moon, squawking bird noises in the distance. So far up the beach that I had to strain my eyes to see it all.

"Tell me you're having fun," he said, whispering in my ear, the force of his breath sending chills down my neck.

I jumped, practically twisting in a figure eight ... almost landing in the ocean now by some bizarre trick of nature "turned" hot tub.

"How did you do that?" A swirling gust of wind made me yelp. "You were over there and now...."

"I'm over here," he called out, his voice more serious.

He was well behind me, leaning over to pick up a shell embedded in the sand.

My eyes watched him as I stepped back. Confusion and panic left me speechless as my mind merged this with what had happened in the parking lot, how he somehow got past me while chasing from behind.

I stifled a gasp as he grabbed my elbow and spun me around. The smile on his lips made me forget how scared I should be.

Without fear, anger was sure to find me. Anger would keep me in my power zone which was where I needed to be when he was around, since his ego wouldn't give up long enough for me to figure out what was going on.

"What's with the Chris Angel act?" I asked him with "head-butting" attitude.

"It's the light out here; it plays tricks with your eyes," he said quietly, as he examined the shell still in his hand.

"I know what I saw," I said.

I removed his coat and handed it to him. I hadn't realized how warm it was keeping me until I took it off.

"I should go," I said, almost moving.

The wind was pulling his hair across his face, his glorious face.

"Stay Genna," he said, placing the shell carefully in my hand. "You know you want to."

4. AFFLICTION

I strolled through the science building hoping to find him, as if finding him was all that mattered. My ramped up senses told me that he was nearby, closer now than a minute ago.

I reached into my pocket to check the time on my cell. Instead, my fingers pulled out the shell that he had snatched from the sand, luminous and white like a pearl. I thought back to the beach, to the things that I thought I saw him do.

It was a long night, getting in late and then surfing the internet till dawn, trying to find out if there was any natural phenomenon that could explain why the ocean was so warm in the middle of one of the coldest winters on record. Even global warming didn't seem to be able to account for it.

Then there was that twisted knack he had of moving from one place to the next. Whatever he was doing, I was sure that it wasn't what it seemed. Like second-rate magic tricks, once you know how they're done, they seem really lame.

I slipped the shell back into my pocket and pulled out my phone, desperate to talk to someone normal. I waited while the call went through, tucking my head inside my locker for privacy.

It was impossible to close my eyes without seeing him prancing around in the sand like the front man for some gorgeous boy band. One illusion, I was sure that he couldn't pull off. No matter what, he could never be Byron.

I waited for it ... that little prick that I always felt when I thought of *him*, his absence washing over me fresh and new.

It was a mystery how I found myself attracted to two guys who rode the opposite ends of extreme. Physical perfection excluded; they were nothing alike. Byron's cool aloofness, matched in intensity with Elon's unrestrained exuberance. Now it seemed that, despite their differences, they were united by a single mission: to make me totally and helplessly miserable.

"Can I see that?" he asked with a mischievous smirk.

Elon walked around my locker door and held his hand out for my cell phone.

My eyes blinked at his sudden appearance. It was never really possible to expect Elon even when I was expecting him.

Nick answered my call, "Hey Genna — what's up?"

"Where are you?" My eyes barely left Elon. "I need to see you."

"Are you okay?" Nick asked.

It was a reasonable question.

No, I wanted to say, *I've never been less okay.*

I'm in crisis-mode, with a new set of extrasensory skills that I can't control, and this "strike me down with a single look heart-throb" won't quit shadowing me.

That was what I wanted to say.

"Give it to me — just for a minute," Elon insisted with a feisty grin, wiggling his fingers for me to turn over my phone.

"I'm talking on it *now*," I said, my voice stressing high as I slipped the phone away from my ear.

"That's okay," he said yanking the phone out of my hand, "I don't mind."

"Give it back," I snapped, trying to grab the phone while he dangled it above my head.

Lifting up on my heels, I struggled to reach his height only to find myself staggering closer.

It was too late to stop myself even if I could. My eyes zoomed in like a camera, adjusting to the view. He was wearing his hair pulled back in a short ponytail, his flawless features fully visible. I could have spent hours obsessing over that face ... loosing myself in the slope of his forehead, the curved lines of his cheekbones.

He looked like an angel, sprung to life from some renaissance fresco.

Finally, my hand caught his arm, the one holding my cell. As I tried to pull it down, his jacket fell open. I noticed the dark blue sweatshirt underneath: *Property of Princeton University Physics Department.*

Dorky shirt, I thought. But there was no missing the way it draped over him.

"Stop it!" I yelled as if I was talking to a six-year old.

He evaded my grabbing hands as he brought the phone to his ear.

"Genna's a little busy at the moment," he said, almost laughing.

I heard Nick grunting, "Who's this?"

"I'll call you back," I shouted, hoping he could hear me since everyone else around us had.

"Your boyfriend's a jerk." Elon smirked as he powered-down my phone.

I didn't bother to correct him that Nick wasn't my boyfriend. I was too busy watching him as he flipped my "nothing special" phone around in his hand, checking it out from different angles before he finally handed it back to me.

"Thanks," I said sarcastically.

"Don't mention it," he said as if he had seriously done me a favor.

My mouth opened with a gasp, "How do you do stuff like that?"

He started laughing, the kind of laughter that tickles you into laughing back.

I resisted partly because I was annoyed and partly because I didn't want to encourage him. We looked at each other until it became awkward. My face dropped as far as it could without kinking my neck. Total anti-flirt move but I had to do it.

I heard a muffled giggle as he crouched down, looking up from under my chin.

"What are you doing?" he teased with a deliberately adorable expression on his face, irresistibly precious, deceptively innocent.

The pressure of him staring made me want to look up.

"Nothing," I answered in a coy voice.

"Are you sure?" He sounded unconvinced.

The fooling around over, I slowly lifted my eyes with a sense of being unglued.

"Are you always like this?" I asked.

His eyes deepened. "Like what?"

"Happy?" I asked.

"Yes," he said, gently. "I'm always like this."

Unable to move, I watched his eyes begin to close as he leaned forward.

Suddenly we sprang back. The rush of the crowd hit the halls like thunder. It was only after we pulled apart that I realized how close we were standing.

Tash didn't force the pace as he strolled behind students trying to text and walk at the same time, his smile reasonably amicable before he caught sight of Elon. I was ready to stop him, maybe comment on the lecture, when he tore through the hall like he couldn't get away fast enough.

"Don't let him bother you," Elon said.

Me bothered? I thought, *I was wired to be bothered.*

"Promise me that you won't get upset," he said.

I quickly realized that he was no longer talking about Tash.

The girls walked in perfect step, like a dance routine. No way to miss the "about-face" turns as they swung out of their paths and into his way with clumsy intention.

The whispers and giggles were enough to make me cringe. Without thinking, I covered my ears as if I could silence their thoughts, posting in my head like a blog.

They hadn't seen him around. Was he new, who did he hang with — not the rocker chic with the blue in her hair...?

I felt for my clip-in extensions while they raved about the new frozen yogurt place. Then someone asked him to a party over the weekend. She probably didn't mean me when she said, "Bring your girlfriend."

His excuses were lame as he wiggled free, the look in his eyes telling me to wait.

Maybe I should take a number, I thought. *Or maybe I shouldn't be standing here like a total idiot while...*

"Sorry about that," he said, sprinting towards me.

My eyes roamed back to the hungry pack of she-wolves strolling away, each of them convinced that he was into her. Seconds later, the girl who didn't know how to wear combat boots came rushing back.

"Don't move," she said, scribbling her number across his hand with a semi-permanent marker.

An uncomfortable expression crossed his face while he said something about losing his cell ... which would explain why I never saw him with one.

"No worries," she said, "I'll find you."

Maybe it was my loud sighs that made him take his hand back, short of the last two numbers.

"I have to go...," he said, fumbling for her name.

"Harley," she said like she expected applause.

He began to back away, but it was too late. In my mind, I already heard the music. Elon turned with me; the light snuffed from his eyes as he followed my reaching arm.

Through the thinning crowd, I saw *him* — an easy stand-out with grunge-hip good looks downplayed by a pair of round shades. The timing was right. Without slowing, without stopping, Nick grabbed my hand and pulled me toward him like we were already a couple.

"Okay?" he asked, wrapping his arm around me with a protective squeeze.

With a faint smile, I snatched his black fedora and dropped it on my head. The curved brim shadowed my eyes as I merged with him into the moving crowd ... like I wanted to be swallowed up and carried away.

5. BACKSTAGE

Nick is such a fierce musician that I could almost forgive him for not being *the one*.

"Gen, that was awesome," he said, leading me backstage.

"I know you are," I giggled.

"I meant the vocals," he insisted, grinning playfully.

Before I could toss the compliment back, I heard an incoming text. It was my mother letting us know that a New York rock station was in the audience to check out the latest wave of Jersey bands.

Too sad that the rest of our crew had already cleared out, headed for an after-party at Logan's. She practically begged Nick to come, but he made some excuse when he saw that I wasn't going.

"Really," she said, "If we're going to be the Jersey Shore's new 'It' band, we shouldn't be seen hanging around after the show. It's cooler to disappear."

I wish you'd disappear, Logan, I thought.

Nick rested his guitar against a wall, careful not to whack it. Then he took both my hands in his and slipped his fingers between mine, rocking back and forth with a rhythm, not unlike the song we just played. The connection was reassuring. Nick was real. I didn't feel him running away from me like Byron. I didn't feel him overtake me like Elon.

"Hey," he said, "I've missed you."

I saw the kiss in his eyes, and I wondered what I would do when the moment came.

The mascara running down my eyes; I let myself look at him, attractive enough to be believable. Not some mega-gorgeous, mind-bending bad boy who didn't know when to stop.

"Straight-up dude...." Elon's magnetic voice broke from behind. "She's so out of your league."

I drew back as if an invisible sword had just divided the space between us.

So he had found his way backstage, I thought; *past security, past the locked doors.*

From the stage, caught up in the music, I might have imagined him, a sprinting figure merging with the shadows. Nick's guitar howled back between verses, his fingers playing from memory while he squinted into the audience trying to see where I was looking ... his eyes asking what was wrong.

Elon was already on the opposite side of the club, hanging loose the way he did, with his legs crossed at the ankles and arms folded across his chest.

I had to think of a way to last until the encore, so I gave up on the idea of stealth moves and paranormal tricks. I told myself that it was the disco lighting, the slow-motion effects stalling the action in spurts and shifting it into freeze-frame.

"Hey man — what's your problem?" Nick swung around.

"Did I say I had a problem?" Elon snarled back.

Nick's eyes narrowed, "You must have missed the sign that said *backstage passes only*."

"No, I saw it," Elon admitted, indifferently.

"Hold off, Nick," I stepped in. "Elon is tutoring me in physics for pre-med next fall."

"Hmm," Nick mused. "Good to know but we're not in school right now so what brings him around?"

"Genna," Elon answered with a willful smile.

Nick turned to me, "Did you invite him or did he just show up?"

"I can't remember," I hedged.

"I remember," Nick said turning back to Elon. "It was your voice on the phone yesterday."

Nick had been stopped in traffic when I called. After Elon had ended our conversation, he turned off at the Princeton exit. Minutes later, he tore through the science building, in and out of lecture halls and labs, until he found me.

His eyes were on Elon when he spoke. "Get a clue," he said with a condescending tone. "Stop forcing yourself where you're not wanted."

I tugged at Nick's arm trying to stop him, but he continued. "There's always the fan club. You can sign up online. Who knows ... maybe you'll win an autographed poster."

I watched Elon react. Anger did nothing to diminish the power of his beautiful face, the slight cleft in his chin overshadowed by barely-there stubble.

If I weren't so overwhelmed, I might have noticed Nick's guitar as it began to slide away from the wall. Nick reacted instinctively, jumping sideways as he grabbed the guitar before it hit the floor.

Elon was strangely quiet, propped up against a wall with a menacing glare.

"Hey, Nick," he said, taunting him like it was his new favorite sport. "Ever gone rock-climbing in the desert?"

Nick scoffed, "Man, you're out there."

Only Elon knew what kind of twisted game he was playing. Or maybe, the power of suggestion was stronger than I thought, because desert images seemed to flash through my head like a movie trailer: red rocks running high into the sky, jagged walls of stone baking in the sun and nothing around — nothing but an occasional lizard, skipping between the black crevices of the boulders.

I held up well. I didn't freak out. Not until my head jerked away like the sun was blinding my eyes.

Elon turned to me, "Whoa!" He lifted his hand over his eyes. "Is it bright in here?"

My mind seized up. Instantly, running wild with impossible thoughts even if he was talking about the dressing room, lit up like Times Square. Still I couldn't shake the feeling that I wanted the night to end.

"I'll call you," I told Nick in a choppy voice.

My cheek grazed his as I lifted up on my heels. Level with his face, my lips pressed together and did this little "air-kiss" thing good night.

"Don't leave," Nick protested trying to catch my face as it pulled away.

My hand fit into Elon's.

"Don't do this, Genna," Nick said, his voice falling with frustration as a girl who was standing there for who knows how long quickly replaced me.

He called out once more as she draped her arm over him.

The smell of the ocean swirled around us, salty and fresh. The feeling of Elon's hand in mine left me disoriented like I was zip-lining into a fog, until eventually, I couldn't tell where I was going *or* what I wanted to do.

We stopped. He released my hand and lifted me from my waist on top of the boardwalk railing, bracing me so I could sit without falling over. The night breeze lifted my hair from my shoulders. My head was still buzzing from the music. I might have heard him ask me if I was all right *or* did he tell me that I was going to be all right.

He dropped one hand to my lap. I thought about taking it.

"From the stage tonight," I said, "I thought I saw you doing these weird moves."

He chuckled, "Weird moves...?"

"Yeah, like the beach," I said.

He arched his brow. "Do you know what I think?" He didn't wait for me to answer. "I think you're watching me *way too closely*."

I felt the heat hit my cheeks like instant blush.

"I should head home," I said, expecting him to talk me out of it, or at least insist that he drive me.

"You should," he readily agreed. "It's getting late."

He pulled me down from the railing; his hands slowly sliding from my hips.

"Good night," I said, looking at him through lowered lashes.

"Be careful driving," he said. "The roads are dark."

I managed an awkward smile before I turned; walking slowly until I was sure that he could no longer see me.

And then I ran, like I was running for my life.

6. Mixed Signals

I was expecting him to track ahead of me, be standing there when I got to my car, or maybe pop up from the backseat while I was driving. I was both relieved and bothered when neither happened until I walked through my front door.

"How long has he been here?" My eyes darted towards the kitchen.

"I don't know ... a while," my mother answered, her voice hushed.

"That's impossible!" I shrieked. "I left before him"

"Speak softly," she whispered, "or don't speak at all."

I sighed, realizing that we weren't alone.

Remi reacted with a colossal frown. "I can see that old habits die hard,," she said.

Now that my telepathic skills had improved, using speech as the primary mode of communication was discouraged.

"Your boyfriend is in the kitchen," Lexa said, hoping that her voice was sufficiently irritating to send me flying from the room.

"He's *not* my boyfriend," I snipped, "And I know where he is, thank you."

I had no intention of going in after him until I figured out what was going on.

"Nothing's going on," my mother said.

"It feels like something," I mumbled.

Lexa was glued to her phone, checking e-mail. "You're dealing with a more active sense of awareness," she said. "You have no idea how to use it."

The attitude in her voice made me defensive.

"If I had it my way," I said, "Wednesday night would come around as often as the winter solstice — once a year."

She barely glanced up. "You were never so bratty when you couldn't read to save your life."

"That's enough!" My mother jumped in.

Lexa flashed an insincere smile. "I just realized that I never congratulated your darling daughter."

I waited for the sucker-punch.

"Never too late to come into your own," Lexa said, reaching for her drink with a ring-studded hand. "Too bad, so sad … that it will never last."

"Of course, it won't," said a woman I didn't know.

It seemed that anyone my own age was at Logan's party.

Harris looked up from his laptop.

"That's not the issue," he said. "She shows a complete lack of judgment."

"Look at how many meetings she missed," Remi said. "If it wasn't for our careful mentoring, she would be hopeless."

"Hopeless and helpless," Harris agreed.

My mother circled the room, anger flashing in her eyes.

"Sit down Arielle," Remi motioned. "Even you must admit that Genna has no clue how to handle a more sensitive skill."

"How quick you are to take credit for the upside," my mother said. "Stop blaming my daughter for stuff she can't control."

"Control is everything," Lexa said.

"No one is asking you." My mother's voice chilled.

Lexa rolled her eyes with an exaggerated huff and waved me closer. I knew what she wanted. She wanted to read me, of course. I hated being read almost as much as when people asked me to pose for pictures. Especially my dad, with his camera-ready, next generation phone lurking around.

"Let's just get it over with," I finally agreed.

The room fell silent. I did some breathing exercises and then waited for her senses to reach me.

"Relax...," she said with her eyes closed, a painful smile distorting her lips. "Everyone's entitled to a few secrets."

In the time it took to open a text, her eyes widened as if she had been suddenly shaken awake.

"I know what you think you know," she said in an enlightened voice.

Remi's hand flapped in the air. "Just tell her."

Lexa pressed her fingers to her temple, "Your impressions are no more reliable than they were before, easily corrupted by strong emotions."

It was a fancy way of saying that I was so physically attracted to him that I couldn't think straight. But Lexa wasn't done with me yet. Her voice warmed as she broke the news.

"You're wrong about him Genna. He's not one of us."

"Of course," "Remi balked, "he's as ordinary as leaves in fall."

Ordinary, I thought.

There were so many adjectives I could use to describe Elon, but "ordinary" never came to mind.

"Back and forth, back and forth," Remi complained. "Make up your mind whether you want to talk *or* think. The boy's mind is hardly worth reading."

That I couldn't argue with ... reading Elon wasn't much fun unless you wanted a crash course on how to split an atom.

The woman who I didn't know weighed in, "Who cares if he's boring. He is so unbelievably hot."

"How old are you?" Remi snapped.

"Not that old," the woman smirked.

"It's official," Remi said, throwing her hands up. "No psychic rock star in the house and here we are talking up a storm instead of picking each other's brain."

Lexa held back a yawn. "I don't know about you," she said. "But I'm picked over."

"Remember Genna," my mother said. "Lightning doesn't strike twice, at least not in the same place."

She was thinking of Byron. Her smile let loose as she lifted her necklace to her mouth.

"I'm totally sick of your boyfriends, Genna," Lexa said. "The last one had the gift, and goodness knows the face, but he was so weird that who knew what he was actually doing."

I held my mother's attention as I managed a cautious smile. One thing for sure, if Elon had the gift, it was unlikely that he would get past their combined radar.

So in the end I was left with one theory: my imagination was on overdrive which meant that I was fooling myself into thinking that stuff was happening when it wasn't.

Translation: *It was all in my head.*

"Really Genna...," my mother said, "that boy in the kitchen wouldn't know how to find his way out of a paper bag. He's so sweet and unassuming."

I stepped back with a total "gag me with a spoon" look on my face.

"Unassuming?" I squealed.

Now I was in serious doubt-mode again. My incredibly intuitive mother had totally missed the mark. Elon was about as unassuming as nuclear war.

I held still as he came strolling out of the kitchen like he owned the place, holding what looked like a fruit smoothie in his hand. I met him halfway and managed to reverse his direction before he reached the living room. Finding privacy in a house full of psychics wasn't the easiest thing to do.

"Lost you back there," he said with a breezy smile.

I wasn't listening. I was reviewing the evening's timeline in my head from the moment I left the club.

"I took a shortcut through Colts Neck," he said as if he wanted to explain. "I saw you behind me on the main road."

"I didn't see you," I said.

"You were driving way under the speed limit," he giggled. "Like someone's grandmother."

I felt momentarily dazed. "What did you say?"

"You were crawling through the streets," he said.

"You told me to be careful," I said, trying to think clearly.

"Oh wow," he said with wide eyes. "You actually listened."

Oh wow, I actually did!

"I noticed a truck on your tail," he said. "So I decided to stay close. Make sure you got home safe."

He pulled out the straw and slurped up the remainder of the smoothie.

It had happened once before — some fan *or whoever* followed me home after a concert and chased me into the battlefield.

"I guess I should say thank you," I said.

His mouth moved towards my ear. "I'm sorry," he said playfully. "Did I hear you say thank you?"

"Thank you," I repeated, breathing in the smell of his skin.

"Oh, you're welcome," he answered with a flirty smile. Then he touched his index finger to my lips. "Shhh...," he whispered, "they're listening."

I followed the stir of voices back to the living room. Remi was at the center of attention, sitting upright on the sofa, her back stiff as a board.

"Are you feeling okay?" my mother asked.

Her lips parted, but there was no sound. The only movement I noticed was in her eyes as they circled the room like a hawk until they found *him*.

Elon responded with an exaggerated, "silly face" smile that made her abruptly turn.

She dropped her face as if she was fainting. My mother caught her head and rolled it back while the others leaned in around her. They didn't notice anyone approaching until Remi pushed back, her eyes slowly lifting.

"Hi," Elon said, coming around the sofa.

There was silence. The first response was in the form of a gushy female voice trying to sound too sexy.

"Sorry, I didn't mean to interrupt," he said. "Just pretend I'm not here."

Yeah sure, I thought. *That'll work.*

I scurried him aside.

"It's one of Remi's monster migraines," I said. "We're like three minutes away from a 911 call."

"You know what?" he asked, changing the subject. "I'm glad you didn't run away from me again tonight."

He sounded like he believed it.

"I told you that I was going home," I said, glancing behind when I heard Remi moan.

"Before you ran," he said.

I avoided his eyes.

Yeah like … whatever, I thought.

"Now aren't you glad I'm here," he said. "Otherwise you would be waiting until morning to tell me how sorry you are."

My eyes came alert, "Hold it right there!"

"Don't worry," he giggled. "I'm not going anywhere."

"You're impossible!" I said.

He flashed a wide grin. "That's a widely-accepted opinion," he said. "Tell me something I don't know."

The commotion behind us forced my attention. Remi was now slumped over, with both hands gripping her head. Several sets of arms held her down as she thrashed against the sofa, whipping sideways as if to fend off an assault.

I began wondering if I shouldn't be doing something to help.

"Genna!" my mother called.

Remi was motioning for her medication that she kept in her bag.

I found the pill bottle, and then struggled to twist off the child-proof cap. Elon came over, which caused everyone to freeze. He took the bottle from me and opened it with one quick motion. Then he crouched down so that he was just over Remi.

I could see the skin on his knees showing through the slashed denim, worn and distressed, and so cool on him.

"Just breathe normally," he told her in a super-relaxed voice.

She looked up, baffled by his interest.

"That's it," he said, placing his right hand against her forehead. "Nice and slowly — I know you can do it."

His eyes held hers until her breathing fell into a steady rhythm, rising and falling at regular intervals. A moment later she bounced up, her face no longer resisting pain, yet something else remained ... something worse than the headache. A solitary tear trickled down her cheek, her eyes unblinking and black with fear.

With shaky fingers, Remi took the pill from my hand. Someone else gave her the water to wash it down. I walked away, knowing he would follow.

"What just happened?" I asked when we were out of listening range.

My eyes pointed towards my mother's totally freaked-out friend.

"I spilled some smoothie on my shirt," he said, looking at a pink splotch on his black shirt.

I resisted the impulse to wipe it away, unable to imagine what it would be like to move my hands across his chest, curved like a shield.

"I meant ... what happened to Remi?" My eyes pulled away.

"I guess she had a headache," he said. "I tried to help."

It was true that Remi was susceptible to migraines, which was why she carried medication. It wasn't unusual that they came and went all in the space of a few minutes and yet....

"Somehow you're involved," I said. "Remi must know something."

"She doesn't know anything." His tone was firm.

Before I could challenge him again, he handed me his empty glass like it was my job to clean up and started for the door. He was about to step out when he suddenly turned as if he had forgotten something.

Slowly he looked up and down — from my eyes to my lips and back again. I felt my face warm.

"I'll be in class tomorrow," he whispered, his breath sweet like vanilla.

I managed to reverse out of the swoon that threatened to pull me down as he walked away, no car waiting for him in the visible distance. Slowly I backed into my house letting the door shut ... while he disappeared into the night.

7. OPPOSITION

I came to class early, hoping to review my assignment before turning it in. Elon slipped in through the back door, the one that shouldn't be opened unless there's an emergency. Even with a stealth entrance, he immediately owned the room. Conversations muted; eyes turned.

From across the room, he noticed me noticing him. He turned from Tash, their words stalling in mid-sentence. His smile widened, and then with one of those amazing blue eyes he winked at me.

I held the side of the desk to keep from sliding off my chair. In the back of my mind, I wondered if a prettier girl was standing behind me, but there was no one there.

He winked at me and with that extreme smile that made me feel more beautiful than a supermodel. I dropped my eyes as the heat rose to my cheeks, like I was ready to burst into flames.

One quick glance and I saw him walking my way, his music video swagger baiting me with every step. I pretended to be intensely concerned with finding the right page in my textbook. My heart was pounding. He was an outrageous flirt, probably the biggest player on campus. He wasn't worth a second thought, much less a third, a fourth....

"Hey Genna," he said.

"Hey," I answered back.

He glanced down at my open notebook. "Did you do your lab assignment?"

I slid the book towards him. He pulled a red marker from his back pocket and removed the cap with his teeth. I half-watched what he was doing: circling, slashing out and subtracting points.

"Much better," he said as he wrote the grade on the top of the paper.

I gasped with disappointment. There was no way that I deserved three points off the second question.

"You gave me the right answer," he explained, "but you didn't show me how you got there."

Tash interrupted with an exaggerated cough as if to summon him away.

"I promised him that I would help him today," Elon said, rolling his eyes. "He can't seem to do anything without me."

I stared blankly, unable to think of anything to say.

"I'll catch you later," he said.

Without turning, he took small, slow steps back, his eyes unwilling to break contact, his smile unrelenting.

The class gathered around, while Elon knotted a piece of string around a pendulum. I recognized the girls on my right, the same bunch that stalked the halls any time he was around.

"Excuse me," Harley said, pushing through.

You're excused, I thought. *Now get out of my way.*

The artificial light highlighted her "natural girl" face, the kind that was almost pretty without makeup. The sweater under her lab coat was total prep and in a color that I couldn't pin down because I wasn't into pastels.

Push me off the catwalk now, I thought.

"I'm Genna," I said, my voice unavoidably cold.

"Genna..." she repeated, her eyes thinking. "You're *not* in that new band that's playing down the shore?"

"I'm the lead vocalist," I said.

It was a simple fact. I wasn't fishing for compliments.

"Wow," she said like she might be impressed. "Princeton must have been a real long shot!"

With a satisfied grin, she drew back, her friends rallying around her like she had scored a victory.

Meanwhile, Elon was improvising, setting up the experiment in a way that looked nothing like the diagram in the book. My eyes followed the lines of his arm as he worked; every muscle visible even through a shapeless sweatshirt. And the way his waist tapered in couldn't be real....

I snapped my head away like I was done watching, but a second later I looked again. Harley whispered in his ear while he was searching for a power strip to plug in a wire. I tried to pick up what she was saying, but my reaction was interfering ... to the point where I would have been better off reading lips instead of minds.

I felt a sudden overwhelming need to flip the page of my book, snapping it so hard between my fingers it almost tore. Then I heard the perky "cheerleader" voice, which made her sound like she wasn't old enough to drive herself to the movies.

When I looked again, Harley had snatched the pendulum from his hand as if she hoped he would take it back. Instead, he reached for another and managed to avoid her.

It would have been enough to make most girls give up, if she had been "most girls." It should have been enough to make me less crazy, yet I was twirling my hair at manic speed with no sign of letting up.

I closed in for a better view probably for the same reason people slow down to gawk at an accident on the parkway: morbid fascination. Then I saw her hand slip under his arm like it belonged there.

I stiffened as if someone had stuck me with a pin. If they had, I doubt I would have felt it. I was lost in imagination, wondering what would happen if he turned to her, if he looked at her the way he looked at me; his delicious smile and those hi-def eyes, wandering over her face as if she was the most beautiful girl *ever*.

All at once, my *inner voice* screamed. The pendulum crashed to the floor as Elon suddenly and inexplicably turned my way. The strand of hair I was holding fell into a loose spiral. The room took off in a wild spin, and a full feeling began to press on my stomach like I might throw up the breakfast I never ate.

I reached for my jacket and threw it over my shoulders. The longer I stayed, the sicker I felt. Finally, I pushed away my book and dashed from the room at topple-over speed.

The water fountain was just outside. Propped up on heels, I positioned myself low enough to reach the spout. Carefully, I leaned forward trying to keep balance, while my hair flipped in my face each time my mouth got near the water.

Suddenly I felt the pull of two hands, gathering my hair together and holding it in place in a loose ponytail.

A smile crept over my lips. The chilled water ran down my throat.

"Thanks," I said blotting my mouth with the back of my hand.

"You're welcome," Elon said. "Why did you take off like that?"

"What difference does it make?" I asked.

He shook his head and sighed. "You don't really believe that I was interested in that girl?"

My eyes popped, offended by the presumption that he thought I cared.

"Whatever," I said.

"Genna," he said firmly. "She doesn't mean anything to me."

"I know the feeling," I said point-blank, as if he had just described the way I felt about him.

"Don't do that," he said.

"Do what?" I pretended.

He was staring again and when he looked at me like that it was impossible to keep a good fight going.

"Don't say things you don't mean," he said.

"I don't have the right to tell you who you can hang with," I answered.

He placed his forefinger beneath my chin and slowly lifted my face.

"I just gave you the right," he said. "So go ahead ... and take it."

I lowered my eyes as his lips lined up with mine.

"Take everything I have," he said.

Something inside me collapsed.

He pushed back a strand of sweat-matted hair from my face. It would have been so natural to give in, to let my head fall against his shoulder, to rest there while his arms circled me.

"I'm taking you home," he said.

"No," I said refusing to give in to my achy, feverish body.

This time I didn't look away. I looked straight into his eyes, and I thought about kissing him — just this one time to see what it would be like. I fought the impulse, and then he threw me a tender smile that brought it right back.

"Is it okay, if I do this?" he asked.

Before I could answer, he brought my hand to his mouth and pressed his lips to my fingers. I felt a slight rocking sensation across my knuckles as he increased the pressure.

The feeling was amazing. I felt breathless.

"I have a boyfriend," I blurted as if the words would catch fire. "It's not Nick," I explained. "He's away but he'll be back soon."

I spoke unnaturally fast, with a sense of urgency that comes when you know that if you don't say it then, you never would.

"Tell me to stop, and I'll stop," he said.

His lips were working their way to the underside of my wrist.

I closed my eyes.

"My boyfriend — he's different," I gasped. "We're the same."

"Are you sure about that?" he asked without questioning exactly what I meant by "different."

My voice weakened, "You don't understand."

"Have you heard from him while he's been away?" he asked. "Has he called you?"

The look on my face made the answer obvious.

"Maybe he's not what you think," he said. "Maybe he's not coming back."

I shook my head, hoping he would stop.

"Whatever he did, whatever he told you...," he continued, "he let you down."

A burst of anger startled me. All at once, the hand he had kissed so gently swung through the air and slapped him hard across his face. It happened so fast that, for an instant, I didn't think that I actually did it.

Half-stunned, I turned my hand over, the redness already spreading across the back of my fingers. The incident drew a small crowd. Through the circle of bodies, I felt someone tap my arm and ask me if I was okay. I don't remember answering.

A look of sadness clouded his brilliant eyes. He lingered for a moment and then turned away.

"Good-bye, Genna," he said.

* * *

I lifted my arms, struck by how light they felt without the weight of studded cuffs and leather wrap-around bracelets.

"What are you doing?" I sighed.

My eyes flickered shut, a movement that only worked to heighten the sensation of his fingers running through my hair, across my face.

"Shhh," Elon whispered, reaching for my hand. "You'll wake yourself up."

I'm dreaming, I thought.

That would explain how I could see myself without a mirror and why my face was bare with no trace of makeup.

"This is so *not* cool," I said, trying to avoid his stare.

"Why?" he asked. "Don't you want to see yourself the way I see you?"

"This is how you see me?" I asked, slightly offended.

"There are different sides to you Genna," he said. "Maybe I should explain that I want them all."

I began seriously wondering if a dream-kiss counted as a real kiss. Once that gushy feeling passed, I questioned whether my subconscious would take me to place without eyeliner or lip gloss.

"I think I want to wake up now," I said even though I felt completely lucid, which made the whole thing scary-wonderful.

"Remember the dreamcatcher," he said.

I returned his smile as I pictured my bedroom, the dreamcatcher hanging from the bedpost, wrapped in suede fringe and knotted with beads and feathers.

My mother's words came rushing back from a time when I was sure that monsters still lived under my bed.

"It'll keep the nightmares away," she said.

I rested my hand on his chest.

"The dreamcatcher, it only lets the good dreams in?" I asked, still uncertain.

The sound of gorgeous laughter fell with the waves as I shielded my eyes from the sun, flashing over sand and broken bits of shell.

The beach was deserted, wide as the sky with waves rushing towards the shore in crested, white-capped sheets. I sensed the wind but for some reason nothing was moving with it. Every turn of my head was caught in slow motion; my legs weighed down as if dragging through sand.

"Sometimes you need to step away from the world," he said, turning back to me. 'Step away from the things people have told you; from the things that you thought were true."

"And I suppose you know the truth?" I asked.

He said nothing as his eyes settled on my face. Then suddenly the scenery shifted gears, backing into reverse before lurching forward.

I fell towards him.

"So much better now," he said with his lips on my face.

We were moving freely, at natural speed. I tilted my face, so that his mouth could easily wander. Then I said something that I would never say if I had been awake.

"Elon, I'm sorry," I said.

The apology came without the immediate urge to take it back; proof-positive that dream logic had won.

"What was that?" he asked.

"I'm sorry," I said again.

"It must be the ocean surge," he said. "Say it again."

The tears caught in my throat as I squirmed in his arms.

"I'm sorry," I shouted. "You'll never know how unbelievably sorry I am."

"Why?' he asked, holding me tighter. "Is it because you acted against your feelings, or because you hurt yourself as much as you hurt me?"

"More," I cried. "I hurt myself more."

"Is that all?" he asked.

My voice broke with frustration.

"No, I think I'm going crazy," I said. "No matter what I say, you don't believe in second chances."

"Of course I do," he said, touching my fingers, watching how they moved with his. "I believe in every chance."

The sweat trickled down my cheek, yet the cold made me shiver as I followed his eyes toward the horizon.

"The sun is either up *or* down," I said. "You can't have it both ways."

"I'll have to remember that," he said.

Whatever part of me I was still fighting; my mind found a way to face him in a re-imagined world where a sun-drenched beach stretched for miles under a night sky. The only thing that wasn't completely twisted around and reversed was the music.

The music was right. The music was perfect.

He turned again, his hand floating over my cheek. "It's good to be alive, Genna."

I felt myself smile. What I wanted to tell him was pressing on my mind.

"I know." He stopped me, the moonlit shadows playing across his face. "I can see it in your eyes."

This time the wind gusted, so hard and real that it pushed us closer.

"Maybe you should come with me," he said, the sun dancing in his eyes.

"Where...?" I asked.

The smile broke fresh across his lips as he lifted his face. Then like an eclipse, the sun bright as high noon winked out ... and the beach flooded in shadows from a midnight sky ablaze with stars.

* * *

The new bed sheets my mother bought me, the ones with peace signs and angel wings billowed over me like splashing waves. For a moment, I thought I saw him there — in my room, sitting on the edge of my bed with his legs draped over the side. But then, I brushed away the sleep from my eyes and saw that I was alone.

8. REPLAY

I sat through first period without hearing a word. The part of my brain that worked without thinking took down the notes, speed-writing at an almost manic clip.

Elon wasn't in the physics lab when seats began to fill. By force of habit, I looked around every corner, my eyes alert as if I expected to collide with him.

"What did you do to chase him away?"

Harley's voice resorted to "mean-girl" twang, more wrenching than the sound of nails on chalkboard. Two friends who looked like sisters stood by her side. The one wearing a sweatshirt with a picture of a cat rollerblading spoke first.

"Maybe you should keep your hands to yourself next time."

The other followed. "I heard you slapped him in the hall when you caught him with someone else."

LOL, I thought.

It was unreal how quickly the story had spread around campus, adding details that never happened.

"How sad," Harley said, pretending to be sorry. "And now he wants nothing to do with you."

"Back off," I said; my voice empty.

"They say that he was tutoring you because you couldn't handle the math?" she taunted.

"Yeah, what's up with that?" asked her friend. "If you can't handle it now, you'll never get through freshman year."

Harley grew impatient. "Where is he?"

I shrugged my shoulders. "Where is who?"

"Elon," she snapped.

Hearing her say his name as if she knew him better than me was beyond infuriating.

"Haven't got a clue," I said.

The truth was that my mind couldn't reach him. My mother went kind of vague when I asked her, sensing only that he wasn't far. I even questioned Remi, but a flash of panic in her eyes made me drop the subject.

Harley grimaced. "I'm *not* saying this because I want to...," she began.

"Then don't," I stopped her. "Don't say another word."

Her eyes moved to my leather leggings. "Oh my goth", she said to her friends. "That look was so last year."

The cackling receded as they marched away. I barely noticed while the images replayed from memory: the way Elon flinched when I slapped him, the light faded from his eyes as he searched my face for an explanation.

After pacing the halls for the longest time, I decided to speak to Tash. I knocked on the door just as I had that first day when I met him.

He held his tiger-cat in one arm.

"Come in," he said, his tone guarded.

He closed the door behind us. It felt awkward, standing there facing him. I held my books against my chest as if they could hold me steady long enough to ask him what I wanted to know.

"How can I help you, Genna?" he asked.

He seemed less formal than usual. Somehow that made it easier.

"I was wondering if you might have seen Elon lately," I said. "I need to talk to him. It's really important."

His expression soured. "I don't usually get involved in my students' social lives." He paused and then leaned in closer. "Elon is *not* someone you should be involved with. *No one* should be involved with Elon."

The last part he said more adamantly, emphasizing each word to make his point.

Before I could respond, the door opened. The deep voice behind me flooded my senses like a long-lasting hug.

"Singing my praises again, Tash...?"

I turned so fast that I almost fell over.

"Hi," I said, my voice weakened. "I was just asking about you."

"Really...," Elon said. "Well I'm here now."

He led me by the arm into the hall. Tash shut his door without a word.

"How are you?" he asked.

We made our way towards the science building courtyard.

"Where have you been?" I asked him, trying to conceal the euphoria.

"Around," he said.

We ducked into a small alcove near an emergency exit, away from the traffic of teachers and students.

"How do you feel?" he asked.

"Better," I answered, puzzled. "You knew that I was sick?"

"Of course," he said. "I came to see you."

The dream flashed in my mind, a starry, sun-lit beach that didn't leave me until the fever broke.

"That's funny," I said. "My mother didn't tell me."

There's no way, I thought. *She would have said something, especially since I was asking for him every two minutes.*

"You know how it is," he said.

No, actually I didn't know how it was. I only knew how it should be.

"This is hard for me," I said with an awkward smile. "I owe you an apology."

He sighed before he smiled. With the lightest touch possible, his fingers ran the length of my arm. Each passing second made me a little more unsteady, and a little more willing to dive into his arms.

I took a deep breath before I reached for his "work-of-art" face. My hand found the place where I had slapped him. I stood on my toes for extra height and kissed him there quickly, gently.

His eyes brightened as he slowly stroked the underside of my chin, following the curve of my throat until his fingers settled on my rub-on butterfly tattoo.

"Let me take you home," he said.

His voice alone was enough to shut my eyes.

He drove my car. I was thinking about Tash's strange remark and wondering if I should be afraid. He probably knew that I was a little afraid.

"It's not like I'm a serial killer," he said turning into a steep traffic circle with NASCAR precision.

The mere mention of the reference made me lean towards the door. I wondered if my psychic advantage would make it easier to be found if I suddenly went missing.

"Tash is a little grumpy these days," he added. "You can't believe the stuff he says."

"What's with the tension between you?" I asked.

"Oh that." He smirked. "He's looking for some technical information for his research."

"What does that have to do with you?" I asked.

He looked at me as if it should have been obvious.

"I haven't decided if I'm going to help him yet," he said. "After all, where's the fun in it ... if I give him ALL the answers."

I suppressed a grin. Even if he acted like he was in charge, it was pretty unlikely that Tash would rely on one of his grad students.

We arrived at the house in record time. I led the way to my room as my mother shouted from somewhere in the kitchen: "Keep THAT door open please."

"I do my best thinking here," I said as I kicked off my boots and dropped to the floor.

Beside me, he stretched his legs, falling easily into kick-back mode. The music was playing. Our eyes were on each other. And the only thing I wanted was here and now.

"Hold that thought," he said, overlapping his hand with mine.

My heart stopped.

What if I was thinking aloud? Hey — that happens to even normal people.

Or, what if he assumes that everything is about him? HE was the type that would.

I yanked my hand away, but he reached for it again.

"You know when you resist me like that..." His eyes narrowed seductively. "It's a total rush."

I'm right, I thought. *He's arrogant, conceited, totally self-involved.*

"Tell me what you really think," he giggled.

This time I went breathless ... as the pieces to the puzzle began to find one another.

Please let this be another lucid dream, I thought.

"In that case...." He winked. "Did you still want that dream-kiss?"

"What did you say?" I gasped.

"I said you were beautiful," he answered, without flinching.

Now I felt the whimper in my throat, like the sound of agony. What affected me more I couldn't decide: the way he seemed to know my thoughts or the sound of his voice when he called me beautiful...?

"Don't," I pleaded. "Don't say anything else."

An objective observer would have pointed out that everything he had said so far was nothing more than a play on words; a series of coincidental statements that seemed to work consistently in his favor. As long as he stopped now, I could go on believing that something less than supernatural was at work.

"What if...," he said, with a glint in his eyes, "there's more to the gift than the way you're using it."

His hand caught me when I jumped.

"It's okay," he said, easing me down.

My mind went racing: *First Byron and then Elon — what were the chances?*

"This isn't happening," I said. "Lightning doesn't strike twice."

"I don't know," he said with a teasing smile. "Things that come out of the sky are just so hard to get right."

The mortified look on my face grabbed his attention as I suddenly remembered the kind of thoughts that had gone through my mind since I met him.

"Mmm...." He moistened his lips. "You are crushing on me big time."

I bounced up, hurling my favorite pillow at him, the one with the pet face and paws, before running for cover under my desk.

"My mother and the others...," I shouted. "How could they all be wrong?"

"Are you asking me?" he giggled. "Never mind; just stay there."

He crawled to my side like a stalking tomcat. I made room for him as he ducked under the desk.

"Why didn't you tell me?" I asked.

His eyes softened as he touched his forehead to mine, skimming my nose gently with his.

"Tell you what?" he asked, distracted.

"You never mentioned that you were psychic," I said.

"What gave you the idea that I was psychic?"

I furrowed my brow. "Well it has to be something," I said, "If it's not psychic ability, then what is it?"

"You make too many assumptions," he said, avoiding the question. "There's more to a person than what you think you know."

"Still," I said, "The others had me thinking that it was me, that I was somehow spinning reality. All the time it was YOU — jumping from one place to the next — playing with my dreams AND the way you scared the daylights out of Remi."

My eyes opened wide, remembering previous suspicions.

"What did you do to Remi?"

"I didn't do anything to her," he said. "She tried to penetrate my thoughts. It's not possible, but she wouldn't quit trying. She gave herself the headache."

I gulped hard. "You were BLOCKING!"

It was the last, worst revelation that I could handle today. On some level, I always suspected it but the confirmation unhinged me just the same.

"If you think about every thought as a computer file," he said. "I simply chose which ones to open."

"There's nothing simple about it," I said. "Besides you left the math files open."

"I was tutoring you." He laughed. "I didn't see the harm."

"What about the chocolate?" I asked.

"Hmm," he said with his eyes playing over me. "Nothing wrong with catching a taste, if it happened to cross my mind."

I caught myself smiling.

"The others said it was impossible," I said, forcing the issue.

I also remembered how they said that Byron couldn't be blocking. Now I was beginning to wonder how much of what they said was wrong. If Elon could selectively reveal his thinking, I wondered if he could restrict the flow of information from others.

"Yes," he easily said.

I paused for a moment while I considered the ramifications. A psychic who didn't call himself psychic because he was more than that; he was someone capable of keeping others from his mind, someone who could keep me from reading others *at will,* so there was no way to know if I was getting the full story.

"In time," he said. "You'll know everything."

"Now," I demanded.

"It's better like this," he said. "Getting to know each other slowly, revealing our secrets one by one."

"Sure," I said. "Now give it up."

He tickled me under my rib cage until I doubled over.

"You give it up," he giggled.

"Stop," I said enjoying the struggle. "I don't have any secrets."

"Really," he said skeptically. "I never would have known."

For a brief moment, I felt his presence inside my mind. I felt his patience, his gentleness and a spirit so unbelievably strong that I didn't want to unplug from it.

"There's a game I want to play," he said.

I gave him a wary look. Somehow I knew it wasn't a board game.

"I promise this will be fun," he said.

The thrill in his voice made me curious. "How do we play?"

"Think of an experience so cool that you wanted to do it again."

It wasn't a hard decision. The "epic" experience was last spring break in Italy.

"Bring it to mind," he said in a softy-commanding voice.

I closed my eyes.

"Say the name of the place," he said. "Say it like you want to be there."

I repeated the name of a world-famous museum. The second time he asked for it, I said it with more force, as if I was pulling it into the present. Then I heard him count in Italian, in an accent as good as born there: one, two, and three....

I was free-falling, like the feeling that you get when you're drifting asleep. It was just like that, including the point when you have to force yourself awake to escape impact.

The security guard stood in front of me.

"*Buongiorno,*" he said, motioning for me to hand over my bag.

For a moment or two, I stood there disoriented. I didn't know if I should be scared. I didn't know what was happening. He glanced at my passport photo and then back at me. He smiled while rambling in Italian. The only word I caught was "*bella*" for beautiful.

I took in a few deep breaths. There was no obvious reason to feel threatened. It was all good, except for the fact that I was doing it over again. Down to the smallest detail, it was exactly the way I remembered: the Japanese tour group with impressive cameras, the French students with bands on T-shirts that haven't been popular in twenty years.

Eventually, I accepted the situation and felt comfortable enough to look around. My hand ran along the cold marble walls. The fact that they were solid reinforced the impression that I was really here.

Once in the lobby, I didn't bother with museum maps. The poster on the wall drew me in: a giant-sized photograph of Michelangelo's *David* surrounded by a daily swarm of visitors — all standing wide-eyed, with gaping mouths because *David* is too incredible for words.

I looked ahead into the corridors, trying to remember which way to walk. My eyes raced past religious paintings and gold-gilt panels from the Renaissance. Then I found it again, the narrow hall that would eventually split into two separate rooms. On my right, the light from an overhead skylight led to a circular rotunda.

The vaulted ceilings, carved into symmetrical squares, created the perfect gallery. There in the center, surrounded by gold pillars and red velvet rope stood Michelangelo's *David*. I paced around the statue, slowly coming back to the frontal view ... elliptical eyes, straight nose and square jaw. His hair was long, with loose ringlets clinging to his face in classic Greco-Roman style.

I felt myself wandering closer while the guards shifted on their feet aware of my proximity. The description on the wall was written in English. It said that the statue captured the exact moment between decision and action. I couldn't bear to look away, but how could I *not*, because the boy standing next to me was more than cold, lifeless marble.

The way he wore his hair was obviously modern. His body was lean, not overly athletic but totally ripped. Now and then, he glanced away from the statue, breaking focus to look back at me. And when he moved, his T-shirt with the university logo fell into view from behind his jacket.

"Now are you having fun?" Elon asked.

No talking, just watching.

He placed his index finger under my chin and drew my mouth to his, our lips barely touching when he stopped. Caught in his eyes, I stayed perfectly still as he fed the kiss slowly, like he could make it last forever.

My lips warmed as he varied the pressure, his mouth opening wider as I lifted up and wrapped my arms around his neck.

The pillows across my bed absorbed the impact of our landing as we fell together. The transition from one place to the next was seamless, but it was impossible to think about that now.

My face was still cupped in his hand as he traced the outline of my lips with his, tapping under my nose, above my chin. I said things that I couldn't imagine. He answered back in tender stares and half-whispers with words too true to take back, and better than a love song.

The second kiss was *more urgent*.

The stubble on his chin scratched my face. Twice I kissed him back when I meant to pull away. Fear mixed with pleasure, it fueled the fire while my face somehow turned sideways; allowing his mouth to slide away, across my cheek, that sensitive place under my throat and then....

The hardest thing that I've ever had to do was to tell him to "STOP."

He rolled flat on his back, totally out of breath. "I'm sorry, Genna."

My fingers touched my lips. They felt different. They felt kissed.

"Tell me that you're okay," he said, panting wildly.

When I didn't answer, he raised me to a seated position. From behind, he wrapped his arms around and cradled me in a way that made me feel perfectly cherished.

My head fell back against his shoulder.

I kept thinking: it's *my first kiss. It's the best kiss I'll ever have.*

"I promise to be more careful," he whispered in my ear. "I should never have gone that far."

"How was that possible to be back in Italy again?" I asked.

"Call it enhanced memory recall," he said, clinging to me.

"What do you call it?"

"It's like a rewind," he said trying to find the right words. "Think of it as an extreme version of a second chance."

"You downloaded my memories," I said, resisting whatever further explanation he was about to give.

"With the right techniques, you can relive any memory," he explained, weaving his fingers through my hair.

I waited, carefully considering my next words.

"Where did you come in?" I suddenly asked. "You weren't there in the original experience."

His eyes strayed.

"I sort of ... spliced myself in," he said, his voice holding back.

"You changed it up," I engaged him. "The way a song track is remixed for a new release."

For a moment or two, I retreated into my thoughts, sitting quietly with my head resting on his shoulder while the winter sun set between the trees. The sky was dark gray, splattered with broad, sweeping strokes of pink and blue. By the time the shadows flooded the room, the window candles flickered on.

Then I turned to him.

"Who are you, Elon?" He held silent. "Or maybe, I should ask you, what are you?"

"Well," he said with a mischievous grin, tucking a strand of hair behind my ear, "I'm *not* a vampire."

9. SPEED TRAP

I peeled my clothes away one layer at a time, letting my jeans bunch up around my ankles before tugging them off.

It was late, but I was too wired for sleep. I threw on my headphones so my mother wouldn't hear. The light in her room meant that she was probably still up. I felt around my bed for my tablet, buried under yesterday's clothes. The screen was smudged so I wiped it clean with edge of my pillowcase before typing in the search box:

Teleportation: The act of moving an object or person without physical contact by psychokinesis.

Psychokinesis: a movement of physical objects by the mind without physical means.

Eventually, manic browsing opened up links with some seriously weird pop-up ads.

I powered-down and pulled my pillow under my neck. Since *he* left, the last thought before sleep was always the same. I was back in the bookstore, and Byron was there watching my hand go through the slow motions of sliding the scarf from his neck. The scene quickly surrendered to other images, more vivid and clear: Elon on the windswept beach with his endless stare....

The faces, the places — they merged into one unbroken stream. There was an instant, a half-second when I had all the answers, when I knew who I loved, what I wanted. It never lasts ... the feeling of everything falling into place because by the time you think you know — you no longer do.

It was my voice next that I heard tearing through the stillness. A splash of watery color suspended in a thick fog began a new dream. I was looking for Elon, my head spinning because I couldn't catch him. He was everywhere at the same time.

"Where are you?" I called out. "I can't see you."

"I'm here," he said.

His voice was a soft whisper in my ear, his breath a warm breeze against my skin.

"Open your eyes, Genna"

It felt like I was swimming underwater, his voice hanging on a thin thread of light leading to the surface.

"Genna," he repeated. "Open your eyes."

I woke with a sudden jolt, turned onto my stomach, teetering on the edge of the mattress with my heart racing — the tablet thrown from my legs, where it had been when I fell asleep. Elon's hand quickly covered my mouth to muffle the scream. The same album was still playing through my earphones, no longer on my ears, so I knew that I couldn't have been asleep very long.

When he felt my breathing slow in the cup of his hand, his fingers slid away. Scared out of sleep, and all I could think about was how much I wanted to hear him say my name, like I needed it to power my next breath.

"Genna," he whispered, releasing the sound so perfectly that it quickened the air.

Slowly a single tear fell from his cheek, leaving a pale streak across his airbrushed, flawless face.

"Sometimes I think that the truth isn't worth risking that look in your eyes," he said.

I resisted the impulse to kiss his face dry because I knew that if I did, I would never stop.

"How did you get in here?" I asked. "The house is tripled alarmed — all the windows and doors." My voice reduced to a high whisper, "If my mother finds you...."

"She's asleep," he said.

He was holding my hand now, sliding his fingers between mine.

"What did you mean ... the truth?" I asked.

The serious look on his face fizzled, and he was "off-the-wall" crazy again with a "rock the house" look in his eyes.

"Do you want to see something really cool?" he asked.

"I don't even want to know what that means."

"Put some clothes on," he said.

He spun around as if to give me the privacy to dress like he could be trusted. With my eyes darting behind me, I pulled some clothes from a chair that looked less rumpled than the ones on the bed, and back-stepped into the bathroom to change.

"I'm not supposed to leave the house this time of night," I said, emerging from the bathroom fully dressed.

I considered leaving my mother a note; a text message in case she woke up and found me gone.

"We won't be gone long," he said.

I reached for my bag.

"You won't need that," he said.

Was he kidding? I slung it over my shoulder. *My whole life was in that bag.*

"Where exactly are we going?" I asked, heading towards the door.

"Stay here," he said. I gave him a skeptical look as I backed away. "You're a brave girl, aren't you?" he asked.

"Why?" I asked, warily.

"No reason," he said. "I just don't want to scare you."

"Can you stop now?" I asked. "You're seriously freaking me out."

"Come closer," he said.

I took two small steps forward. I was still in my own room, in my house.

"Closer," he giggled.

I leaned in, my weight partially resting on my heel, ready to pull back at the first sign of trouble.

"You're going to have to trust me," he said with an impatient sigh as he took my arms and pulled me against him.

I felt myself yelp.

"How does that feel?" he asked.

I wanted to say *amazing*! But instead, not quite recovered from the sudden gush of pure pleasure, all I managed was an overwhelmed "Okay."

"Hmm ... good," he said. "Now close your eyes and don't open them."

I felt his breath against my face as his lips hovered over mine.

"No matter what happens, hold on to me," he said.

The warning alone was enough to trigger a tremor in my gut. I took a deep breath, reminding myself that my mother was in the next bedroom. The idea that he may have intended to harm me never entered my mind.

"You're absolutely safe," he said while his fingers caressed my face.

My mouth parted as he went on touching ... until his hand covered my eyes. His other hand reached over my shoulder and held me.

"Man, where did you come from that you can make me feel like this?" I asked. My head fell against the natural curve of his chest.

"You're about to find out," he said.

If anything was going to happen, it had already started. A feeling of intense pressure pushed out from the center of my chest as if all the air had suddenly been sucked out of the room.

I began to struggle.

"It's nothing more than walking from one room to the next," he said.

With my head still buried in his chest, I winced and then gasped for air.

"You're okay," he said feeling my panic. "I've got you."

Like a fish pulled from the ocean, I thrashed and flailed.

His arms tightened around my shoulders as I felt my ears pop, the kind of feeling that you get on planes during altitude changes. Then a ringing sound shattered my ears, high-pitched and relentless.

"Make it stop." I felt myself scream.

"It's normal," he said with a voice that managed to stay above the noise.

Beneath my face, I felt his heartbeat, steady and strong. If only I could only see what was happening.

"There's nothing to see," he said, pressing his hand over my lids.

I coughed once and then started to choke.

"I can't breathe."

"The feeling will pass," he said. "Just breathe normally and it'll be fine."

Gentle, reassuring words spoken in the same super-calm voice, overlapped my memory of Remi writhing in pain as he stood over her.

"Stop it," I cried, the noise rising above my voice by several octaves.

Suddenly I realized that my mother must be hearing it too — worse than if every smoke detector went off in the house. I pictured her checking the alarm panel, calling the emergency number.

My face clung to his chest as his arms came around and lifted me up. Then I felt the feeling of his lips floating over my face.

"I can't hear you," I said.

"Genna, I love you."

My back arched back into his arms as if I was letting go into a pool of warm water.

"Did you hear me?" he asked.

"Yes," I said. "I don't know."

The noise was suddenly distant, growing fainter. Whether he actually said, it wasn't important because just the idea was enough to unravel every sense in my body. My thoughts danced to the remembered rhythm of his voice as a feeling of perfect joy ... beat down the fear.

His hands held on. He spoke to me the way my parents did when I was little and everything I did was wonderful. His comforting voice made me quiet, reminded me to keep still. Then the spinning began, and I thought I was going to die — really going to die.

I screamed again.

"I'm here," he immediately reassured. "I'm right here."

We were turning with speed that I could never imagine, horrific speed that gave me the sensation that I was moving outside of my body.

"Don't move. Don't open your eyes," he reminded.

"Make it stop," I cried.

I tried to free myself, but he held me back.

My thoughts began to ramble, the way they do when you're too scared to live in the moment. I was flashing back to my first sleep-over in fourth grade and my middle school graduation. I never did thank my mother for helping me start the band. Desperately, I tried to remember the lines to one of Nick's songs.

The speed was something that I felt inside. I knew that if I didn't lose consciousness now, there would be nothing worse to endure. Eventually, I was able to open my mouth. My voice ... I couldn't be sure that it would be there until I tried.

"I don't go to church a lot," I said, "just on holidays."

I screamed again as we spun around a steep revolution. He held the back of my neck as my body tilted sideways.

"Let me guess," he said. "Now you wish you would have gone more."

I nodded against his chest.

"I don't really pray," I said, "Only when things go wrong."

"I know," he said. "So that must mean that most of the time things go right."

"Not counting this very moment," I yelped like I had to get my point across while skipping over hot coals. We were moving crazy-fast.

"It's all good, Genna," he said in a way that bore unshakeable confidence. "Hold on to your faith because there's really nothing to be afraid of — not now, not ever."

The spinning never slowed. It didn't sputter or reverse. In an instant, every force that was in play, the extreme speed and movement came to an immediate, screech-less, evenly-paced STOP.

We fell together in a heap. I heard myself groan as my body slammed against a hard surface.

"WHAT in the world was that?" I yelled.

I was on the floor; my limbs turned outward like I had been making angels in the snow. He was kneeling over me, petting my head like a sick child. The movements felt familiar, but there was no doubt in my mind that this was definitely first-time.

He helped me up, making sure I could stand before he let go of me.

"All right?" he asked.

I shook my head, feeling that I might collapse.

"Rest for a minute," he said supporting my shoulders as I spread across his lap.

"What just happened?" I gasped. "I thought we were going somewhere and then everything went hyper-virtual on me."

"Not exactly," he said. "But you did really well."

I looked at him curiously. "There was this 'swoosh' and then it was like running down a tube at a water park."

He smiled as if my description amused him.

"I know," he giggled. "I was there."

Slowly he raised me up. I thought back to what I possibly heard him say during the worst rollercoaster ride imaginable. Had he really said it, or was it just my own mind projecting back what I wanted to hear?

Either way, I was looking at him differently just because he might have said it.

Then my eyes moved to my room. After all the scary sensations, I had been here the whole time. He was still holding me while my eyes focused on personal stuff; the little things that made me feel safe.

I was so glad to be home that it seemed like my room never looked better; my bed made up neat and orderly without piles of clothes thrown on top, underwear usually stuck in my turned inside-out jeans.

He held me tighter as I glanced over his shoulder to my bathroom, so uncluttered that I could actually see the swirling pattern of the marble counter. His fingers worked their way to the back of my neck, the massage so relaxing that I almost quit staring at my bedroom door. It was closed, my calendar hanging from a hook with a million things scribbled in.

I pictured what was on the other side, the hall, the staircase. My mother had to be awake by now. I had screamed louder than a horror movie. Her first impulse would be to roll out of her bed and run to me, with bare feet pounding the carpet.

In fact, I was sure that I would collide with her if I just....

"No!" he shouted, pouncing on me. "Don't open the door."

"Why?" I asked him.

"There's no easy way to say it," he said.

"This isn't my room." I said it for him. "It's different. It's *all different.*"

He lifted me to my feet.

"Where are we?" I shouted. "What is this place?"

I felt an odd mixture of anger and fear bubble to the surface. Before I could get to my next thought, he walked to the door and opened it himself. He stepped aside as the door itself disappeared; the room that we were standing in — gone in a flash — morphed into some other place.

* * *

My hands lifted up as if I was trying to defend myself. Endless curved walls as far as I could see without an obvious exit or entry. He knew my thoughts before I did, and he felt me pulling away, slowly edging back as he approached one step at a time.

I let out a small cry as my back met the wall, cold metallic gray.

Nowhere to go, nowhere to run, I pressed against the surface as if I could expand the distance between us. I trembled as he brushed his hand across my face. It was unnatural to fear pleasure, his touch so light and tender yet I couldn't control the fact that I was completely and utterly terrified.

"Genna," he said sadly. "Don't...."

My face pulled away from his hand, poised to brush away a solitary tear.

"Tell me where we are?" I insisted; my voice straining to be heard, caught between varying states of sadness, anger and fear.

"Where do you want to be?" he asked.

I looked into his beautiful eyes. "That's not fair."

"Would you rather be home?" He asked the question knowing the answer.

The nod was an involuntary reflex, although I knew that *home was not where I was going.*

Instantly, the empty space became my room, poster-covered walls, my desk and computer just as they were moments ago. The scene was liquid, wet like paint on canvas. My trembling fingers reached out to touch my bookcase. Like inserting my hand into colored gelatin, the image shimmied.

"The longer the images are projected, the more solid they become," he said. "Your mind fills in the details."

I was too much in awe to answer.

"Maybe, you would rather be at school," he said.

The features of my room collapsed into a messy swirl of color that quickly rearranged itself into wood-paneled halls.

"Or even better ... the beach along the Jersey Shore," he said. "That's your favorite place, isn't it?"

I felt the sun hit my face, and the wind pull my hair back. Elon's unnaturally bright eyes seemed translucent in the glare.

"Stop," I said holding my hand up.

The walls seemed to respond, returning at once to a generic shade of gray.

"What is this place," I asked, "when it's *not* pretending to be something else?"

He raised his eyebrows and exhaled deeply like he wished I had never asked.

The walls dissolved away. What I saw next defied explanation.

10. THE GUARDIAN

"A picture is worth a thousand words," he whispered into my ear, pressing his cheek to mine as we both stared ahead.

"That's *not* real," I said reacting to the panic in my voice. "There's no way that can be real."

Against my face, I felt Elon's lips flex into a smile.

"Why?" he asked.

"It's everywhere." My voice strayed. "I can download it ... in hi-def digital."

He said nothing. He was away from me now, stretched out across a thin sheath of a chair, pensive as he looked on. Without turning away, I whipped out my phone. Pressing it to life, I held it up for him to see the iconic image on the default wallpaper.

"That's why I know it's not real," I said.

"Keep looking," he said, hardly impressed. "And then tell me how it makes you feel."

There was no way to describe the feeling — looking across a sweeping vision of space illuminated by a confetti of stars, and the earth ahead, slowly-turning in living color.

"This is wilder than 3-D movie," I mumbled.

We were standing on the edge of what seemed to be transparent flooring. It gave the feeling of being in a fish bowl with an unimpeded, almost limitless view.

"Man, you're good," I said.

"I know," he instantly agreed.

"Okay," I said, turning away. "What's really going on here?"

I was in my own room just a few minutes ago, and now he wanted me to believe that we were orbiting the earth.

He shook his head. "Follow your senses and decide for yourself."

I lifted my cell. I was going to call home, but I noticed no bars.

"I can't get a signal," I complained.

He shrugged his shoulders with an amused grin as he gestured with his hands toward the earth-image and back to us.

"I don't think your service in New Jersey can reach out here."

I ignored the attitude and moved closer. It was a breathtaking projection, the sharpest, most realistic image I had ever seen. The continents, they floated on the globe like swirls of lace, speckled with blue, tan and white. And the atmosphere halo shimmered against black space.

"I'd be totally impressed if it wasn't such a sick joke," I said. "What's that little thing over there?" I pointed to a small blip near the earth.

Eyes squinting; he leaned in. "GPS satellite," he answered matter-of-factly, before settling back again.

"That's it," I snapped.

For me, it was the tipping point, when the illusion flew so hard in the face of reason that I had to stand up for what I believed — for what I knew to be true.

"Forget what you know," he said.

Each look was more convincing, so I decided to stop looking.

"You know what!" I said, exasperated. "I'm out of here."

I felt for my bag, hanging over my shoulder as if I was about to sneak out through the back door.

"Wherever this is," I huffed. "Make sure that the next stop is New Jersey because I'm getting off."

A voice, *not* Elon's spoke from somewhere else.

"It's a lot further than it looks," he said.

A man approached, from where I couldn't say.

"Can I help you?" His tone was careful yet not unfriendly.

Elon's eyes narrowed. "You look like someone I love to hate."

The man ignored him as he turned to me.

"Perspective changes things, doesn't it," he said motioning to the earth-view. "No worries. You'll be home before you know it."

I got a better look as he came around to face me. He was older, probably around my mother's age, but he was the best looking middle-aged guy I had ever seen, dressed in stylish black clothes.

"Who are you?" I asked him.

"I don't actually have a name...," he began, as if he was anxious to tell me more.

"He isn't real, Genna," Elon cut in.

The man reeled back. "Really, Elon," he said. "That's just rude."

"If he's not real — what is he?" I asked, walking around him as if I expected to find a power strip behind his overly-handsome physique.

"Don't believe him," the man said with a quick smile. "I'm as real as that cell phone that you can't let go of."

I dropped the phone in my bag.

"Elon knows me as the Guardian," he said.

"The Guardian," I repeated, vaguely intrigued.

"Someone has to protect the integrity of the mission should things go wrong," he said.

"Go wrong," I said sarcastically. "What would give you the idea that something has gone wrong?"

Here I was stuck in the eye of a telescope with a couple of guys that looked like they had just stepped out of a men's cologne ad. Maybe there was a lot that I didn't understand, but on one point I was certain: I wasn't on a spaceship.

To think that I could be convinced otherwise was frankly an insult to my intelligence, not to mention absolutely preposterous.

Any idea I had of what spaceships were like said that they were small, cramped places where the default position was upside down, knees to the chest. The place I was in felt enormous, with no sense of movement, no hum of engines, no wires or mechanical devices that I could see. I was free to move, to jump up and down, to dance if I wanted, to breathe normally, with no bulky anti-gravity suit or oxygen supply.

Yet it might be easier to enjoy the illusion ... if it wasn't for this weird feeling that kept riding me every time my eyes hit the 360 degree panoramic view of space. The longer I looked, the more there was to see — across the largest, wide-screen imaginable with lights flickering in and out like a live video feed.

I blinked, forcing myself to look away.

"What are you guys trying to say? That you're from another planet?" I kidded.

Unfortunately, my sense of humor didn't have the strength to stand alone. What was left of my smile surrendered ... to a silent room where the only sound was my own tortured breathing.

"Nothing but slick special effects," I mumbled. "Give me a break here."

"Speaking of breaks," Elon said with his hand on my shoulder. "I have to leave for a little while."

The thought of him leaving me alone in this place was unbearable.

"Where are you going?" I asked, my voice breaking up with fear.

"I'm looking for something — *someone* down there," he said, his eyes motioning towards the earth-view.

"How can you do that?" I asked.

"G-ggle Earth," he said with a wink.

* * *

I found myself locked in a deep, penetrating stare with "the Guardian."

"So Gen," he said folding his arms across his chest, in a way that reminded me of Elon. "Tell me what you think? I want to know."

He gestured towards the space-view.

"I think it's fake," I said defiantly.

"No you don't," he said. The persuasive spark in his eyes made me turn. "If you did," he said, "You wouldn't find it so hard to stop looking."

He walked around me.

"Don't you want to know?" he asked.

I kept deliberately quiet.

He fell into a comfortable heap beside me.

"Haven't you ever looked up at the sky and wondered what else might be out there?"

Before I could answer, he pushed through my thoughts. *Would you rather we communicate like this or should I use speech?*

"Neither," I said sharply, startled by the spontaneity of the connection.

The first attempt to read him triggered a type of security system that stopped me cold.

"Let's try that again," he said. "When one door closes; another opens."

I pressed my temples with my fingers while he re-routed me to the places he wanted me to go. The access was still limited, the details fuzzy and yet I got the answers to the bigger questions, the ones that nagged me since the day I first met Elon at Princeton.

Elon was different.

I knew that better than I knew my own name. I just couldn't imagine how different. Now I got it. Within seconds, I knew who he was and worst of all, *I knew where I was.*

Instantly, I reeled back as if I had been brought to the edge of a cliff. Only my eyes moved — to the awesome blue planet in my visual.

"Hey Gen," the Guardian said, waving his hand in my face. "I'm still here."

I struggled to find my voice. "How can this be possible?"

"Let your senses catch up," he said. "Don't over-think it."

"My senses are unreliable," I choked.

"They'll get better with practice," he said. He sat with one leg casually crossed over the other. "If you were willing to open your mind, shed your biases and preconceptions, you could have picked up the truth sooner."

"I want to go home," I said, sounding like a kid on the first day of school.

"Don't be afraid, Gennie," he said.

Unthinkingly I smiled, because the face staring at me was the safest face I knew. Byron's face, his sad, beautiful eyes farther away than the planet I was musing after. He stretched his legs over the seat and motioned me towards him with a finger curl.

"Gennie' he repeated with his magical voice. "I've missed you."

He was only a few feet away. I moved forward so abruptly that I stumbled. The fall left me stunned. When I looked up again, the face was no less handsome ... but it was no longer Byron's.

The Guardian flexed his arms if the shape-shifting had fatigued him. I was still on the floor, braced by my arms and legs and as angry as a deranged animal.

"You're *not* a man," I groaned. "You're *not* a machine."

'No," he answered, casually. "I'm something in between."

"You ripped off his image from my mind," I shouted.

"I'm sorry," he apologized.

In his eyes, the shadow of Byron remained.

"Why are you here?" I asked.

"There are others," he said. "They went missing. Elon will find them. It's as simple as that."

"And as soon as he does ... you'll leave?" I hoped that the answer would be both '"Yes" and "No."

"Yes," he said, "There's no reason to stay."

Refusing his hand, I leaned my weight on one leg and pulled myself up. I was careful to avoid him as I began pacing back and forth in an almost straight line; a few feet forward and back again. I did this more times than I could count until Elon stepped in.

I startled, his impossibly gorgeous face inches away like he was standing there the entire time. But then instinct took over. My hands began beating him back as if he was this repulsive monster that had to be driven away.

"I thought that you were a powerful psychic," I shouted. "That would have been bad enough."

He grabbed me by my wrists.

"Stop," he said in a calm, but firm voice. "You'll hurt yourself."

"Don't touch me!" I screamed. "Don't ever touch me again."

I tried to avoid using the "alien" word even though it was pushing at my tongue. So was the word "abduction." How easy it would have been to put them together as in: "alien abduction."

Elon locked eyes with the Guardian while my accusations traveled between them like instant messaging. And still, most of the thought-transfer between them was out of my range. Suddenly Elon flashed an angry look when he realized how my time with his strange companion went … including the part where he clued me in to the whole "alien thing" and changed up his face for Byron's.

The Guardian turned to me, "You've been negatively influenced by popular culture."

In between, other comments reached me which made me feel inadequate, as if I had just emerged from a prehistoric cave.

"Back off G-man," I shouted.

Elon tried to get hold of me without dislocating my shoulder. It was no use. A few forceful yanks did nothing against his strength but bring me closer.

Finally, in a moment of impatience, he did what he could have easily done from the beginning if he wasn't so worried about hurting me. He pulled me around with a single move that felt more like dancing than fighting. There was a slight "ouch" reflex when I felt the strength in his hands. Then my back fell against his chest as he slipped his arms around my waist from behind. I felt myself respond, my hands braced by his as we fell into a rocking motion.

"You were saying?" he asked, as his lips ran the length of my neck.

11. STRAIGHT TALK

Until now, it wasn't my favorite subject: UFOs, extraterrestrials.

Most of what I knew or thought I knew came from the movies. The more popular images ran through my mind ... from the clearly laughable to the super-horror extreme where they have to blow up the space station to get rid of the alien, but the heroine manages to save the cat.

It took a few days of obsessive searching before I finally realized that there wasn't any intelligent view of extraterrestrials. Still the stuff online had me thinking.

"You can't believe everything on the internet," he said, slipping into the seat next to me.

I scrambled to keep my belongings from flying off the table.

"Do you have to keep doing that?" I shrieked, forgetting my indoor voice.

We were in the library, and I could feel eyes drifting.

"Look at me," Elon said, lifting my face.

I jerked my head away even though it frustrated me to lose his touch.

"Resistance is futile," he teased with a robotic voice.

I began to wonder if we didn't watch the same movies.

"What's wrong?" His fingers reclaimed my face. "Don't you like my 'spaceman' voice?"

I mouthed an uneasy "No."

His eyes hit my laptop screen. "All those stories are made up."

"There's so many," I said, my voice wilting as his hand roamed.

"Talk about stereotypes." His eyes narrowed on the image of a particularly gruesome alien with seething jaws.

"Doesn't seem like a fair representation," I agreed, the face of Adonis staring back at me.

"It isn't," he said. "Still, the truth *is* stranger."

He threw me a playful wink, waiting for me to laugh first. Normally, his sense of humor, however infuriating, was one of the sexiest things about him.

I started to pack up my things, slamming stuff together so hard that I was sure something would break.

"Sorry," he said. "I'm not being romantic enough."

My shoulders hunched as I felt a kiss land softly on my lips.

"Take my hand," he said in a quiet voice.

I fell back into my seat. If he kissed me again, I'd have to kiss him back which probably meant that we'd both be thrown out of the library.

"Your hand," he repeated, reaching for my right one.

He clasped it tight and brought it up to his chest.

"I'm human," he said. "I'm as human as you are."

My head spun around trying to check out who might be listening.

"How is that even possible?" I asked, trying to look busy as one of my teachers walked by.

"If this is about not being born on earth...," he began.

"You know," I said super-sarcastically, "I think that may be it."

"Man," he sighed. "How do we get you past this?"

I wanted to say with another kiss, but I didn't dare go there.

"All these crazy ideas about alien life," he said, as he wrapped a strand of my hair between his fingers. "Our DNA is practically the same."

"What?' I blurted.

"DNA," he said, emphasizing the letters as if he was about to walk me through a molecular biology lesson.

"When it comes to DNA," I said with a confident voice, "practically the same isn't nearly as good as exactly the same."

The benefits of studying hard were never more obvious.

"Agreed," he said, unexpectedly impressed. "But you have to admit that it's a game-changer."

Did he really believe that he had found a way to make us equal — as if from here on, everything would be all right...? We were going to be a normal couple — hang out, go to the movies on Friday nights, have silly fights when he didn't call or when he went out with his friends instead of me.

"The differences are not as significant as you think," he said.

Even if I wanted to listen, I was too obsessed with looking over my shoulder, hoping that no one was catching any part of our whacked conversation. I rose from my seat and motioned him to follow. We tucked into a book aisle, full of huge, outdated reference books. With the exception of one squirrelly-looking guy, we were alone.

"What are you doing here at this school?" I asked.

"It's a safe haven while 'operation recovery' goes into full swing," he answered.

"Do you think you'll find them ... your friends?" I asked.

"I found you," he said.

He was flirting again, his hand wandering over to mine. I liked it too much to want to move.

"Go ahead and ask me," he whispered in my ear with a massive grin. "Ask me what it is to be human?"

"Okay," I sighed, trying to appease. "What is it to be human?"

"Depends," he said. "Here on earth, at this stage of development, every human is a wild-type. It's the upgrades that set you apart."

I tried to process what I thought he meant.

"Upgrades," he repeated, like he was talking about the latest software, "or, otherwise known as *Extrasensory Perception.*"

He anticipated my next question but let me ask it anyway, because it can get annoying when someone constantly beats you to the next thought.

"What's a wild-type?"

I wondered if it was a politically correct way of acknowledging my inferior status.

"All it means is that you haven't been genetically altered," he answered.

"No," I agreed, smirking. "And I haven't been cloned either."

He leaned against the bookshelf behind me, enclosing me in his arms.

"Evolution alters genes through a process called natural selection...," he started to explain.

"Take what's best and discard the rest," I interrupted. "You don't have to dumb it down for me."

He nodded with a smile.

"The gift is nothing more than a glimpse into the future of human evolution for this planet," he continued. "There will come a time when everyone will have it, many times more powerful than it is now for you and your friends."

"So these genes are just starting to turn on," I said. "And my mother and I, we have the beginner's version."

"That's a great way of thinking about it," he said. "Natural selection is always working. I just didn't realize that these genes were activated yet ... in a human society that's still so technologically primitive."

"Ouch," I said. "Looks like I'm back in the cave again."

"Oh, please," he said, rolling his eyes. "Let's lose the Neolithic references."

The guy who resembled a backyard rodent looked up from his device, wrinkled his face and walked away.

"One question," I said. "How did you get ahead of the game?"

He laughed. "Why wait for natural selection when there are ways to jump-start the process."

We were in my room now. If we weren't in the middle of such a deep conversation, I could have almost enjoyed the pure exhilaration of being in the library one minute, and home again in the next.

I plopped myself down on my bean bag chair and ingested the information from a reclining position.

"Now I understand why you didn't call yourself psychic," I said.

He sprawled out on the floor beside me.

"There's no such thing," he explained. "The whole concept is driven by cultural superstition."

"All this time...," I said with a disillusioned pout. "There was a genetic basis."

"For the most part," he said. "But like any skill, some people will always be better than others."

I delayed my next question, wondering if the answer would drive a gap between us so wide that even he wouldn't be able to close it. Of course he was blocking, preferring instead to lead me towards carefully vetted responses.

"How long would it take?" I asked.

He seemed relieved that the question left him plenty of wiggle room. So I quickly rephrased. "How long would it take natural selection to produce someone like you?"

"Like me?" He played dumb.

I nodded insistently.

"Why think about that," he said avoiding my eyes.

"I won't break," I said, "If you tell me."

"It doesn't matter," he said, glancing back.

"Are you sure?" I asked.

"In terms of actual years, who really knows," he said. "One thing the universe has is time."

"Time as in ... thousands of years?" I persisted.

"No," he said flatly.

He answered so fast that I almost missed what he didn't say.

"There's no way you're millions of years more advanced," I insisted.

If that were true, one thing was certain. There could be nothing between us.

He knelt over me. "Don't let your mind run away without me."

I felt his lips on my hair.

"I don't believe you." I argued with myself.

"Don't," he said. "Just believe that I love you."

His voice trailed in a wave of emotion as I tried to hold myself straight, but my eyes were already closing as he kissed my forehead.

"I love you," he repeated, kissing the top of my nose.

"I love you," he said with a deeper, softer voice as his lips moved in circles, barely missing mine.

If there was any doubt left as to whether I had heard what I thought I had heard, that doubt was now unequivocally shattered.

Just three words, they had the power to do what I expected them to do — expand my concept of what was "normal." It was normal that alien visitors should be here on earth. It was normal that I should be so attracted to him. It was normal that I should expect him to do all the normal boyfriend things.

I kissed the corner of his mouth quickly. It was an unthinking reaction, restrained compared to the first time we kissed ... with a full-on lip lock that nearly went too far.

"What did we come through when it felt like the sky was falling?" I asked.

His mouth disappeared behind my ear. "It's called a portal," he said. "Well, it's not really called that but in a way, it's a door."

I encouraged him to continue.

"The physical reality that you experience every day is actually divided into layers or dimensions ... like a stack of pancakes," he said

"I'll never eat pancakes again," I said.

His smile faltered like he was momentarily confused.

"An open portal allows you to move through the layers, so it's possible to move from one place to the next — anywhere on earth or from earth to orbiting space."

"It was easy moving from campus to home, not scary like it was when we left the planet," I said.

"More distance, more layers to jump through," he said, "More layers, more barriers to break and the rougher the ride."

"What about the noise?" I asked.

"The sound barrier," he said, inhaling the scent around my earlobe.

"And that feeling I had of not being able to breath?"

"G-forces," he said. "Most of the trip was limited to a high-altitude excursion but it takes a lot of energy to break through the earth's gravitational field."

"What about the replay," I asked, curious to know the truth about our return trip to Italy.

"Oh that," he said like he had forgotten, "That's something different."

That was all he said.

"How does the portal work?" I backtracked, my eyes on his lips.

"Quantum mechanics," he whispered as his mouth drifted towards mine. "It just means that we end up somewhere else … really fast."

12. CURVEBALL

Some secrets are better left that way … a protected to the last breath secret.

Like the truth about him, like the truth about us.

"Try this," I said, tearing off a corner of bread and dipping it into a bowl of chutney.

Elon's lips parted as a crusty piece of dough slipped into his mouth.

"So good," he said, his eyes staring like I was part of the meal. "It's sweet and spicy at the same time."

"That's why I like Indian food," I giggled.

"Wow," he said, suddenly pleased. "Is that you laughing again?"

Whether it was the sheer magic of being with him, I couldn't tell. Sometimes I had to force myself to remember who he was and where he was from — because most of the time I was just too incredibly happy to care.

He kissed away a crumb above my mouth. Totally immersed, I startled when the sound of a deep cough interrupted. We seemed to forget that we weren't alone.

Nick swept back the jagged bangs from his face.

"Why are you here?" he asked Elon. "This is a band meeting … and the last time I checked YOU weren't in the band."

Elon's eyes didn't leave me. "I think he's talking," he said. "But I don't hear him."

"Really," Nick mused. "Do you hear me *now*?"

Logan screamed as dishes and silverware crashed to the floor. I felt my arm slam against the edge of something hard, probably the table.

Liam bounced up. "Okay man," he said, restraining Nick. "It's chill-out time."

Elon rotated my arm back and forth. "Are you okay Genna?"

"Yeah, I'm fine." I said, wincing.

Nick reached across the table. "Gen, I'm sorry."

"Keep away," Elon growled.

Meanwhile, Josh told the waiter that the overturned dishes were an accident.

"Our guitar player is a little clumsy." He smirked at Nick.

The waiter replaced the table setting and promptly walked away.

"Nick has a point," Josh said, turning to Elon. "You can't just show up without clearing it with us first."

Elon was massaging my arm and didn't answer.

Logan was only too happy to chime in. "I would have said okay if someone asked me."

Liam threw her a sharp glance. "No one would have asked you."

As a general rule, Elon had a way of making other guys feel invisible when he was around. Logan normally went weak at the sight of Nick, Liam, and Josh in that approximate order.

Stop staring at him, I thought.

She rolled her eyes, flaunting her ability to ignore me.

"Back to band business," Nick said, whipping out his new high-tech device.

Liam leaned over his shoulder. Then suddenly, Nick said something about not being able to handle the schedule because "some of us" were not committed enough.

"Are you talking to me?" I asked, defensively.

"Do you think so?" he fired back, his eyes unwilling to engage me.

Just as my face pulled away, Elon whispered into my ear, "Over there."

The hostess was seating customers. The sari she wore made her movements appear more graceful as she placed menus on a table, the bangles on her wrist catching the light in her eyes, still fresh with the memory of her wedding.

Under the tablecloth, Elon's hand found mine. At the moment we touched, the surrounding images fell away like tissue paper, caught in a whirlwind of colors and shapes as they morphed into the next thing, like a screensaver gone wild.

The music was slow at first. From where I was standing it looked like dancing, gentle gliding movements. Steadily, the rhythm picked up. The dance moves became energized and repetitive, building faster until a high-pitched crescendo signaled an end point.

It struck like a bell.

There was silence as eyes turned to the center of the room, softly lit by a fountain of floating candles.

Elon was wearing a gold brocade Nehru jacket. His hair was pulled back in a short ponytail, the way he sometimes wore it, with just a few wavy strands dangling at the sides of his face. My hand was still in his, painted with henna, the tattoo markings of a bride.

We stood under a sheer canopy, as sheer as the veil over my face; it draped over my shoulders, over the tightly-wrapped sari I was wearing.

He lifted the veil.

I couldn't do anything but smile. It was the kind of smile that came from the deepest place imaginable, a place where I wasn't afraid to face my feelings.

The waiter blinked. He had read the specials and was waiting for my order.

I told him I wasn't hungry.

I looked back at the hostess, pouring water and acting vaguely disturbed like someone had shoved her from behind. She couldn't have imagined that Elon had tapped into her memories like an interactive video, edited her out and the groom and replaced them with us.

"Hey, maybe you guys want to be alone," Nick snapped.

"Really," Liam agreed.

"Excuse me," I said in a choked voice as I left my seat.

Nick jumped up, regretting the way he had upset me.

"I'm okay," I said placing my unused napkin on the table.

I gave Elon a hidden smile as I walked towards the rear of the restaurant and through a beaded curtain that led to the restrooms. The sense of "letting go" was overwhelming when I got behind the bathroom door. Alone for a moment, I closed my eyes and relived the experience of looking through the veil into his eyes.

When I finally opened the door, there he was waiting patiently. With a growing smile, he pulled me towards him … and then froze. A faraway look invaded his eyes like he was listening to someone else.

"They're leaving," he said.

The look on my face forced an explanation.

"There's a launch scheduled at Cape Canaveral within the hour," he said. "We have to leave orbit or they'll see us. I'll be back in less than twelve hours."

"No," I said, jumping into his arms with the full force of my weight. "Separation is *not* an option."

His laugh triggered my own as he spun us around, waiting for inertia to drag us into the portal. The countdown was the fun part. I heard him recite in my head like an old-time spaceflight broadcast: *Ten, nine, eight.…*

He never reached seven. We were already moving too fast. There wasn't time to be afraid beyond the initial moments of paralyzing terror which really didn't seem too bad. As long as he was holding me, and with my eyes tightly shut … I didn't actually see anything that would reinforce the fear.

Minutes later, the earth was shrinking from view, and I was trying to hold on to my newly-found courage as it grew more distant.

"It feels weird." My voice broke.

His hand brushed my arm, lingering at places where he wanted to linger.

"It's hard at first," he said. "But it gets better."

"I want to go back," I said, my voice floundering like a child pulled from something safe and familiar.

"You will soon," he said.

My arm reached out until the last bit of the image disappeared.

"It's still there." He shushed me quiet. "We'll come around Neptune, orbit one of its moons and then be back before morning."

"You make it sound like a trip to a theme park," I said.

"You know," he said with a light-hearted smile. "I have a feeling that it's a whole lot easier than that."

* * *

"I have a gift for you," he said.

We were sitting together, our knees touching. He was obviously holding something behind him.

"What is it?' I asked, trying to see around him.

"First you have to close your eyes," he said.

I braced myself as he lifted my hand and held it gently. Anything was possible including an unexpected, last-minute, high-velocity experience. My eyes opened when I felt something enclose my wrist.

Of all the possibilities that ran through my mind — jewelry certainly wasn't one of them. It was a super-fashionable cuff bracelet made of some kind of soft, flexible metal if there was such a thing. It draped so close to my skin that it almost looked like it was tattooed on.

"It reminds me of karma-inspired jewelry without the message," I said.

"The message is *us*," he said, exposing his own wrist to show me that he was wearing one too.

"So cool," I said.

They were each changing color, first deep blue and then moving to jewel-toned purples and reds, kind of like a mood ring but more sensitive, more alive.

"What are the colors?" I asked.

"They're our auras," he said, "Our combined life force, the visual perception of our hopes, our dreams, everything that makes us unique ... everything that makes us stronger together."

"They're changing," I said.

He brought my hand to his mouth and gently kissed it.

"We change each other," he said, "Into something more than we could ever be apart."

"Change isn't my thing," I said, thinking about my family.

"I know," he said. "So this is my promise to you that at least one thing in your life won't change —I will love you always."

I forced my eyes shut until I was sure that they were dry again.

"How does it come off?" I asked, searching for the clasp.

"It's part of you now. It won't come off unless either one of us wants it off."

"*Or*, unless you're separated." The Guardian's steely voice interrupted as he walked between us, materialized from nowhere.

"Hey Gen," he said with a strained politeness. "Long time no see."

He was dressed differently than before, wearing a baseball cap with a team shirt. In his hand was a ball cupped in a glove. I wasn't much of a sports fan, but I thought I heard him call out scores. Then he yelled "Play ball!" and the vision of a stadium with a roaring crowd flashed in front of my eyes.

I reacted, jumping aside as the ball flew past me and then disappeared in mid-flight.

"She shouldn't be here again." He turned to Elon, his otherwise perfect, camera-ready face marred with disapproval. He was getting ready to throw again.

"Look out —curveball!" he shouted.

Elon barely flinched as he snatched the ball from the air ... so easily that for a split second, it was as if the ball slowed and then came purposely towards him. Then, with a casual maneuver that seemed to confound the G-man, he tossed the ball straight up in the air.

Somehow I knew that it wouldn't come down and yet, my eyes looked up twice still expecting something in this place to obey the natural laws of physics.

"Be back soon," Elon whispered, giving me a super-slow peck at the corner of my mouth.

It was a sudden near-miss kiss, and it left me flat-out dazed.

"Hey, "Elon called to the Guardian as he walked away. "Stick with your own face this time."

I watched as my extreme boyfriend simply vanished. I didn't ask him where he was going or what he was doing. Somehow I knew that he was on the verge of finding them — the people he came here to rescue. I didn't know why they were here. I only knew that they were important enough for him to come. Once he had them back, what could keep him here?

Meanwhile, I stared my strange companion in the eye. He was stretching and yawning like a kid caught indoors on a rainy day and itching to be somewhere else ... or in this case, someone else.

The costumes changed, but the face remained his, strong and masculine and fit to rule every woman's fantasy.

"You think that I might be willing to tell you stuff that Elon won't?" he asked.

My eyes fluttered. He was wearing dark green doctor's scrubs. I had seen my dad wearing them in the hospital. His hands were pointed upwards in that "don't touch me, I'm sterile" way.

I shrugged my shoulders. There wasn't any point in giving in to this circus act.

"You think you can manipulate me that easily," he said, removing his helmet, gleaming white like his racecar driver's jumpsuit, covered with the names of expensive Italian cars.

"Are you really millions of years more advanced?" I asked.

I waited for him to tell me that it was a ridiculous exaggeration.

The music was ear-splitting. The guitar he was swinging over his head was red and black and in the shape of a triangle. As he let it go, it dissolved into a haze of colored smoke.

"You must feel cut off from him," he said, gasping for air.

The leather pants that he was wearing discreetly vanished.

"You're further from him than you think," he said.

Now I felt like I was at church in a confession booth; the man sitting across from me, wearing a priest's collar.

"Enough," I said, throwing my hands in the air.

The role-playing was riding my nerves.

"There's no one like him, Gen," he said, shuffling a deck of playing cards. He was back in basic black just as I had seen him the first time. "Even among us, he's practically a miracle."

The spirited glint was suddenly gone from his eyes as he inched closer.

"He can't stay, Gen," he said in a soft, precise voice.

I didn't care if he saw me cry.

"He can't stay and you can't go ... and there's no power in the universe that can change that," he said.

I felt for my aura band, touching it as if he was already gone. Gone like Byron ... gone like everyone I might have loved.

The Guardian's hand tugged at my arm. I never saw him actually move towards me, so I jumped back when suddenly he was there. He waited for me to get used to the idea. When I did, the hug felt paternal.

"You may be able to access my thoughts, but you'll never be able to feel what I feel," I said, holding on.

"Untrue," he said with a quiet smile. "I can feel exactly what you feel."

13. INTERVIEW

It starts now ... living each moment knowing that he'll eventually leave. Somehow, no matter how much I fought against it, the best things in my life were always on the verge of ending.

My mother wasn't home when I staggered into my room and fell across my bed. Elon had gone back to Princeton. I resisted the fear that any random "see you later" moment could turn out to be our last.

"I'll be back soon," he told me.

The sulky look on my face remained.

"Hey," he said, almost getting me to smile. "G-man — you can't take him seriously."

"Don't go," I said, using the same voice that I used when my father left, the same voice that didn't stop Byron.

He pulled me into his arms. "Everything will be fine."

The words rang familiar. Too many people had said them to me when the world was crashing around us.

"Tell me how we stay together," I said, "without one of us having to give up something."

With the back of his hand, he wiped a tear from my face.

"You'll have to trust me," he said.

The conflicted look in his eyes was impossible to miss. Even if he wanted to avoid the subject, this was more than just the average set of relationship complications. He was from another world, a place I had scarcely any sense of....

"I bet it's completely different — where you're from?" I asked, clinging to him.

"No," he said, unconvincingly.

We studied each other for a speechless moment.

"Yes," he slowly admitted.

"What about me?" I asked. "I must seem really different."

"Some things can't be more than they are," he said with his eyes on my face. "No matter what, they're perfect."

His mouth pressed my forehead, where he stayed. I couldn't pinpoint the moment he finally pulled away. I hung on for so long that it felt like he was still there even when he wasn't.

The texts that I didn't get while in orbit came all at once.

First, my mother: *In big trouble now. Wait until I find u.*

Then, Josh: *Okay, I give up. Where are u?*

About four texts from Nick; the text box with dots meant he was still typing:

Hey, I'm at rehearsal.

Rehearsal over. Bunch of us going into NYC. Miss u.

Can't sleep. Please call.

Gen - r u ok? Your mom called.

I answered them all with the same one-letter reply: "*K.*"

It let them know I was still alive, which was the best I could do at the moment. Unable to sleep, I tossed around until the sheets knotted up between my legs. I was reaching for some music when I heard the front door. I called out to my mother, but she didn't answer. I called her telepathically and still she didn't answer. I grumbled a bit as I pulled myself out of my comfy bed and started for the stairs.

The footsteps were heavy. I backed up as the moving shadows of two large figures flashed across the wall.

I thought back to fifteen minutes ago, when I pulled into my driveway. The SUV parked near the house didn't belong to the neighbors.

I crept along the hall, my eyes darting. All the best hiding places were down on the first floor. The linen closet was the only option within easy reach. I crouched behind plastic bags flattened with winter blankets, pulled my knees to my chest, and bit my lip to silence my panting.

From behind the closet, I heard the muffled sounds of doors slamming and floorboards creaking. First they checked my room and then my mother's. Finally they backtracked as if they were done, or so I hoped until the light seeping from around the door blacked out. Someone was standing there just on the other side.

In my mind, I called to Elon, sending him a psychic "flare." It flashed a two-word message: *Help me!*

I was proud of myself. I didn't scream when the door flew open. I threw pillows instead, towels … anything within reach. The struggle was kind of pathetic. My 105 pounds matched against two rugged, over-built types. My only saving grace was that, apparently, they weren't interested in hurting me. I was doing a fine job of that myself as I thrashed and kicked until I finally felt myself lifted up. The tape over my mouth went on quickly once my hands were tied.

I nearly broke free while getting into the back seat of the truck, now waiting at the top of the driveway. Somehow while resisting, I almost fell. One man stopped and said he was sorry while the other moved him along. They took seats on either side of me. There was a partition between the front and back seats so I couldn't see the driver. The windows were tinted, dark enough to cast shadows where there should have been sunlight.

The ride seemed endless, miles of wind-whipped, straw-colored farmland in the middle of nowhere. I sat quietly, hoping to pick up whatever thoughts might be out there. Trying to read information that wasn't readily coming through was a sure path to a headache and apparently, I was scared enough to send my extrasensory perception into shutdown mode.

When I closed my eyes, I suddenly had the sense that I might be safe. It was worth knowing, and still no amount of psychic reassurance could change the fact that I had been forced out of my house against my will. I didn't know the reasons. I didn't know if I was in some kind of trouble.

"You're trembling." The man on my right offered a smile.

Slowly he removed the tape from my mouth. I took a deep breath as the last bit of it tore away.

"Did that sting?" he asked, reasonably concerned.

"Where are you taking me?" I asked, rubbing away the burn on my upper lip.

"It won't be much longer," he said avoiding the question.

"There's nothing out this way," I said, my eyes glued to the rural landscape.

"I know it must look bad," he said.

"Really," I said, turning back to him. "I think it's called kidnapping."

"Stay calm," he said. "You put up quite a fight back there."

His face was almost friendly, getting friendlier by the second. I relaxed somewhat, and suddenly my mind wasn't such an empty vacuum.

"What did you expect Major___?" I dropped his name with a mischievous smile.

His bio was an open book, code for an "easy read." He was only twenty-six, yet his credentials were a mile long. His current title stood out among the rest: Intelligence Operations Officer.

I waited for the reaction. On cue, he turned to me with a perfectly stunned look on his face. "What did you say?"

I smiled sadistically. "You didn't know about me —did you?"

"No," he said, frowning. "I'm just glad you didn't decide to run into the woods this time."

The other man shook his head and signaled him to stay quiet.

"What do you want with me?" I asked, remembering the battlefield.

He leaned back in his seat and closed his eyes. Fear once again weakened my resolve, and when it did, my ability to read anything promptly failed.

I jumped up when I felt the truck slow and then jerk to a stop. We were passing through a checkpoint, some sort of gate with uniformed guards. Then I saw the sign: *McGuire Air Force Base.*

The other man, wearing a phone clipped to his ear mumbled into the headset with a monotone, clipped voice.

"Target delivered, ETA on schedule."

The vehicle drove down a long road lined with gray metal buildings. Finally, we stopped. The men got out of the truck and came around to help me. They braced my arms so I couldn't bolt as they led me into the largest building, down a dark hallway and into an elevator.

The Major flashed an ID badge over an electronic eye and punched in what seemed to be a pass code. The elevator doors swished open, and we entered. I noticed only one button on the panel. The other man pushed it, and the elevator began to drop quickly and smoothly.

The ride lasted for a long time. I tried to imagine how many levels underground we had descended. The elevator doors opened.

A modern office space came into view, with uniformed men racing between desks, phones ringing; fax machines bleeping. Several people turned to look as I was hurried into a back office. The door closed behind us. My escorts took seats.

An enormous desk stood at the center of the room, decked out with family photos; kids and pets. The walls were covered with glossy plaques, service medals with shiny gold emblems and satin ribbons. One particular photo caught my eye: a picture of a former President in a golf cart, his partner grinning beside him with a thick cigar clenched in his teeth; an intimidating, unpleasant kind of man.

The door opened.

The two men bolted from their seats and saluted as he walked in with barely a nod, removing his coat and carelessly tossing it on a chair.

"At ease, gentlemen." He waved them back.

I watched as he came around the desk and fell into an over-stuffed chair, as if he had gone through the motions many times before. He opened a humidor on his desk and retrieved a cigar. He slid off the label.

"Nice to see you again, Genna, he said. "I'm General Langdon Ross." He offered his hand. "My friends call me Ross."

"Then I'll call you something else," I said, defiantly.

"Ouch," he said, losing his smile. "You don't seem at all surprised to see me."

"I recognized you from the pictures on your desk," I said.

He glanced over. "You're an observant girl," he said. "Maybe that's why you have such a keen appreciation for art."

"Don't forget music," I said, referring to the last time I saw him, when I couldn't believe it was him, hanging around the club.

While he rambled, questioning my musical preferences, I wondered about my phone. It was in my bag if I could just get to it.

"Is there a rest room around here?" I asked, matter-of-factly.

"Come now, let's *not* play mind games." Ross laughed. "It doesn't take a crystal ball to know that you're trying to dodge me."

He whistled quirky sci-fi music as he eyes lowered to my hand, slowly creeping towards my bag.

Spare me, I thought, returning my empty hand to my lap.

"Don't you want to know why you're here?" he asked.

"I already know," I said, sarcastically. "I'm the one with the crystal ball."

"Hmm," he mused. "Abrasive, but I like it! That is — up to a certain point."

He reached over his desk, coming within inches of my face.

"You're here darling," he said, "because your perfect boyfriend ... is an alien."

I considered my response carefully.

"I don't believe in aliens," I said point-blank.

"Really," he said, doubtfully. "That's quite remarkable because the one we have here believes in you. In fact, he's 'head over heels' over you and just about worthless to us."

"He's here?" I asked, skeptically.

He nodded with a smirk.

Since Ross had been tracking me before I met Elon, I wondered about the circumstances that led him to me.

"I won't help you unless I see him," I snapped.

"First I want you to meet someone," he said. "And then you'll see him ... maybe."

* * *

The woman was a recent graduate from a military academy. Her hair was pulled back. She wore menswear; a white shirt tucked into blue pants. If she was pretty, I couldn't tell.

"Where is he?" I asked.

She said nothing as she flopped into a chair opposite me. The table wasn't very wide which meant that we were within striking distance. She turned on her digital recorder and adjusted her headset. She went through a laundry list: her name and rank, the date and time, recited faster than a rap star.

Somewhere in the middle, I heard my full name: Genna Ann Savoy.

"Subject's height is approximately 5 feet, 6 inches," she continued half-mumbling. "Weight estimated at 105 pounds, hair blonde, eyes brown."

"They're more green than brown," I corrected.

She turned up her voice without pausing.

"Age seventeen years old, born New York City, USA, resides Freehold, New Jersey, USA. Occupation: Student.

Academic major: Pre-med. School: Princeton University. No prior arrests or convictions. No history of substance abuse. Psychiatric history remarkable for anxiety disorders attributed to teenage angst. Hobbies and interests: rock music, fashion culture, environmentalism, romantic literature and the paranormal pseudo-sciences."

My eyes lowered to the flashing green button on the side of the recorder.

"If you had to use one word to describe him," she asked. "What would it be?"

I rolled my eyes. "Hmm...," I smirked. "Excessive."

She blinked, a bothersome feeling riding her.

"What about him is excessive?" she asked.

"*Everything* about him is excessive," I said trying to unnerve her with provocative suggestion.

"Fine," she stammered, her face flushed. "One way or the other, you'll open up to me."

I pulled back, unexpectedly surprised.

They had sent in their own psychic. She was so borderline that I almost missed it.

"What do you think you're doing?" I hissed.

She reached for her head, pressing her forefinger to her right temple. The headache was a sure sign that Elon was blocking any information I had from reaching her — and probably, vice versa.

"You won't find out anything he doesn't want you to know," I said.

"Answer the questions," she snapped, rotating her neck and bracing the top of her shoulder with one hand.

"If you quit now, you'll feel better," I said.

"Your relationship with this being," she said, wincing. "It's a breach of national security."

"Guilty as charged." I presented her with my overturned wrists in handcuff-ready position. "Why not just take me to him now?"

She sneered. "The only reason you're here is to provide us with facts."

"What facts are those?" I said with my best "brat" voice.

Her eyes narrowed. "We're looking for specific information, something that you might have seen or heard."

"I hear lots of things," I said, letting my mind drift to my new favorite song. The music was a kind of shield. Behind it, I could think straight, figure out a way to help him.

"You have no right to hold him here," I said. "He's as human as we are."

She stared without blinking, letting her pen slip through her fingers.

"Bring in the sponsor," she groaned into her headset. "I'm done here."

The door opened.

The man pulled up a chair beside the woman, a.k.a. "rookie psychic."

"Genna, you have to tell them what they want to know," he said.

He was sitting with his hands folded on the desk looking more uptight than usual.

"You knew all along," I muttered. "You tried to warn me."

Tash looked at me if a single thought occupied his mind.

"He must have told you something," he said. "Maybe you thought it wasn't important. Maybe you forgot."

"What did I forget?" I asked.

He unfolded his hands and pressed his palms together "prayer-style." Without separating them, he gestured to me as he spoke in a quiet, deliberate voice.

"A series of mathematical equations," he said. His eyes turned more serious as he pushed a hardcover book across the table. "Have a look," he said.

"I'm sorry," I said, flipping the pages. "I don't know what you want."

The interviewer walked around the desk and stood behind us.

Tash turned, abruptly. "I can't be expected to question her with you breathing down my neck."

Hastily, she picked up her belongings and left.

The door slammed as he turned back to me. "Talk to me Genna."

Talking was the last thing I wanted to do, especially when it led to countless dead ends and almost never the truth. This time, I wanted to rummage through his thoughts, the ones that Elon felt the need to block, the ones he was still blocking.

"How do you know him?" I asked.

He slid back in his chair and sighed. "He showed up one day after the others left."

"He's been looking for them," I said. "What were they doing here?"

"It wasn't in my interest to ask." He shrugged. "I provided them with basic essentials, a place to stay ... so that they could do whatever they were here to do without raising suspicion."

I thought back to my first impressions of Princeton ... how the study lounge in the science building seemed like the perfect tech haven for people too smart to register normal.

"I couldn't tell you what happened to them," he said. "I hardly saw them, together or alone and when I did ... they didn't exactly lend themselves to conversation."

"Not like Elon," I said.

"No." He almost laughed. "Not like Elon. "There was always something different about him."

Cool, capable Elon, I thought. *How did they manage to keep him here against his will?*

"You seem like you admired him," I said. "I thought you hated him."

"It was a little bit of both," he said, his eyes drifting.

"When did you hate him less?" I asked, hanging on his every word.

"When I was working," he said, thinking back. "He got me to think in a new way, see what I couldn't see before." He paused. "I wouldn't expect you to understand."

Even without the ability to read him, I already understood.

"You were using him," I accused. "You breathe physics like it's some kind of religion, and somehow he got you closer to what you were looking for but it wasn't close enough —was it?"

"We were using each other," he snapped. "As my graduate student he adapted to campus life easily, in a place where his unique nature would go virtually undetected."

"The interviewer called you the sponsor," I said. "How does a high-tech extraterrestrial find someone like you?"

"It was something I posted online," he said. "Like anyone, I couldn't be sure that they existed but if they did and if they were here, I wasn't ashamed to admit that I would be more interested in acquiring knowledge than interfering with their motives."

"It must have gone viral," I said.

He shook his head. "It only had a handful of hits, but technically...."

"Technically," I interrupted. "Signals travel through space at light speed. So any alien civilization within listening range would have known where the party was ... and who was running it."

"Elon was a better tutor than I gave him credit for," he sneered.

"Have you seen him?" I asked, ignoring the insinuations.

"No," he answered, baffled. "I can't believe that they actually got him." His eyes widened. "Tell me," he said. "What has he told you?"

I didn't answer.

"He wanted to impress you," he said. "Maybe you didn't pay attention at the time, unable to fully appreciate higher mathematics and physics."

"Can you stop now?" I asked.

His eyes rolled. "Okay," he said, huffing slightly.

"Really...?" I asked, waiting for stronger confirmation.

"I'm sorry," he said louder. "I'm being unfair."

My eyes lowered, just remembering that he left the math files open.

"Since he was tutoring me," I said. "He didn't bother to selectively block everything connected to math."

"You mean to say that you had full access to those equations." His voice spiraled higher, like he was ready to explode.

Quickly, I cupped my hands over my ears.

"Do you realize that those equations would explain everything?" he shouted. "How the universe works, where Einstein left off ... *everything*."

I spoke quickly. "The first time I tried reading him, I saw numbers and symbols. They were jumbled, upside-down, sideways — they didn't mean anything."

"Maybe you better let the Professor be the judge of that," Ross said.

I was so busy remembering that I didn't notice at what point he came into the room and filled the seat beside me.

"Let me handle her," Tash said.

"Handle her?" Ross snickered. "If I didn't know better, I'd say that she's doing the interview."

Tash ignored him. "Genna, there's a missing sequence to a formula that I've been working on for most of my career." He blinked nervously. "It has strategic importance. That's what the military is looking for ... and that's why they have us both here."

"I can't think anymore," I said, my voice fading.

Tash turned to Ross. "Maybe you should let me talk to the boy."

"Excuse me Professor," Ross said. "But your 'live and let live' alien sympathizer routine is getting old fast."

Tash gave him an incensed look. "You dragged me off campus in the middle of the day, blindfolded and tied, and now you barge in here and hurl accusations."

"Yeah, well," Ross said. "Stuff happens."

My fingers dug into my lap. "I won't help either one of you," I said, "unless you let me see him."

14. Identity Crisis

The corridor was barely lit. There were two guards outside the door, standing at attention, hardly batting an eye.

"The girl goes in alone," Ross said.

"No way," Tash objected. "You can't stop me."

Ross threw a nod to the guards. On cue, they lunged forward and sent Tash in retreat with his hands in the air.

"Okay darling." Ross turned to me. "There are surveillance cameras inside that room. Whatever happens will be recorded. The guards are posted here at all times. They're authorized to use lethal force if necessary."

"He isn't … he won't." My voice trembled.

Even if it was an overreaction brought on by fear, it still unraveled me to think that the greatest military force on the planet considered Elon a threat.

Ross put his hands on my shoulders and looked me in the eye.

"Whoever you think he is, whatever he's told you," he said. "By now, you must have considered the possibility that it may *not* be that way."

How was it then? I didn't know for sure because I was being blocked from every direction.

"When your little reunion is over, I expect answers," Ross said. "I want to know why they're here. And I want the rest of that formula."

Tash squeezed my arm. "It'll be okay Genna," he said.

"You never told me." I turned to him, my voice wilting. "All the time that you were with them — how did you get over being afraid?"

Tash forced a smile. "I didn't."

The door shut behind me. I heard the lock slide into place.

The room was darker than the hallway, more long than wide. I inched forward slowly, stopping midway. In the shallow light, I recognized furniture, a round table and two chairs. The space felt abandoned, as if whoever had been there had long since gone.

My eyes focused on a motionless silhouette sitting on the floor, with his face lowered towards his knees. His arms were draped around his ankles, like he had resigned himself to that one position and didn't have the will to move.

He didn't turn as I came closer. The hooded sweatshirt he was wearing was pulled over his head so I couldn't see his face.

I dropped to my knees.

"Hey," I said.

He didn't answer.

"It's going to be okay," I said, lifting my face to see if I could spot the surveillance cameras.

Still he didn't answer.

"They think you're a security risk." I reached out to touch his arm.

Now would be a good time, I thought, *for one of his bright smiles, for a reassuring wink.*

"Tash is here," I said, hoping to comfort him. "They know that he's been covering for you."

My hand remained on his arm.

"It's that formula they want," I said, "The one that's supposed to explain everything." I rolled my eyes. "Seriously," I giggled nervously. "I think they call it the *Theory of Everything.*"

I waited for his infectious laugh. If anyone could find the humor in this situation, it was him.

"What they want doesn't matter," I sighed. "The only thing that matters is YOU."

He shifted uncomfortably as if he didn't want to listen.

"Why are you being like this?" I snapped. "At least look at me."

My hand hesitated. The olive drab sweatshirt he was wearing belonged to the Air Force with the name of the base printed across the front. Slowly, I leaned over and pulled the hood down.

I looked once. And then, I looked away.

"It's okay," he said, turning my face around.

"Is it you?" I gasped. "Are you really here?"

Byron moved my hair to one side. "It's me," he said.

"All this time…," I cried, patting down his face.

His eyes lowered to my aura band.

"I missed you," he said.

I started to stand, but he pulled me back down.

"No," I said, my mind racing. "I have to get you out of here. They have you confused with someone else."

"I know you guys are listening!" I screamed to the ceiling … to the walls. "Hello," I called out, waving my hands over my head. "It's *not* him. You have the wrong guy."

Byron didn't react. He didn't speak. His lips were on my hair which made it impossible to stay on track. The only way to get his attention was to physically push him away.

"Byron, are you listening?" I shouted. "There's someone else — he's *not* from earth."

"Let me look at you," he said as if every word flew over his head. "You're so beautiful."

His fingers circled my cheeks, like a substitute-kiss. The feeling I had was like dissolving head first, into a puddle.

"It's still there," he whispered, floating his face over mine. "The fire in your eyes…"

Imagine, in the middle of all this — I was getting a text. Well, it didn't exactly come through yet, but it was about to….

"Whoa," he said, sensing the improvement in my skills. "When did *that* happen?"

I reached into my pocket and pulled out my phone. Fortunately, Ross let me keep it after they were satisfied that it didn't contain strategically relevant information.

Bill's name popped up with the message: *Byron's plate: NJ Registration - Henry J. Tashimoto - Princeton. Sorry took so long. Give luv to your Mom.*

I froze for a half-second, the phone still in my hand. Then my eyes flew to him.

"It'll be over soon," he said, a sad smile pulling at his lips. "We'll be out of here."

"I don't understand," I said, afraid to hear more.

"Elon will be here soon," he said.

My head reeled back.

"Elon...," I repeated, dazed. "That must mean..." My voice fell, "that you're the same."

I looked at him like I was seeing him now for the first time.

"So which is it?" I asked. "Are you friends ... or enemies?"

"Neither," he answered. "He's my brother."

* * *

I collapsed beside him, my body lifeless. Nothing was what it seemed except for my tangled emotions.

"Why didn't you tell me?" I asked.

"I tried once," he said. "But how do you say something like that without sounding..."

"Crazy!" I finished his sentence.

He nodded back.

"Elon...," I said, reluctant to use his name. "He never told me about you."

Byron's face drew nearer. "Tell me that you never stopped thinking about me," he said. "Tell me that whatever else happened means nothing now."

I could easily agree to the first part. "I never stopped thinking about you."

His eyes pulled away. "He's manipulated you, Gennie," he snapped.

I felt tears coming, and then I stopped.

"What are you seeing?" I asked, reacting to the sudden awareness in his eyes.

He shook his head.

"Don't block me," I pleaded. "Whatever you're seeing, I want to see it too."

"Elon...," he said reaching for my hand. "He's already here."

He was walking towards the main gate, having materialized in mid-stride at a point where there was no one around to see. Every few feet or so, he did this little dance-spin, stopping to pick up a stone or twig.

At the sight of him, the uniformed serviceman stationed at the guard post came alert.

"Whoa," the guard said, blocking his way. "Hold it right there."

Elon decided to play along. "Nice weather we're having."

"Where do you think you're going?" the guard asked, indifferent to his charm.

Elon turned to the sign at the entrance. "McGuire Air Force Base," he answered.

The guard stretched his neck towards the private road.

"Someone, drop you off?" he asked.

Elon folded his arms across his chest, proud and defiant.

"Look here," the guard said more impatiently. "There's no way to get up here unless you came in by vehicle or chopper."

Elon let loose his smile. "Don't count on it."

They never tell me anything, the guard thought. *He has to be one of the officer's kids.*

"Actually my father sent me," Elon said with a rascal smirk.

Satisfied, the guard pulled out the guest list from behind the booth.

"Name?" he asked.

"Elon," he answered.

The guard ran his eyes down the list. "Last name?"

"Let's use yours," Elon said, eyeing the man's ID tag. "It's easier to pronounce."

The guard had no time to respond. The objects in his hand dropped as he slowly backed away like he had seen a ghost.

Elon approached the gate and extended his arms fully. The sensors blinked green, the gate slid open, and he simply walked through.

The next checkpoint was fifty feet ahead. The armed sentry asked to see his visitor's pass.

Elon patted down his pockets. "Left it in my dorm."

The man pulled out his phone. "You're not moving one inch from this spot until I can identify you," he said.

The phone slipped from his hand and hit the ground. With his eyes still on Elon, he leaned over and then suddenly froze; his face blanched with fear, as if he was staring down a wild animal ready to pounce.

The base was divided into three sections. Elon headed towards an area that resembled an oversized trailer park, with rows of hangars, large enough to house planes. He stopped when he came to the unmarked one: no numbers, no letters. The officer at the entrance saluted him. Elon nodded, and the man stepped away without breaking pose.

He entered the elevator and depressed the pass code. The retina-scan failed the first time. One more try and a blue light blinked with the words: *Access Accepted.*

The girl was waiting patiently; her nose pressed against the door. She backed away when she was sure that it was his hand on the other side. Lightly his fingers tapped the door in two places. The seal quickly released, allowing the door to slide open and disappear into a pocket-groove in the wall. At the sight of him, she immediately flew into his arms.

There was a twisting feeling in the center of my chest that made me want to cry and scream at the same time. She was pretty. Probably, one of the most beautiful girls I had ever seen with long, red-purple hair that lightened to pink at the ends.

The hair color was on-trend, but certainly not the most unusual thing about her. Her eyes were doing this "chameleon thing" ... changing from blue to green to amber-brown. It was like she was switching out color contact lenses every ten seconds. The fact that it made her look less human, only added to her beauty.

Just when I brought myself to an inconsolable state, the remote-viewing quit. Byron decided to unplug from the action, and in doing so, completely cut me off.

"Who's the girl?" I asked, trying to sound barely curious.

He said nothing as his eyes detached, a hard frown set across his mouth.

On the other side of the door, the guards snapped their heels and grunted: "Sir."

Elon came charging into the room with a carefree smile so confident that you would think he owned the place.

"Genna...," he said moving toward me, his arm brazenly around the girl with open affection.

She glared my way while her eyes were changing, so that one was green and the other still blue. He released her, but she stayed close, as he slipped his hand around my waist and pulled me against him. He kissed me on the side of my head; quick "glad to see you" kisses. The last pressed harder, lasting longer than the others.

"What's wrong?" he whispered anxiously into my ear.

I didn't respond. His eyes followed mine to the gorgeous creature standing at his side.

"Genna," he said, his voice astonished. "This is my sister."

It was something I should have easily picked up if my emotions weren't fighting me. Suddenly I was beyond embarrassed.

"Daria," he said, gently. "Say hello to Genna."

"Hello," she said; her voice timid.

Then Byron stepped forward, and she quickly sprinted around me and rushed into his arms.

Elon pulled me aside. "Are you okay?" he asked, thoughtfully. "I hope you didn't get too scared."

"No, it's fine" I said, sarcastically. "It's every day that I'm kidnapped from my house, and I find out that the guy who might qualify as my 'ex-boyfriend'... is really an alien and your brother."

"About that...," he began.

"You made me think he wasn't coming back." I stopped him. "You hid the truth over and over again. I should totally hate you."

"Maybe," he said. "But you don't."

I groaned loudly, failing to find the words that could explain my frustration.

"You're controlling information," I said. "I don't know what the truth is anymore."

"I don't want to talk about anything that isn't us," he whispered against my face.

I felt his hand in mine, and all I wanted was to touch him, kiss him.

"Oh man," Elon sighed as Byron walked over. "Don't you know when to knock?"

"You didn't need to come," Byron said. "The problem was about to be handled."

"Really," Elon said, taunting him. "Tell us how it happened. Explain how you opened the portal using the wrong frequency and left Daria behind."

Daria's eyes flickered as she looped her arm under Byron's and rested her head on his shoulder.

"It happened so quickly," Byron said, his eyes thinking back. "The helicopters were landing one by one."

I had the feeling of dusk approaching. They were standing in a clearing. Around them, the ground shook and the earth kicked-up. My head pulled back, reacting to the remembered sound of propellers spinning.

"You're somewhere in South Jersey," I said. "It could be the Pine Barrens."

"They tracked us there, the UFO hunters," Byron said. "They had military backup, some sort of special operations task force. It was overkill: the fire power, the night vision goggles."

"You were here to look for other aliens," I suddenly said, as he allowed me access to other details.

"Preliminary reports suggested that they were here," Elon said. "My father was concerned that they found a way to assimilate into the local population, so he sent Byron to check it out. It was a low-risk scouting mission, safe enough to allow Daria to go along."

"Who are *they*?" I asked.

The answer to that question wasn't coming through.

"The reports were wrong," Byron said, turning to Elon. "If they were here, they must have moved on."

"You were getting ready to leave," I said, accepting new information. "And then they surrounded you."

"I told Daria not to move," Byron said.

The images played out. She was wandering around like she had been dropped into a fun zone, wearing a baseball cap, her two-toned hair spilling out from the sides, a pair of dark glasses to cover her eyes.

"She was moving too fast." Elon glared. "You didn't compensate when you opened the portal."

"I was already through when I realized it," Byron sighed. "Before I phased out, I saw the look in her eyes."

"She saw you disappear," Elon growled. "She saw you leave her."

"I didn't leave her," Byron shouted. "I never would have left her. I was waiting for the right time to take her back."

"In the meantime," Elon said. "You hung around Princeton. Oh, and I forgot, you joined a rock band. That is … when you weren't running around shopping malls and filling in at the local psychic meetings."

"They were chasing me," Byron said. "I tried to lie low. I tried to blend in."

I thought back to the first time I caught a glimpse of him. He was flying down the road near the mall with a rush of sirens behind him. And another time, when I was followed into Battlefield Park, and he miraculously showed up.

"The band, the psychic group … they were a better cover than even Tash could arrange," Elon said. "But maybe hiding out in the open wasn't such a good idea once you decided that you liked your new life a little too much."

"I wanted to stage a rescue without stirring up a military response." Byron ignored the accusations. "The base is protected by some kind of anti-missile defense system. It uses a high-energy magnetic field that interferes with the portal."

The memory of Cassie harping on the magnet as the reason why Byron couldn't come back flashed through my mind.

Elon shook his head. "You should have signaled for help," he said. "Instead, you answered a cell phone in the middle of the rescue and ended up captured yourself."

Byron succumbed to a long sigh.

"Hang on," I said, turning to him. "I gave you the phone, and when you didn't come back, I called you."

"It wasn't your fault, Gennie," Byron said.

"It was totally my fault," I insisted. "The ringtone went off — it must have been so loud, so distracting. If I didn't call you at that exact moment, you never would have been caught."

"It really doesn't matter," Elon said; a jealous edge to his voice. "He should have called for help."

"No," Byron said. "Just this once, I wanted to handle a problem without the need to dispatch the 'chosen' son."

"It's more than that," Elon said. "You knew that if I came to get Daria, you would have to leave with me. Guess what?" He grinned. "That's exactly how it's going down."

Byron clenched his jaw. "You would have had Daria back. I was going to signal a space cruiser to bring her home."

"So you could continue in Genna's world?" Elon snarled. "Impress her friends, play in the band...?"

"It's *not* like I would be missed," he said, his eyes lingering on me. "And for sure, no one would come back just for me."

Elon suddenly turned to me. "Stay close to me."

Before I could ask why, the first alarm sounded. Over the loudspeaker, a computer-generated warning repeated.

"This is not a drill. Repeat, this is not a drill. Code 5 security breach; Special Operations Task Force: Report to lower sub-levels."

General Langdon Ross argued with his guards before they finally recognized him. He pushed them aside impatiently and entered the room.

"Don't," he said, raising his hands as if to surrender.

The guards rushed in behind him and nearly stumbled as they held back.

Elon cocked his head and smiled. "You know my father," he said, his eyes on Ross. "I can see that you've met before."

Ross groaned. "Please."

"Please what?" Elon asked, menacingly.

"I had no idea," Ross said. "The others were nothing like *him*. But you...."

"I'm not interested in what you think," Elon said sharply.

Ross cleared his throat. "Your father...," he stammered. "Is he here with you?"

"No," Elon answered. "But I'll be sure to tell him that you're asking for him."

"No, don't do that!" Ross snapped, raising his hands again.

The stir of voices and the sound of boots clamored behind the door.

"Looks like the cavalry is here," Elon said.

Ross glanced behind his shoulder.

"Have them stand down," Elon said calmly, but firmly.

Ross hesitated, weighing his options.

"There were never any options," Elon assured. "Do as I say or it won't end well."

Ross inhaled deeply. "Stand down!" he yelled through the door just as it opened. The combat team instantly surrounded Elon. "I said — stand down!" Ross repeated, more insistently.

Tash bolted through the door. His eyes moved between Byron and Elon and then, finally to Daria. "When they started talking math," he said, turning to Elon. "I assumed that they had you."

Ross gave Tash a harsh glance and then looked to Elon. "Now what...?"

"Now we go," Elon said, motioning me closer.

Ross shook his head. "I can't let you take the girl."

"Genna trusts me," Elon said. "And don't think about pursuing — or you'll regret it."

"The girl belongs here with us," Ross persisted, his tone gently pleading.

"I don't believe she would agree," Elon said, breaking his superior demeanor to give me a smile.

"The magnet," Ross reminded. "It can't be disengaged."

Elon grinned. "It's about as strong as tissue paper and even easier to blow through."

His arms opened wide enough to hold his sister with one arm, and me with the other. With my face pressed against his chest and his heartbeat in my ear, I watched Daria's eyes blink and change color, until his hand closed over my eyes.

On my right side, Byron drew closer.

"Hey Tash," Elon said, his voice almost sad. "Sorry about the mix-up. Thanks for everything."

15. Sacrifice

"Kiss me," Byron said.

He was suddenly facing me, where he wasn't a second ago.

"Kiss me the way you kissed him."

My eyes darted past him.

"Looking for someone?" he asked.

"Elon," I said, setting my eyes on the earth-view. "He'll be back soon."

"I've seen it Gennie," he said. "...The way your face lights up when he walks into the room." I took a small step back. "And when he's gone..." He leaned closer. "Everything inside you pines for him."

I let out a small cry as he reached for my arms. It was the beginning of a struggle, a few tugs back and forth which ended when our eyes met. He wasn't in Air Force clothes anymore. He was wearing straight-legged jeans, a shirt styled with wings and guitars. He looked the way he always did, the way he lived in my memories.

The smile started at the corners of his mouth.

"Hi," he whispered into my face.

I felt my arms go limp around his neck.

"Hi," I repeated, half-stunned as his lips drew dangerously close.

"Get away from her." Elon's enraged voice broke from behind and stopped him cold.

I heard myself scream.

Byron moved me aside and then pushed against him, springing back at once like he hit a brick wall. Elon exhaled, and with one hand barely trying, sent him crashing to the floor.

"No," I shrieked loudly. "Don't hurt him."

Elon reached for my face. His eyes held the perfect semblance of vulnerability and menace.

"If he so much as looks at you again…," he said.

I caught his hand and pressed it to my mouth. "It's okay."

Every moment spent touching weakened his anger, until his smile cautiously returned. Then Byron called out, and my hand slipped away.

"I can't move, Gennie," he said, his voice deathly low.

He was no longer sprawled across the floor. He was standing with his back pressed to the wall; his face turned sideways.

Elon's beautiful smile fell. "Look at him, Genna," he snarled. "The veritable black sheep of the family."

My mouth opened, but I was too shocked to speak. Byron's boots were rising above the floor, dangling in mid-air as he was slammed against the wall repeatedly, like an invisible hand was picking him up and throwing him back.

My eyes flew to Elon. "I'll do anything," I cried. "Just don't hurt him."

A look of astonishment flickered in his eyes, his face so wounded that it made me tear up.

"Anything…?" he asked.

"He's your brother," I said, swallowing hard. "You can't hate him that much."

"It's driving him crazy Gennie," Byron said, fighting for breath. "He knows that no matter what he does, you'll never forget. You'll never be his."

Elon stepped within inches of his face.

"Actually Bro," he said. "What you began, *ended* before it happened because YOU were stuck in a military base for weeks."

Byron avoided his eyes.

"Gennie," he called again. "You think you're torn between us but you're not. You're feelings for him — they're all about me."

"Last warning," Elon threatened.

"Stop it!" I shouted, holding my ears. "Both of you stop it."

"He hijacked your feelings," Byron snapped. "You were waiting for me while he worked his way into your life. He made you think I wasn't coming back."

"You're *not* coming back," Elon said with a sadistic grin.

Byron smiled, not happily. "Either are you."

* * *

"Whatever you're feeling now," I said. "Don't shut me out."

Elon turned, his gaze lost in the endless sweep of space around us.

"Is that what I'm doing, Genna?" he asked, his voice distant.

I knew that I had no right to demand it of him; his irrepressible energy, his sparkling smile and the kind of laughter that would reboot me out any crisis. It was selfish to need him like that, to need him now ... so much.

The sound of painful gasping startled me.

"What are you doing to him?" I turned back to Elon.

"It's my father, Gennie." Byron stopped me. "He won't let me go back with you."

I shook my head, trying to understand. Besides the three of us, there was no one else in sight.

"He's using a mind-reach," Byron said, as he thrashed against the wall trying to break free.

Suddenly the air turned icy-cold, swirling faster around us until we were caught in a raging wind, the space between us ignited by a rush of pure energy — capable of good, bad and everything in between.

"Let me stay," Byron shouted. "You have Elon. You don't need me."

"Leave him alone," I cried, unsure of where to direct my outburst.

My hair whipped around my face while I tried to keep from toppling over.

"Help him!" I shouted to Elon.

Elon didn't react. He was still sidetracked, watching the earth as if something compelling had his attention. He was stronger than Byron, and yet the way he suddenly reeled back made it clear that his father was forcing a telepathic exchange, one that he would never have agreed to if he had the choice.

A moment or two passed before he dropped his eyes, his face shaken. He looked once more at the earth and then looked away.

"My father," Elon said unfeelingly. "He's made his decision."

I sighed deeply while I lifted my eyes, hoping *he* was still there to hear me.

"No!" I shouted. "Leave him alone or take me too."

The force behind his father's will shattered through me like shards of broken glass. I knew in an instant that they wouldn't take me — even if I had the courage to go, even if it was what Elon had wanted from the beginning.

Quickly, I backed up as if something all-encompassing was approaching. Byron was still pinned to the wall. Somehow he managed to catch me as I raced by.

"It's okay," he said, shielding me with his arms. "My father won't hurt you."

I felt a kiss press against the top of my cheek.

The contact was enough to make me long again for what I had been missing when he went away, for what I would have continued to miss — *if not for Elon.*

I looked up to find *him* pacing, a volatile mix of anger and hurt filled his eyes.

"Look at you," Elon said, suddenly towering over me. I flinched.

"Look at you," he repeated louder this time.

"Give me a chance to explain," I said.

"Why?" he asked bitterly. "Is it because you're afraid?"

"I'm *not* afraid," I said, trembling under the weight of his outrage. "I'm only afraid of losing you, of losing us."

My perfect boyfriend ... his balance faltered like he was too weak to stand ... like he was resisting his next move to lunge forward and pull me into his arms.

"Why are you saying these things?" Byron asked; the color drained from his eyes. "He's got you totally confused."

"I'm sorry...," I told Byron, while watching Elon.

"Don't tell me you're sorry," Byron said. "I don't want to hear that you're sorry."

I shook my head, turning over past feelings like they were crushing me again.

"Did you miss me?" Byron whispered; his voice deliberate. "What was it like when I didn't come back?"

My eyes stayed on Elon.

"I know how you felt," he continued. "It must have been punishing, putting up with all those questions from the band about where I was?"

I shook my head to deny it.

"How many times did you wait by the window?" Byron grinned. "How many times did you check your cell phone?"

I shut my eyes.

"When you called that night, Gennie," he said. "I couldn't think of anything else. All that mattered was hearing your voice one more time."

Finally, the hurt held inside let loose. If I didn't confront it, I would never be free.

"I thought that you weren't coming back," I cried, the memory still raw. "I thought that I would never see you again, and it was the most horrible feeling that I've ever felt."

It was as though my confession had the power to transform the situation, instantly giving him the strength to free himself. He tightened his grip around my waist with the full strength of his body. There was a moment when I felt him overcome, before he slipped really fast.

"Don't go," I choked.

"Remember the bookstore," he said with a weepy smile. "Remember every time that I said I was going, and then came running back."

"It'll be okay," I said, looking around for a way to help him.

"No, it won't," he said, his fingers on my face. "So let me look at you until I can't."

"Hold on," I said, demanding it. "Byron, you have to fight back."

Desperate, I called out to G-man as if he would actually come. From somewhere he was watching, unwilling to run interference. In the back of mind, I had clung to the idea of a friendship that wasn't real.

"Don't move," I whispered into Byron's eyes. "Don't let go of me."

I felt his arms release.

"No!" I screamed hard.

His face began to pull away.

He whispered quickly: "Never give up on you, Gennie."

I held on until there was nothing to hold on to. I don't think that I actually saw it happen, "the leaving part." There was no winking out, no fading into white static, no sense of the visible turning invisible. I only knew the one moment when he was no longer there.

A feeling of petrified numbness came over me. I don't remember turning, but I must have because Elon was now facing me. And there was NOTHING — absolutely nothing that I dreaded more.

"You're everything," I breathed hard.

"Everything," he repeated. "Are you sure about that?"

"Yes," I answered. "You know it's true, so why isn't it enough?"

His lifeless gaze drifted.

"I can't change what happened before we met," I said. His fingers quivered as I reached for his hand. "All I know is how I feel now."

He said nothing.

"Okay," I said, drawing strength from a deeper place. "All those feelings I had for Byron, all those memories ... I realized I had to let them go because everything that I am — wants you more."

He squeezed his eyes shut and then reopened them.

Slowly, my arms lifted around his shoulders and neck. For a second or two, he didn't move. I felt the tender pressure of his hands around my waist, as his arms reached up and *pushed me away*.

"Don't," I whimpered.

His face hardened as if he had to find the strength to stay angry.

"I'm sorry, Genna," he said.

Even the way he said my name felt different. I didn't want to hear it like that, the way everyone else said it.

"Don't read me when you're upset," I said, anticipating.

"I'm not reading you," he said, his voice empty. "So it's okay...lie to me. Tell me what I want to hear."

"I can't lie to you," I said. "I love you."

His eyes met mine and then, he froze.

I leaned in with a full smile on my lips.

"I love you," I said, my eyes wide. "Just when I think I can't feel more, it keeps coming — so fast and hard that I think I'm going to die."

He winced, and then closed his eyes.

"I love you so much," I repeated, lifting the tone of my voice higher.

Now that I had said it, nothing could keep me from saying it over and over again.

He reopened his eyes. Did I see it ... the beginnings of a smile, before he realized that even this couldn't make him happy again...?

"Tell me why it hurts to hear it now?" I asked. My hand pressed the side of his face. "Is it because you can't love me again *or* is because there's no way for us to be together?"

His lips parted, as if he was about to answer.

My hands ran over his chest, along the length of his arm. "Have you ever been so attracted to someone that it scared you?"

His face didn't react. But he let me talk.

"The first time I met you at Princeton," I said. "You smiled at me so hard that I couldn't even look at you."

"You didn't meet me," he suddenly said, distracted by my hand. "I met you."

I shook my head, confused.

"Think back," he whispered with a "cresting and falling" sync to his voice. "Think back to the plane ride that morning."

Suddenly I was streaming live.

The explosion was bright and loud as thunder. I was on the ground, face down. There was a smell of fire, burning fuel.

"I'm cold," I said in a low, weak voice.

The wreckage sizzled around me. The heat distorted the background and made things wavy. I could barely make out his face, but I knew that he was there, bending over me, turning me around.

"I'm here Genna," he said.

The smoke cleared and for the first time, I saw him: the square jaw, the impossibly blue eyes.

"I'm sorry," he said, his eyes on my scarf. "I'm looking for my brother. I think you know him."

Suddenly the action stalled. Elon and I watched the scene from a distance while he explained.

"We crossed into your flight path," he said, his eyes remembering. "I latched onto your thoughts. They were full of Byron."

He sighed before continuing. "G-man tried to abort the maneuver, but I managed to override him even though I'm not supposed to be able to do that. We followed for a while. Air Force radar picked us up. They scrambled fighter jets."

"A dogfight," I said.

"Your plane was small and light," he said. "The pursuing aircraft created turbulence and brought you down."

"I would have been rescued," I said.

He shook his head. "You were already dying."

He fed me the images slowly, rewinding to fill in the missing parts.

I saw him walk past the pilot who was unconscious with minor injuries. He found me on the other side of the field.

Again, I saw the image of him turning me over, his hand moving past my scarf — to my face. He kept apologizing as if there was nothing he could do.

"I'm so cold." My voice trembled violently.

"I'm prohibited from interfering," he said.

His face sickened as he began to turn away.

"Hospital...," I called out.

It was just one word but enough to stop him.

"There isn't time," he answered.

He stepped towards me again. I saw his jeans and black coat. Even through the thick smoke, he was beyond handsome.

"Let's see," he said with a voice that already decided.

He knelt beside me and lifted my head and shoulders. In his arms, I fell limp like a rag doll. He brought me to his chest, his hand petting my head like something to be fiercely adored. I felt the pain increase for a moment — searing through my body until I was thrown into spasms.

"Is this what it feels like to die?" I asked.

"No," he said, gasping. "This is what it feels like to live."

There was a jolt.

I pulled back, suspended for a moment with my back arched. Then I felt the release, sudden and forceful as he accepted my injuries. Barely aware, I watched him flinch as the first pangs of pain reached his nervous system, his sapphire eyes fading to gray.

Gradually my strength returned, but there was something more, something that I didn't have before because it was a part of him.

"Can you feel it?" he asked.

He followed with a soft, rolling giggle, the kind of laughter that makes you wonder how you'll ever live without it.

I turned away from the scene, back to him.

"So I didn't come into my own?" I asked, recalling Remi's lame explanation for my sudden spike in extrasensory ability.

He shook his head. "It isn't enough to change the course of the world, but used correctly, it could be totally amazing."

The sound of approaching sirens wailed in the distance. He cradled my head and slowly lowered my body to the ground.

"I need to leave," he said.

I felt sleep overtake despite my attempt to resist it.

As the sirens grew louder, he whispered: "Princeton." Then he kissed my lips, holding the pressure as I drifted. "I'll wait for you."

"All this time it was you," I said. "We were about to crash when I heard my name. I thought it was Byron, but it was you."

"I'm *not* your hero, Genna," he said, unplugging from the memory. "The decisions I made that day caused the accident."

"You were trying to find your family."

"I didn't need you to find them," he said. "I would have found them anyway. What I was chasing was your love, your tenacity — the way your thoughts clung to my brother, the way you woke up in the middle of the night, crying over him when he didn't come back."

"Did you think that I could feel that way about you?" I asked.

He almost answered.

"Elon, it's time." The Guardian strolled towards us with his hands clasped behind him.

I caught my stomach, feeling suddenly sick. Elon veered forward as if he wanted to reach out, but then some thought triggered in his mind ... and held him back. I raised myself on my toes to reach him at eye level. I didn't think twice — I didn't think at all. I kissed him on the lips; a full-on kiss that lasted longer than it should have, especially with the G-man staring us down.

He let the kiss happen but didn't return the pressure. For just a brief second, I thought I saw the light return to his eyes, but then it was gone so quickly that I wasn't sure if it had ever been there.

"Genna...," he stammered, a helpless look floundered in his eyes. "Give me your hand."

I felt a rush of excitement.

The aura band unclasped.

"No," I groaned.

Underneath, the skin was blanched with a ghostly indentation of what was once there, something fluid and alive.

The band was gone, but his hand was still in mine.

"Elon," G-man said, forcefully.

He actually startled at the sound of his name, his eyes suddenly moistening.

G-man turned to me. "You'll be back on earth in less than thirty minutes. What can I say Gen ... only good thoughts and wishes." He glanced behind him. "Now Elon..."

Slowly his hand left mine, despite my eagerness to grab it again.

One more look before he turned, and his eyes sent me there, to the better version of my room. Probably the best place to wait out the next half-hour, to wait to be sent home.

I sat on the foot of the bed and started to cry — the kind of crying that eventually turns into convulsive sobbing, tearless frustrated vocals that bring you to an inconsolable, twisted mess.

From the corner of one watery eye, I noticed my sound equipment. Maybe *not* exactly mine, but it looked identical to the stuff back in my real room. I hit the power, unsure that the simulation would follow through. To my surprise, it did. The first track on my playlist came blasting through the speakers like on-demand endorphins.

I drifted around the room, all "dawn of the dead" like, flashing back to the small moments, the first time I saw him, the magazine dropping away from his heaven-sent face.

That restless feeling that I struggled with before I met him returned with a vengeance. I circled my bed, the one I never slept in, and began messing up the pillows, tearing off the bedspread and sheets. It didn't matter if time and space conspired to separate us, or if he never wanted to see me again. My mind refused to shut down the images of his hand lifting my face for that one slow and perfect kiss.

The epic kiss!

I reached for my books, paperbacks from grade school that never found their way into a good-will box. That shelf was easy to clear. All it took was one wave of my hand. Next up, the teen fantasy series that I should have bought online; one by one, I threw them so hard the bindings split.

Anything Jane Austen, I skipped.

With nothing left to destroy, I found myself trying to shake off the memory of my hand sliding through his hair, past the sexy sideburns underneath. That was where I wanted to kiss him … over and over again.

I spun around looking for something — anything — a trophy from my bookshelf. I never liked that dance competition anyway. So I used it to knock down the other trophies, in true "rock band gone wild" style.

Suddenly I felt the strength of an arm, as the trophy was taken from my hand in mid-swing. Elon said nothing as he tossed it across the room. It crashed somewhere unseen and then he fell flat, sprawled out across the bed, oblivious to everything.

I stretched out beside him, both of us staring intently at the ceiling.

"Tell me again," he said.

I turned to him; a smile slowly emerged across my lips. "I love you," I said.

Carefully his face lowered to mine.

"Let's go," he said with a feisty spark in his eyes.

I was caught between shock and pleasure as he reached for my mouth and kissed it.

"Aren't you coming?" he asked.

He tasted my mouth again.

The excitement was overwhelming.

"You're going back with me?" I asked, kissing him hard.

"I thought I lost you," he said, holding me in his arms. "I never want to feel like that again."

My hand was in his when I felt something catch my wrist. The aura band fit snugly between my other bracelets, pulsing with the wildest colors.

"We haven't much time," he said, lifting me up. "We're going to jump through the portal." He kissed my hand. "But it won't be like the other times. It won't be as easy."

My eyes widened. "You can't be serious?"

He threw me a reassuring smile. "It's a short window in order to get through unnoticed," he explained. "We need to jump through at the exact instant that they break away from the planet. I'll be able to block G-man. By the time he's aware, it'll be too late for him to stop us."

"And if we miss it ... the window?" I asked him.

"The gravitational force of the earth will crush us."

I looked up at him, a raw, nervous fright driving my reaction.

"I won't miss it," he said firmly, his forefinger tapping me on the nose to make his point.

I caught the apprehensive look in his eyes. He was the guy who was fearless — ready for anything with a "bring it on" attitude. If it was true that he was even a little bit worried, it had to be worth worrying about.

He steadied my shoulders with his hands and pulled me out of a hasty retreat.

"Genna, I've asked you to trust me before," he reminded.

"A thousand times," I said.

"Okay," he agreed. "Then trust me once more. Trust me *now*."

My head moved up and down and then sideways, unable to decide. I thought back to the intent look on his face when he was staring at the earth in space and wondered if he knew then what he was going to do; how we were going to get away.

"You tried to convince G-man that we broke up," I realized. "You weren't sure if it would work, so you took the aura band from me."

He didn't answer as he looked around, absorbed in thought as if he was mentally calculating.

"Our landing site should be someplace rural," he said. "But hopefully, still in New Jersey."

He moved me in a specific position. Then he placed himself beside me at a right angle.

"When did you know? I asked. "When were you sure about us?"

"I might have been a little jealous," he said. "But I was always sure."

"That's what you call 'a little' jealous?" I asked; my expression comical.

"Okay," he said. "I was beyond jealous. But I should have known better because you told me something that you never told my brother."

I lowered my eyes.

"There comes a time when thinking through feelings isn't enough," he said, picking up my chin. "You either have the courage to say it *or* it isn't real."

"I love you," I said.

"On second thought...." He threw his arms under my legs and lifted me in his arms. "Okay," he said, with an overwhelmed voice. "Same rules apply: hang on to me and keep your eyes shut." He paused to lean in for a kiss.

"Promise me...," I said.

"No matter what," he said. "We'll be together."

"Tell me when," I said, accepting another kiss before burying my face in his chest.

His answer was immediate: "Now!"

I remember the upward motion as our feet left the ground. As we started to come down I realized that there was no landing ... just down, like falling into a bottomless well. We were tumbling, smashing against unseen obstacles with such force that it seemed as though we were thrashing the surface of a rock wall; the sound like sneakers bouncing around in a clothes dryer.

I can't say for sure when I noticed that he was no longer holding me because I never felt the moment of separation.

I called his name. The sound of my voice skipped.

I waited for what felt like eternity. Then I broke one of his rules. I opened my eyes, just enough so I could see what was happening.

But how can you see ... when there's nothing to see?

I was in total darkness, not the kind of darkness where you can make out a shadow or outline, not the kind that picks up the light behind your eyes. This darkness was pitch-black, without even a sliver of light to guide the way.

The sense of fear was so extreme that I didn't realize when I was no longer moving in a high-velocity tail spin. I was drifting in a see-saw motion. Things were beginning to slow. I wondered if this is what it was like before death. So I did the only thing that I could possibly do, the only thing that made sense.

I prayed.

I prayed for my life ... and to find him again. They were the same prayer.

Take me home. Please take me ... home.

I heard a voice inside me say: *Hold on. You're going to be fine.*

There was a quick acceleration. The hard bumps rippled through every fiber of my body. Just when I thought I couldn't take anymore ... it stopped.

Then out of the dense night, out of the empty darkness came the stars.

16. HIGH POINT

I knew I was lying on grass because I could smell it, fresh like green mint.

My eyes opened against the sun. There were clusters of trees around me with the first hint of leaves. I sensed the elevation as the breeze circled my face, as it fanned my hair across the hard, wet ground.

It didn't feel like a dream. Even so, I feared that this perfect forest, a place that in every way screamed "earth" would soon vanish, leaving me still out there, alone in space.

When I was reasonably sure that the passing moments had no effect on my surroundings, I brought my hand up to my cheek. My fingers were trembling, but I was definitely HERE.

I rolled sideways. No one was lying next to me. My head pulled up, the movement triggering a shooting pain down my arm. Still on the ground, I kneaded my elbow as I called out.

Only natural sounds pierced the silent hum, birds in flight, falling branches. Had Elon been there, I would have heard his boots crushing pebbles and leaves; the clanging of the zippers on his jacket as he skipped over puddles.

"Hey," I shouted into the distance. "Where are you?'

No answer, so I tried to move my legs. They were stiff. I felt the bruises through my jeans. Slowly, I stood myself up, my eyes on the sky, clear blue like his eyes.

"Quit playing games," I yelled. "You better not be hiding."

It would be so like him to spring out from behind a rock or tree. I waited while my hand brushed past the bulge in my hip pocket — my cell phone. I pulled it out and then drew back almost as fast. The wallpaper photo of the earth in space gave me a sinking feeling.

"Please," I muttered to myself, trying to get a signal.

It never occurred to me that the place would be a "dead zone," and the likely reason why Elon chose it for a landing site — to help cloak our escape.

Waving the phone in the air, I gasped when I saw one or two bars flash, only to see them disappear as quickly. When I tried again, my aura band caught the light. No longer a kaleidoscope of living color, it seemed "switched off" to the dullest shade of gray.

I called his name, desperately loud, before a single thought struck so hard that it stopped me in my tracks.

I didn't have to find him, I thought.

If Elon was here, he would know where to find me. He would know that my arm was probably broken and that I was virtually helpless in a part of New Jersey that looked like anywhere *but* New Jersey.

I blinked away the tears as the next thought crept in. What if he never actually went through the portal with me, what if he just made me think we were leaving together? It seemed like we were pulled apart, when he never jumped through with me. And all the hype about it being the worse portal-ride ever, that was just to prepare me for going through alone.

My first instinct was to fall to my knees, curl myself into a tight ball until someone eventually found me. But I didn't have the discipline to keep still. I had to move, as if running through open wilderness could drive back the truth.

Like a wounded animal, I ran recklessly with my dangling arm sending sharp twinges of pain to my fingertips. My boots pressed into the ground, treading past trickling brooks, the musical sound of water against rock mimicking human voices. Twice I stopped myself from looking behind; convinced that he was there, maintaining distance, stalking me with his laser-blue eyes.

I would rather feel the pain from my arm, I thought. *I'd rather feel that pain than lose the part of me that left with him.*

The air stirred under my legs, kicking up a cloud of dried leaves and brush. The sound of wild birds filled the air with a vague menacing feeling that made me run faster. I never saw the branch that caught my ankle. It happened so fast. For an instant, it felt like I might recover, but then gravity won out, and I fell flat on my back.

The thumping sound of the impact made me groan. My hand fell across something that didn't belong there. I patted it down before I looked.

He was lying on his side, his photo-shop flawless face half-hidden between tufts of overgrown foliage. I took my time looking. If he had been the product of wishful thinking, I would never have imagined him this way, breathing shallow, skin so pale.

I raised myself up fighting against pain, wondering how long I could keep from fainting, long enough to turn him over.

My fingers reached for his hand, heavy and limp. "Elon can you hear me?"

His eyes were closed. I ran my fingers across his face; his skin cool to the touch. I brushed the bits of broken twigs from his shirt.

"Hey," I said, losing my voice to tears. "You got us here. We're on earth."

He didn't answer. He didn't move.

"Wake up," I said, caressing his face. "Please wake up."

Looking at him now, it was hard to believe that there was a time when I was afraid to tell him....

"I didn't want to say anything that I couldn't take back," I confessed, leaning closer. "Want to know a secret?" I whispered. " The longer it took to tell you, the more I felt it."

My hand stroked his head.

"I kept worrying that something would change if I told you," I said. "When maybe, I had to change; maybe there was no way to stay the same."

If I was right, then all I wanted now was to be transformed into to this seeing, thinking creature who knew his love.

I slipped my hand inside my shirt and pulled out the shell that he had given me. It was too cool not to be jewelry, so I had it strung on a fringed, leather cord.

"When you gave me this," I said, holding the shell to my lips. "I don't think there's a way to describe how it made me feel."

I thought I saw him stir, but I wasn't sure.

"I have to get help." My eyes lowered to his aura band, as frozen and colorless as mine. "I should have believed in you," I cried. "I should have believed in us."

The sunlight flashed across his face. His eyes fluttered before they opened: the irises transparent, ethereal blue. There was a brief moment of weakness, and then he sprang to life.

"Now was that so hard?" he asked with a wakening smile.

"I thought you left me here," I said.

"How could I do that?" he asked, reaching for my face.

"I was so scared," I said. "I let my imagination run away."

"Actually," he said with an exceptionally rakish grin. "I was awake for a few minutes while you were freaking out … saying all those heartfelt things. So I figured that I would just listen for a while … see how far you would go." He stopped. "Man, you went pretty far."

I don't know what I hit him with, my hand or a stick.

"How could you?" I yelped, reaching over him.

He quickly flipped me around, so we reversed positions.

I felt myself respond, as his lips dragged circles around my opening mouth. He pressed closer, and then I screamed as he touched my shattered arm.

"I think I broke my elbow," I said, wincing as a prickly sensation reached my shoulder.

The pain fired in unrelenting bursts as he set me down. When I looked up, I noticed the trees misting over, their billowy tops swaying with the wind. Even his shining eyes began to blur out, as if a low-lying cloud had passed over the sun.

"Tell me again," he said.

He was holding my arm out straight, bracing my elbow from underneath with his other hand.

"I love you," I said, the power of speech quickly leaving me.

The last glimpse I had of him was his face leaning over me with a sympathetic pout, and then he caught me.

The burn began at my fingertips; the kind of burn you get after a work-out. It was another moment before my entire arm felt like it had been doing a hand-stand. It burned; it cooled. It burned again, and then it was over … and I felt nothing.

"You can move it now," he said.

I flexed my elbow as strength returned, the motion smooth and fluid.

"Whoa…," I said. "Good as new."

"Better than new," he said with a surefire grin.

'Something happened in the portal," I said, wiggling my fingers.

"That was one rough ride," he said gripping the back of his neck as if he had pulled a muscle. "I don't know how we got separated. It shouldn't have happened. Something interfered with our reentry."

His eyes darted sideways as if he had caught movement in the woods. I looked over and saw a large bird swooping down, finding its way into the rustling trees. His eyes broke away when the bird emerged.

He rose to his feet and lifted me up.

"Let's go," he said, slipping his arm around me.

About two hundred yards ahead, arrows nailed to a tree pointed in different directions:

Los Angeles: 2,770 miles

London: 3,463 miles
Rome: 4,288 miles
Tokyo: 6,686 miles

The more official-looking sign staked in the ground read: *High Point State Park, One of the Seven Natural Wonders of New Jersey, Elevation 1800 feet.*

"How are we going to get out of here?" I asked; my voice discouraged.

The suburban girl in me, the one who never wandered beyond New York City, wanted to get back to civilization even if I was grateful to be back on earth ... anywhere on earth.

"Keep walking," he said. "It's just a little further."

"Walk?" I asked. "It's at least a two hour drive home. I hope there's a ranger's station nearby."

We passed the entrance to the Appalachian Trail. The radiance of midday flooded the woods; the shaded canopy pierced by thin streams of hazy light made everything in its path shimmer in constant-green.

His eyes changed too ... in shades of blue, they reflected the light. As we walked, the trees and bushes that filled in the hilly terrain became more familiar, more pruned back. The ground flattened as we came around the bend of the cul-de-sac, treading the steep incline along the driveway.

My mother's truck was parked outside at a lopsided angle; the green bumper sticker slapped on her rear door just as lopsided read: *Jersey Tough.*

"Told you I'd get you home," he said, walking me to the front door.

I looked up at my house like it wasn't really there. I never asked him how we just managed to walk out of the park, crossing over a hundred miles within minutes. I was caught in his stare ... and the music was playing in my head again.

"What am I going to tell my mother?" I cringed.

"Maybe she won't remember," he said, smiling. "Maybe she'll think that you were here the entire time."

"What about your father?' I asked. "What if he comes after you?"

"I doubt he will," he said reaching around my neck. He pulled out my shell necklace and held it between his fingers. "He'll be so furious with me that he won't want anything to do with me."

I lowered my face as the sun moved in and out of the clouds; casting shadows between the trees, so that day seemed to move into night and back again.

"Tell me." His eyes sparked. "I want to know what you're thinking."

The push-pull feeling in my eyes told him to follow. The trees near the gazebo were perfect for playing hide-and-seek. In between giggles, I could hear the thunder in the distance; feel the cool, moist air heavy with the scent of earth.

He staggered towards me, too eager to walk straight. I smiled back while he took hold of my arms and pulled me against him; his lips expanding into a perfect overbite, too delicious to taste all at once.

"What did you give up to be with me?" I asked.

It wasn't something that I realized until just now, a vague sense of some spectacular destiny changed forever.

"Nothing," he whispered against my face as he took my hand. "Nothing compared to what I would have lost if I left without you."

He leaned in, his eyes on my lips.

A thousand pictures I could see behind his eyes; all the things that he had seen in me, the things I never knew.

"What's next?" I asked.

"Read my lips," he whispered, while his mouth slipped over mine.

Are You Breathless for More?

Coming Soon
The Irresistible Sequel:

Starcrush: Beyond Perfect

For more information on the *Starcrush* Series, including
sneak previews for upcoming books, visit:

www.StarcrushStory.com

To stay up-to-date on all things *Starcrush*, follow us:

Facebook: Starcrush Story

Twitter: @starcrushstory